INHABITANTS

BY

N.A. CAULDRON

Text copyright © 2019 by Deborah Johnson
Cover illustration and design by Debby Johnson copyright © 2019
Wiggling Pen Publishing, 1328 Virgil Beaty Rd, Clarkrange, Tennessee

Printed in the USA

ISBN paperback: 979-8-9867839-2-5
ISBN ebook: 979-8-9867839-3-2

https://nippi1.wixsite.com/nacauldron/

Each one of Brandon's classmates hunched in the same position he did, under their desks with their arms wrapped around their heads. The surrounding walls rumbled like boulders rolling down a mountainside.

"This is not a drill," the school's secretary commanded over the intercom.

"No! Really?" Kevin shouted back from the rear of the classroom. His buddies chortled at his sarcasm.

Brandon's neck ached in protest from its seemingly never-ending position of bending over. He could only stare at his sneakers as the floor shook beneath them.

His desk banged into his fingers. "Ouch!" One girl squealed. Another one cried. A bottled drink tipped over before falling off a desk. Brandon watched the yellow fizz inside of it expand as it rolled across the shifting floor.

And then it was over.

"Alright, class," Ms. Gordon called as she stood from her own crouched position. "Drama's over. Let's get back to work."

She habitually tidied up her desk. Brandon picked up the drink bottle and offered it to its rightful owner, the crying girl, Kristy. As she pulled herself up into her seat, she used her black, stringy hair to hide her face. She was still sniffling when Brandon realized his gesture would remain unnoticed. He gently placed the bottle on the corner of her desk and then sat in his own. On the way, he saw Kevin plop onto the seat of his chair, cross his ankle over his knee, and shake his hair out of his eyes. Kevin's friends did the same, afterwards resuming their usual slouches.

Twice this week, thought Brandon. This was the second earthquake since last Monday, and who knows how many since they first started. They continued to grow in intensity too.

"Now. Who can tell me the answer to number fifteen?" Ms. Gordon asked as though their so-called protective positions while being shaken to death was a normal part of their day, which it had become.

The usuals raised their hands. Brandon's eyes gazed unfocused at the cover of the unopened trig book on his desk, unable to concentrate on class at the moment. Last night the news had said the quakes were part of Earth's normal cycle, that this happened every few thousand years and not to worry about it. Some politicians even claimed it resulted from man-made climate change. Brandon scoffed at their explanations. He doubted anyone knew what happened thousands of years ago, and earthquakes and climate change went together like ammo and salt water as far as he was concerned.

"X is equal to the cosign of y times seven," said Peggy, the girl with the high-pitched voice who always knew everything.

Ms. Gordon asked another question. Brandon didn't hear her. His thoughts had drifted to his parents, Cynthia and Michael. As geologists and professors at the local college, it was part of their job to keep up with all the latest details, and last weekend they left to go study some site they said was important, that it had something to do with their work. Brandon wished he'd paid more attention now. Usually when they talked about work, he phased out, much like he was doing right now to his trig teacher. But with the quakes getting worse and him home alone, he was worried about them.

A light aftershock rippled through the classroom. Another girl squealed in surprise, and a book fell to the floor with an ignored thud.

He did remember one detail his parents mentioned before they left. Something about sinkholes, but they weren't like normal sinkholes where the earth opens up and swallows everything on it. They were places where the ground was getting lower, dipping down in a kind of depression but not cracking open. Like a part of the ground where the land suddenly dropped below the surrounding area, but in a place it hadn't before.

"Brandon?" Ms. Gordon called, expecting him to answer some question his thoughts had kept him from realizing the existence of.

"Um… I don't know," he stumbled. "I'm sorry."

Ms. Gordon huffed a sigh and placed her fists on her hips before addressing them all at once. "Really! Class, I know the quakes can be disturbing, but—"

The bell rang. Brandon grabbed his books and joined the more eager to leave than usual current of classmates.

He emerged from the flood of bodies into a hallway filled with a mixture of excited and terrified students, along with every emotion in between. Brandon was one of the between ones, one of the tolerant ones, waiting for it to be over. The quakes, at first alarming, had become routine, even annoying to him and others like him.

It hadn't always been this way. When the quakes first started, students remained excited for days afterward. Not anymore. While some, like Kristy in trig class, fought not to let the fear consume them, others, like Kevin, allowed the excitement to build within. Brandon sometimes wondered if it was all an act for Kevin. He noticed some of Kevin's friends put on a cool act around their buddy, but their faces always paled a little more than his did.

"Hey, Brandon!" Jason called from somewhere at least twenty feet back.

Brandon turned around and waved in acknowledgment. The progression of pupils around him made any other action impossible.

"We still on for tonight?" Jason was one of Brandon's online gaming buddies and should've known better than to ask that question. This weekend was the competition on the newly released Quantum Mass. The winners earn a scholarship for one year each with the American Coding University, the most prestigious online programming school in the world. Jason and Brandon had been preparing for two weeks, and tonight was their last chance to practice. Brandon wouldn't miss this for the world.

"Yeah!" Brandon yelled back over the other heads.

"We are *so* going to beat you!" a familiar voice shouted from the other end of the hallway.

Blade2043. A member of a rival team and one of the excited ones. "Not this time," Brandon said confidently not caring whether he was heard.

The other boy made no response.

As Brandon unwillingly bounced against the talkative tides of backpacks and shoulders, his thoughts were forced back into the present situation, and his body to his next class, English. He sighed. He hated it even more than math. Math was one of the better ones. It made sense. It was easy, comprehendible. But English was subjective, ambiguous, vague. There was no exactness to it, just opinions piled onto opinions.

"Did anything fall in your class this time?" Abigail, a nearby redheaded girl, asked another. Her voice quivered from nervousness and fear, not excitement.

"No." Her black-haired friend's voice held the same tremor. "But water splashed out of the aquarium so bad it took two rolls of paper towels to clean it up."

Abigail didn't respond. The girls faced forward with washed-out faces and stiff bodies, unable to look at each other lest that make it all too real to handle.

Abigail's friend rubbed the goose bumps from her arm, then added without turning her head, "Madison said a piece of their ceiling fell onto one of their desks in her class." Her voice was almost a whisper.

What she said piqued Brandon's interest. The quakes had been getting worse, but never so bad as to cause real damage. He tried to listen unnoticed to the rest of their conversation, but they had none. Abigail had clamped her mouth shut after hearing about the falling ceiling, and the other girl had no more to say. They were two of the terrified ones.

Brandon sat in his seat in English. The desks were slightly off from their regular spots. While it was possible Mr. Stockton, their English teacher, had them do groups, Brandon doubted it. It was more likely another result of the recent quake.

A few more quake questions emanated before the bell rang, indicating class should start. "When will the next one be?", "Does anyone know when they will stop?", "What happened in your class?" No one knew the answers to the first two, and Mr. Stockton shut the door two seconds after the bell rang, the clear sign to get quiet. There was no more discussion.

English felt longer than usual, and not merely because of the recent excitement. It was time to start their research report. Mr. Stockton passed out their schedules. Each section included its own due date. They could choose any topic, but they had to have approval first. Brandon raised his eyebrows in optimism. Maybe it wouldn't suck as much as he thought. He knew exactly what he would write his on, the history and future of the gaming industry.

Next, Mr. Stockton gave everyone a sheet of paper with three lines on it to write their subject choices on. Their decisions weren't due until Monday, but he instructed to spend the last few minutes of class thinking about them anyway. Few people did as they were told. Each clique did its own thing, from still discussing the last quake to conversing about their weekend plans. Brandon handed his choices to the teacher on the way out. He knew Mr. Stockton wouldn't let him get away with just one, so he filled in all three. Besides, there was a good chance he wouldn't be allowed his first choice. He put geology and computer programming for his other two. Programming was close enough to gaming he felt comfortable with it, and he could use his parents to whip out a geology report without too much trouble. They're always trying to get him interested in their work anyway.

Oops. The realization of what he just did made him grimace. If he *did* wind up doing his report on geology, it would probably just encourage his parents even more in their ultimate plans for his future, something he'd been fighting against for years. In retrospect, he realized he shouldn't have put that topic down as an option. He hoped he wouldn't be forced to use it.

Spanish was next, and thankfully his last class for the day. It was another one of the better subjects, absolute. By now, the excitement had faded. No more quake talk in the halls. Life had returned to normal.

Brandon turned in his homework along with everyone else and listened to the lesson. There would be a quiz Monday. He made a mental note to study tonight after their gaming runs.

When the end bell rang, he pushed against the flow of students to get to his locker. He heard Jason scream, "Six o'clock, man!" from the other side of the sea of students. Brandon thrust a thumb up into the air in response.

After weaving his way outside, he jumped the steps and headed home. The walk normally only took about ten minutes, long enough to forget about school, short enough to not get boring, but with his parents gone, he was obligated to check on his uncle first.

Technically his mother's uncle, and therefore his great uncle, Uncle Gus had a tendency to be … absent minded. He also had a tendency to push others away. Not that he was rude or purposefully inconsiderate, he just got so caught up in whatever he was doing at the time he didn't want to be disturbed by things like eating, phone calls, or his fifteen-year-old great nephew whose job it was to check on him every day after school.

Brandon looked both ways before crossing the street to his side of the pavement. With his thumb hitched under the right strap of his backpack, he trotted to Gus's house, right next door to his own. Overgrown shrubbery and tall grass made Gus's home stand out of place in their neighborhood.

Brandon rapped one of the small windows of the door with his knuckles before turning the knob. It was locked. "Uncle Gus?" His voice echoed against the corner of the jam. He knocked again, longer and harder this time. "Uncle Gus!"

Light footsteps made their way from the rear of the house. Bolts and locks turned from the inside before it cracked open, revealing a short man with greyed hair, thick glasses, and a small LED light strapped to the top of his head. "Brandon! Is it that time already?"

The smell of dusty air overpowered by the aromas of machine oil, metal, and lubricating sprays emanated from the hallway. The whir of a machine purred softly in the background as Brandon asked, "How are you, Uncle Gus? Do you need anything?"

Gus kept the door mostly shut. "No," he replied hastily before looking over his shoulder, preoccupied. "Thank you, Brandon." He began to close the door.

Brandon stopped it with his foot. He was more than certain his parents' request that he check on his uncle was a ruse for his uncle to check on him, but he still wanted to make sure Gus was OK. Just in case. "Are you sure? Do you have something for supper?"

An expression of surprise flitted across Gus's face before he answered, frustrated with such an irrelevant question. "No — er — yes! Yes. I have food. Thank you."

He shut the door again, and this time Brandon didn't stop it. Gus's response was unexpected but not unusual. He was what his family called eccentric. The rest of the world had deemed him, "The Nutty Professor." He was neither.

Gus had made his living as a machinist. Unlike most, his career was also his passion, and he continued it throughout his retirement. He was also somewhat of an inventor, making anything from his own light bulbs to perpetual motion machines. His family had grown used to his piddlings and reacted to them much as a bored parent would to their third child's finger paintings, with fake fascination and tolerance. And while Michael and Cynthia obviously felt Brandon needed checking in on, Gus realized he could take care of himself, providing there were enough leftovers and pizza money.

Brandon dug into his pocket for his front door key while he walked across the lawn. He went inside, threw his backpack over the back of the couch so it landed onto its cushions, and locked the door behind himself. After grabbing the last bag of almost empty chips and a canned drink from the fridge, he plopped into the recliner and opened his laptop. He adjusted his headphones and mic while it warmed up, then entered his password. When his desktop loaded, he doubled clicked on the game's icon, throwing a handful of the chips in his mouth. They crunched noisily in his ears as he went through the ritual to join a chat party and the familiar words appeared across the game's opening screen.

Loading...
Connecting to Network...
Joined Sniper26's party
Party chat open

Brandon called into the mic, "Hey, Sniper. How's it going?"

The other end was dead. Brandon checked the group. Nobody else had joined yet.

He watched a short YouTube video on a few tricks he wanted to try during practice tonight before the feathery scruff of the sound of headphones and a mic being put into place came through his phones. "Sniper, is that you?" asked Brandon, certain someone was there this time.

"Yeah." Sniper's breathless voice answered. "Sorry. We had another quake."

"We had ours a couple of hours ago." Brandon crunched some more potato chips. "Are you joining the tournament this weekend?"

"Um … yeah I don't know, man."

"Are you OK?"

"Um…" Sniper's voice shook when he spoke. "This one was bad, bro. I'll have to talk to you tomorrow. OK?"

"Yeah, man. Whatever you need."

Sniper26 has left the party

Brandon stared at the screen. Sniper sounded pretty shaken up. He had never sounded that way before. When a quake had hit in the past, Sniper always blew it off like it was nothing. Brandon didn't know what to think.

Jason, aka PearlDiver93, and the others wouldn't be ready for at least two more hours. Brandon closed his laptop and turned on the television, knowing every channel would be showing the same thing. News. Maybe one would show what happened in Sniper's neck of the woods.

As the TV warmed up, a man's voice gradually rose from its speakers. "Another quake rippled through the state measuring at 5.4 on the Richter scale. So far no significant damage has been reported." The screen showed footage from a red light cam a few miles from Brandon's neighborhood. He watched as the image jerked from the quake's effect. The reporter spoke over the video. "This footage of the quake was taken from outside the Food Market on Broadway and Clinch Street. Experts say this is the strongest quake to hit us since the main one six months ago. Our own Julie Lovesay is with Professor Mansfield from the East Ridge Technological University. Over to you, Julie."

The screen changed to a heavily made-up woman dressed in a crisp red suit with white frills bulging from its V-neck. It made her look like a stuffed Valentine heart that had burst its seam. Brandon snorted at her ridiculous outfit.

"Thank you, Carl." Julie turned to a man with peppered hair pulled into a tight, low ponytail and a black Slayer T-shirt which stretched over his middle-aged gut. "What have your findings told you, Professor Mansfield?"

"Basically, what we're finding is that this is nothing more than an extended version of a regular quake. And what I mean by that is … if you think of a regular quake, you think of one big shake followed by several little shakes. We call those aftershocks. While aftershocks are famous for causing more damage than the original quake, it's not because they're stronger, it's because the main damage has already occurred. Take the block of wood. If I were to split it down the middle, that would represent the first quake."

He held up a two short pieces of wood stacked on top of each other to demonstrate.

"As you can see, when I slightly bump the block of wood, the top will move as opposed to before the block was split in two."

He tapped the piece of wood, causing the top to fall off.

"That tap was obviously far weaker than what split the wood. So, what we're seeing now, what the whole world is now seeing, is a type of aftershock resulting from that original quake six months ago. Any damage already done by that quake has been repaired, so there's no reason to worry about what these smaller quakes will do. I mean, most people don't even feel a 5.0 quake." He chuckled.

The camera panned to a computer screen. Faded black lines waved up the TV in resistance.

Professor Mansfield's finger pointed to a red dot on a map on the screen. "The epicenter—"

Brandon furrowed his brow. None of this made any sense. The quakes were getting stronger, not weaker, and the first quake wasn't even noticeable. He just happened to know about it because of his parents' discussion of it that morning over breakfast. When the other quakes followed closely thereafter, the media mentioned the first one, claiming it was bigger than it was. Everyone else suddenly knew about it and talked like they had all along.

"One point three last night," his mother had said while pouring her cereal that morning six months ago.

His father's eyes lit up with the same excitement they always did. He never tired of hearing about them, no matter how many times it happened.

"It was deep, too." His mother placed the milk back in the fridge. "Over four hundred miles down."

His father's eyes expanded even further. "Quakes around here rarely reach that level. I might could write a paper on this one!"

Brandon remembered the conversation continuing from there with theories as to why it was so deep and his father bouncing from the table with the joy of a five-year-old due to the prospect of a new study.

Brandon turned his attention back to the news report. This time, a popular daytime psychologist was being interviewed in the news studio by the original anchorman.

"Reports of suicides and depression are increasing all over the world, especially in more developed areas. What are your thoughts on this Dr. Bill?"

The psychologist tugged at his suit and wore a professionally friendly face. "I agree with Professor Mansfield. Parts of the world that are less developed than others are more in tune with the earth and therefore less affected by its … quirks … if you will." Both men chuckled slightly at Dr. Bill's pun.

Brandon didn't think suicide was a joking matter, and he didn't think Dr. Bill was anyone to consult on something as serious as this.

As if he heard Brandon's thoughts, Dr. Bill's face sobered. Carl mirrored the expression.

Bill continued, "The real danger, Carl, comes when we suppress our emotions. When we suppress our emotions, they build until they eventually burst out in potentially dangerous ways. And that's what we're seeing here. The people affected by the original quake who tried to shrug it off instead of dealing with their emotions are now facing the consequences of their actions. When the aftershocks continued, new stress built on the old stress causing what I like to call the stack of dirty dishes." He smiled at his metaphor. "When no one does the dishes, they pile up until they eventually fall over." He turned serious again. Carl's face mimicked Bill's change of expressions with near perfection. Bill continued, "Increased stress can make us sick. It can cause hives, heart strain, and can eventually lead to depression, or even suicide."

The thought of Sniper freaking out ran through Brandon's head. They had never seen each other's faces, which was probably a good thing at the moment. Flashes of the faces of the terrified kids at school replaced Sniper's in his mind.

Brandon knew better than to use the television as an escape method. It would undoubtedly display over-dramatized inaccurate reenactments and interviews of "interesting" people like it had been since this all started. For whatever reason, he kept holding onto the false hope it would show something about the sinkholes his parents were studying. But of course, it never did.

He turned off the TV and reached for his backpack. Monday's Spanish quiz wasn't going to take itself. After pulling out his book and notes, he grabbed the house phone and ordered a pizza. Normally his mother left him strict instructions for supper while they were gone, including pre-made casseroles in the fridge, but they left on such short notice this time she gave him permission to order out if he needed to. He hoped she wouldn't mind if that meant five out of the seven nights he had been alone.

While waiting for the pizza, he studied his notes. Thirty minutes later, he had finished both pizza and homework and was leaning back on the couch, arms stretched wide and sighing at the ceiling. The excitement of being home alone had worn off by the end of the second day. Now it was just filling time.

He got up to grab another canned drink from the fridge, replacing it with a warm one, and saw the chore list his mother left for him on the fridge door. *Dust house. Clean bathroom. Keep dishes done.* He glanced at the shelves hanging on the kitchen wall. They held cast iron novelties and looked perfectly fine to him, especially compared to Gus's house. The sink was only half full. Surely he should wait until it was completely full to save on water. He gritted his teeth. Keeping the bathroom clean was one of his regular chores, and it was his normal day for doing it. Excuses for the dishes and dust might stand, but he could think of none for this dreaded activity. Fifteen grueling minutes later, he finished and was back to killing time, providing that didn't include another chore.

Swigging the last of his drink, he tossed the empty can in the recycling bin and reopened his laptop. After checking his webmail, he visited his favorite programmers' forums. Gaming wasn't a mere hobby with him; it was a passion. He started programming in middle school but hadn't been able to take it seriously until recently, when he received his own computer. The programming for his first real project was nearly complete, but he was still searching for a graphics designer. They didn't have to be amazing, just cheap, as in free. If he didn't find one soon, his baby would have stock images for its playable characters.

No luck. He answered a few newbie questions then opened his engine's text editor along with his most recent save. His program so far was a simple platformer, one where the main character collected particles of light then used them to lighten a darkened world. He wrote a few more lines while waiting for practice.

When the sun lowered behind the mountains, the reduced lighting in the living room told Brandon it was time. The next three hours kept him busy killing giant demon spawn with his buddies from around the world as they trained for their big weekend. After logging out, he closed his laptop one last time, took a shower and brushed his teeth, and crawled into bed.

His arm felt for the tablet on the nightstand. Its brilliant glow nearly blinded him in the darkness when he turned it on. After turning down the brightness, he used it to browse a few online videos. Even though his parents left a week ago, his dad's viewing history still affected the recommended feed. Conspiracy theories about aliens living under Antarctica, Earth really being flat, and falsified Moon landings made Brandon groan with embarrassment and picture his mother's eye roll with spot-on accuracy. Finally he found a favorite show to sleep to and after propping his tablet up against the wall, he pulled the covers under his chin and went to sleep. The weak evening quake didn't wake him.

"You can't tell me you don't see this!" Cynthia Humphries yelled at the scientists before her. A single brown conference table was all that separated her and Michael from their colleagues. Upon the table lay a map. Someone had drawn red dots all over the Nebraska/Colorado area. "The dropped spaces lie so precisely around the southwest, it's as if someone … *put* them there!" Her straightened brown pony tail jumped in place as she leaned over the table, her finger pounding on the map. The dots had formed a perfect circle, with the label "Ash Hollow" in the center. "And there's another circle just like it in Russia."

A man sitting near the front rose from his chair to examine the map more closely. As he did, his eyebrows creased his golden skin until they nearly disappeared into his conservatively short haircut. "You've confirmed this with Russia?" he asked, his eyes now searching her face.

Although they had never worked too closely together, Cynthia had always thought of Dr. Kumar as a helpful and friendly colleague. And so it pained her even more to admit her fallacy, as though she were letting him down personally. Still, prideful as always, she refused to break eye contact when she answered,

"We're having difficulty confirming all the points in Russia."

One of Dr. Kumar's eyebrows fell, allowing his other to remain cocked in a curious, now superior expression. A few utterances of dismissal scattered throughout the room, giving more relevance to his reaction.

He picked up one corner of the map. "Have every one of *these* spots been confirmed?" He indicated the red dots encircling Ash Hollow.

Cynthia hesitated, knowing her answer would be the last nail in their coffin. "No."

Murmurs exploded throughout the room, along with a few chuckles.

This time Kumar's brows did disappear into his hair. "Where did the others come from?" He waved his hand in the air. "Your imagination?"

The insult was too much. No longer feeling camaraderie for the man, her next words nearly forced themselves through her teeth, but she found the strength to make them sound professional before that happened. "I extrapolated them."

Susan, a middle-aged seismologist from Indiana, spoke over the now disinterested room. "Dr. Humphries — Cynthia, we can't take action when there's missing evidence."

Susan had worked in the same building as Cynthia for years, giving her data and advice when needed. Her words sounded like a betrayal. Cynthia's jaw slackened in response. "Over seventy percent of the indentations have been confirmed and plotted. *Over seventy percent.* I've seen less confirmation than that in most of your all's articles!"

"Dr. Humphries, you know this doesn't fit the scheme of modern accepted Earth models." The speaker wore a Hawaiian shirt and khaki shorts, his sandaled foot crossed casually over his other thigh.

Cynthia jerked the map away and rolled it up in her hands as quickly as possible, swallowing her words as she did so. There was no talking sense to these people, but she knew not to burn her bridges.

Michael kept a professional distance from his wife as he addressed the room. "I know this sounds preposterous, but our data is sound. The quakes are getting worse—" Disapproving grunts combined with the sounds of suddenly uncomfortable bodies being repositioned filled the room. "—and— Oh, come on! This isn't CNN!" It was one thing to reject the ideas of another scientist, a whole other ballgame to deny the truth while in a closed room surrounded only by those who knew it already. "We can be honest in this room. The quakes are getting worse, and the sinking spots are increasing in formation along with them—"

"Dr. Humphries," began an older woman in the back with large, squarish glasses and short, black hair which encased her head in giant circles. She was cool, collected; the uncomfortable air in the room didn't reach her. "What you're suggesting is science fiction, nothing more. It is simply impossible, not within our accepted standards, if you will."

Cynthia started to say something in response. Michael put his hand on her back and infinitesimally shook his head. Her anger obeyed, but her voice still tremored slightly from it when she said, "Thank you. I'm sorry to have wasted your time."

Michael smiled and nodded his thanks as well, worried his wife would have an outburst before they could exit.

The older woman stood up. "This was not a waste of time. The discovery of facts should be shared with the scientific community. Just because we process it differently than you doesn't mean this information isn't valuable."

There was a slight pause where Michael plastered a fake smile on his face while watching his wife with hopefully well-hidden apprehension.

Meanwhile, Cynthia thought of only one word she was too polite to say in public, or outside the cattle pasture where it usually lay. "Thank you," she said instead, her voice under complete control.

Michael opened the door for her and guided her though it, trying to appear more cordial than relieved. Once it was behind them, Cynthia said, "I don't know how you kept your cool in there with those idiots. If it hadn't been for you—"

"Shhh." He held his finger to his lips and motioned for them to leave. Muffled laughter broke through the conference room door. They left the university in silence.

"Why are they being so stubborn?" she yelled once they reached their car in the parking lot. "They can't accept anything that goes against their precious doctrine!"

Michael opened the trunk of their black sedan. "I know, honey. I know. We knew this was a long shot."

"But this is so close to their faces, it's practically slapping them!" She threw the map in the trunk. "Impossible to deny." Her voice lowered, and she placed her hand on the top of the trunk lid. "How can they not realize something else is happening here? Something big."

Despite his wife's recently lowered volume, the topic of conversation made Michael uncomfortable. "Can we discuss this in the car?" He scanned the area for anyone within earshot. "I don't want to make a scene in public."

Cynthia slammed the trunk shut and stood by the passenger side door, waiting for her husband to unlock it. Once they were both seated, Michael started the engine and reversed out of the spot. "Your research is sound. I agree with you," he said.

"I'm not upset with you."

"I realize you're not upset with me. What I'm saying is ... I think we should continue our work on this independently." He drove them through campus security, waving at the guard as he passed.

"With what? We have no funding." That was the whole point of today's talk, getting funding for more research. They needed to dig next to one of the dropped spots, visit some epicenters.

Michael took them through a traffic light and then up the ramp to the interstate. "I've been contemplating one of the hot spots. It's next to something I found very interesting."

"Really?" Her arms remained crossed, and her tone still resonated with anger. "What's that?"

"The Grand Canyon."

She rolled her eyes and sighed, but immediately regretted her actions. He was being very supportive, and she didn't want him to think she wasn't appreciative. "I know," she said, forcing her voice to sound pleasant. "That was the first one I disregarded because of all the cave systems and the area's history of sinkholes. I didn't even bother mentioning it today because I realized they would throw it out on those items alone." She propped her elbow against the door and her head against her fist. Her anger was subsiding despite her efforts to keep it going.

They passed a yellow Volvo before sliding back into the right lane. "How much of the canyon's history did you look into?" he asked her.

"Enough to understand its Karst topography makes it unstable enough to disregard the divots that have formed around it," she said as though her answer should have been obvious. "Why?" Her eyes narrowed. "Have you found something? Has something else happened since then?"

"Nothing else has happened there, that I know of anyway, but it fits the pattern of the others perfectly. It's the center of another circle for Pete's sake!" His hands left the steering wheel for a brief moment, intensifying his statement. "I understand why you didn't mention it today, but there's no reason to throw that spot out of the equation. I want to go there."

"To Arizona?" Her bewildered gaze shifted to his face.

"We can grab our stuff and leave tonight."

"Tonight?" She screamed, and shifted in her seat so her body completely faced him. "Michael, Arizona is *days* away. We would need to fly there. Do you honestly expect us to find a flight this late in the—" Michael's expression stopped her question dead. Her eyes narrowed into tiny, suspicious slits. He was holding back something, and she demanded to hear what it was.

His gaze darted to her face, and he sighed in surrender. "I already booked us a red eye flight. We leave at ten."

"You *what?*" This seemed treacherous, or at the very least deceptive. "Why would you do that?"

Guilt he had been holding back all day cascaded over him. His answer would only hurt her, but he couldn't keep it from her any longer. "I … had a hunch."

She sat back and faced forward, her arms crossed again. "Of?"

He continued to sneak glances her way when traffic allowed it. "I love you, honey, I really do. But… I just wanted to plan for … you know … in case it went the way it did." There. Maybe he said it in such a matter that it didn't hurt her as terribly as it could have.

The corners of her eyes prickled. He didn't have faith in her. Her own husband expected her ideas to be rejected. "Why did you let me go then?"

"What do you mean?"

"If my theory was so preposterous, if you sided with them—"

"I did not side with them!" His voice blared in the car. He didn't mean to yell at her. "I'm sorry." His hand reached over to hold hers. She didn't pull away; that was a good sign. "I believe in you, honey. I just knew, well we both did. We knew going in they might react that way."

Yes, they had both acknowledged that fact. She hadn't wanted to though. And no, she didn't believe he sided with them. She knew better. He was her greatest supporter. This planned flight behind her back was just him looking out for her.

"What about work?" Her voice was timid, defeated.

The weakness in her tone nearly killed him, but he ignored it. "Midterms are this week. We don't have to be there. An aide can give our students their tests."

That might work, she thought. It would require several long nights for several days afterward to catch up, but it might work. "I guess," she said, unsure. "But why now? Why not mention this before coming all this way and wasting all this time?"

"I wanted the others on board. I wanted... Well, it doesn't matter anymore." He wanted recognition for their work. He didn't want to spend their personal money to do the research. And most importantly, he had hoped the discussion with the others would expose new ideas, new theories. But mentioning that now would only make Cynthia feel worse.

She pursed her lips, unhappy the unwelcome reception they had just received made her husband feel the way he did but knowing there was nothing she could say to make it better. Their recent announcement of their findings had lowered their reputation within their tiny corner of the scientific community. There was no mistaking that. Maybe a field trip would give them some confirmation, something to bring back and show the others, something to validate their positions as geologists. "Do we take Brandon with us?" she asked.

Michael grimaced. "Brandon's more into gaming than caving. Besides, he would add to the needed supplies and whine more than help." His eyebrows rose significantly with the last sentence.

"True." She rubbed her finger against her bottom lip thoughtfully. She knew he was still just a kid, but she had hoped by now they would have found a shared interest, be able to spend time together doing something one of them didn't loathe. "What are your plans?" she finally asked.

"What do you mean?" Traffic slowed as the vehicles in the right lane tried to make room for the cop and his pulled-over vehicle.

"The Grand Canyon's awfully big, Michael. You do have plans, right?"

"Yeah," he answered, not wanting to share the more intimate details lest she laugh, which he was pretty sure she would. "I have plans." He glanced once more in her direction before scrounging up his courage. "I'll ask you one more time. How much of its history did you look into?"

She squinted her eyes and stared at him.

The several hours it took to return home gave Michael plenty of time to turn her opinion around from thinking he was a lunatic to wondering if he might be on to something. They spent the rest of the trip discussing the finer details.

"We're home!" Cynthia called out upon entering through the side door. Excitement filled her voice now instead of defeat, causing Michael to smile.

The sounds of a teenage boy playing with his friends online wafted into the kitchen where they were, but Brandon never responded to her hail. "He *knows* not to wear headphones when he's home alone!" she said to no one in particular. Her feet pounded the wooden floor as she stomped back to his room and leaned around the corner, giving him a glare only a mother could.

He took off his headphones and muted his mic. "I'm sorry." His sheepish voice was in far contrast to the commanding one he had just used on one of his teammates.

She held up her index finger in a meaningful gesture. "One more time, Brandon. One more time."

Worried about becoming grounded, Brandon quickly placed his laptop to the side and rose from his chair. "I'm sorry, Mom. I know I'm not supposed to have them on when—"

"Save it, Brandon." This was becoming a ritual between them, and she knew she was guilty for not having stopped it sooner. "Come eat."

Brandon watched his mother until she was far enough away he felt safe to get back online. "Hey guys," he said in a low voice into his mic. "I've got to go."

"What's the matter, SoulReaper?" HeadlessHorseman417 jeered, using Brandon's handle. "Mommy making you go clean your room?"

"Leave him alone, Headless," PearlDiver called.

"What, Swims-with-Sharks, you got a date with him later or something?" Headless sneered.

"I use that name because—" Jason started.

Headless interrupted, "Yeah, yeah. Your grandfather was one."

Brandon didn't have time for this. He muttered a quick, "See ya," and then signed out and shut his computer before jogging into the kitchen in hopes of not getting into any more trouble.

Whenever Headless acted like that, it ruined everyone else's night, which really sucked because he was otherwise an excellent gamer. Brandon didn't know too much about him, not even his real name. Uttering a person's actual name over the server was too unsafe and went against gamers' code. So they always used their handles, even when they knew each other in real life like Jason and Brandon did. But he did know Headless wasn't always a jerk. He just got jealous when someone else's parents cared enough to be parents.

Grabbing some dishes from the cabinets, Brandon began to set the table, furthering his "good boy" behavior for the evening. "How was work?" he asked.

"Interesting, to say the least." Cynthia used a spatula to break apart the ground beef she had thrown in a skillet.

Brandon folded the paper napkins in half, laying each one to the left-hand side of the plates. "What do you mean?"

Michael filled a pot with water and placed it on the stove to boil. "We took a trip to meet with some colleagues of ours." He wasn't sure how much he should divulge to Brandon. They had to tell him they were leaving, of course, but exactly what they planned to do while they were gone…

"I remember you saying something about that," Brandon said while making buttered toast. And he had remembered something … about their work … and today. Maybe.

The crackling sounds of spaghetti noodles breaking in half before falling into the boiling water competed with the sizzling beef. "Brandon…" started

Michael, "your mother and I have to go on a trip for work."

"Is that what today was about?" asked Brandon.

Spaghetti sauce glopped onto the browned beef from out of a glass jar. Cynthia turned down her stove eye. "Yes and no." Her voice came out taut; the anger was still holding onto her. Although she and Michael could investigate their theory anyway, it wouldn't be anywhere near as in-depth and detailed as they had wanted. They needed more manpower and tools, neither of which they had now. But the most influential trigger for her anger was her pride. That meeting severely wounded it, and only a great deal of time would heal that.

Michael turned off his stove eye, grabbed a metal strainer, and drained the noodles in the sink. "We've found some evidence that links to a site, and we need to visit it. That's all."

Brandon sat at the table. "What'd you find?"

A prolonged glance passed between his parents, who had both stopped halfway to the table with their food held out in front of them. Cynthia bit her lip. Wanting to be sure at first, and then later not wanting to scare him unnecessarily, they hadn't told their son anything about the divots they discovered weeks ago, not yet, let alone the new theory they were acting upon tonight. Even now, when the facts could no longer be ignored, Cynthia hesitated in her explanation. "There are … symmetrical pits which have formed in certain places of the earth's crust. We want to investigate one of them."

"Pits. What d'you mean, pits?" The news stations had mentioned nothing about the earth opening up anywhere due to the quakes, not yet anyway.

"Calm down, Brandon," said Michael. He then placed his napkin on his lap in a manner so as to show the pits were nothing to worry about. "They're only slight depressions and hundreds of miles away from where we are."

Something about his father's overly casual actions told Brandon they were a façade. "So what are they then?"

Cynthia answered with a soothing yet excited smile, "That's what we're going to find out."

Brandon let his empty fork hang over his plate as his mind filled with pictures of his house falling into a giant sinkhole, its pipes and wires sticking out from where the other half had broken off. Several holes had opened up in Florida a few years back, filling the news with videos of broken homes and buildings, where one part fell in and the rest sat cracked and exposed on the so-called stable ground above. One hole swallowed a man while he slept, his wife unable to reach him in time. A shudder rippled through Brandon's shoulders, making him wince.

"Brandon," said Michael, not noticing his son's unease.

Brandon snapped back into the present.

"Eat your supper," Michael said with a flick of his chin.

Brandon put his napkin in his lap. "Where are these, 'depressions'?" he asked expectantly. Then as slowly as possible, he twirled a bite around the tongs of his fork, not because he was still picturing those sinkholes, but because he was too stubborn to take that first bite until his father answered his question.

"Where we're going isn't one of the actual depressions," answered Michael. Technically, even though the particular spot in the canyon they planned to visit was the center of a circle several of the pits formed, it wasn't a pit itself. "It's several miles from the nearest one." What he said was true. He scooped some noodles onto his toast and bit into them before continuing, "We're leaving tonight so we can get an early start in the morning."

Brandon scraped the bite off his fork with his teeth and chewed it slowly. The answer sounded legit. He took a drink of water. His parents had gone on working trips ever since he could remember, and they usually lasted the whole weekend. Before leaving, they always dropped him off with relatives, mainly his uncle Gus. It was rare he ever traveled with them. This past year, however, they had been leaving him alone at the house while they were gone, with the stipulation of checking on his uncle at least once daily. With the tournament next week, having the house to himself, even for two days, was like a gift from the gaming fairy. "How long will you be gone?"

Cynthia sighed. "At least the weekend, maybe longer."

"And we won't be able to contact you every day, because there's no signal where we're going," added Michael.

Brandon tried to hide his smile with another bite.

Cynthia wasn't fooled. "No parties."

Brandon dropped his fork on the plate with a clatter and raised his palms in questioning surprise. A few chews later, he managed a swallow before getting out, "Since when have I ever partied?"

That was true, Cynthia realized. Brandon had never been one to party. "You just had a Cheshire smile on your face that made me concerned. That's all." She went back to eating.

Brandon widened his eyes and rolled them in exasperation.

"I'll leave you with a list of chores that need doing, and I'll need you to check on your uncle every day after school, if we're gone past the weekend, and twice each Saturday and Sunday." Knowing the chores wouldn't get done, Cynthia at least found some comfort in knowing Gus would keep an eye on things. Brandon was good about obeying that rule.

"What about your jobs?" Brandon asked. "You can't leave in the middle of the school year. If you're gone longer than the weekend, who'll teach your classes?"

"It's midterms, Brandon." Michael said, refusing to look up from his plate so as to give the appearance of this being just another boring old trip his son wouldn't be interested in.

But the fact the trip was so last minute, the fact they were acting far more casual about it than they should be, the fact the quakes were getting worse and were the main reason for this spontaneous announcement, Brandon was most curious indeed, even if he didn't want to admit to it.

"So tell me about it." He concentrated on his plate, acting like his question was merely an attempt at polite conversation. If they could pretend it was boring, he could too.

Cynthia and Michael both froze. A sauce-covered noodle hung from Cynthia's lip in the most undignified way.

Brandon looked up when they didn't respond. "Seriously?" His voice cracked. "How many years have you been trying to get me interested in your work? You're going to clamp up on me *now*?"

"Well, son," started Michael. "What more do you want to know?"

Cynthia choked a little on her spaghetti but quickly recovered. "I'm fine. I'm fine," she responded to their worried expressions. She wanted to tell Brandon what they were doing and why. She wanted to so bad, but she couldn't. Even if he didn't laugh at the idea, he might tell someone. University towns are small, and another professor's child was sure to hear about it if he did, and they might tell their professor parent, and then... No, she couldn't chance telling anyone they didn't have to.

Brandon shrugged. "I don't know. Where are you going...?"

"We told you," Michael interrupted. "The divots."

"Yes, but where *are* these 'divots'?"

"How come you're all of a sudden so interested?" asked Cynthia.

"How come you're all of a sudden not wanting to tell me?" He could play this game too.

Her eyes narrowed, daring him to keep pushing, but he knew he had the upper hand this time and gave her an expectant expression which said so. Cynthia knew she shouldn't take his insolence, but with them leaving she couldn't very well ground him. Besides, his behavior just gave her the excuse to button up. She hardened her jaw and answered, "We're done. Eat."

Brandon turned to his father, who raised his eyebrows in a manner which said, "You know not to disrespect your mother like that."

Brandon realized this wasn't him being punished for being disrespectful. His whole life, Cynthia had tried to tell him about her work, their travels. Normally, she would have jumped at this opportunity no matter how he had acted towards them. The fact she didn't, proved she didn't want to, and the reactions of his father showed he didn't either. But why? Didn't they trust him? Who was he going to tell? The news? Social media? He wasn't a girl, he thought. It wasn't like he would blab all over the internet, "Hey, my parents are going to blah blah to study the quakes blah blah. Ohmygosh! How should I wear my hair and makeup while they're gone, and isn't Gevin so cute?"

They all three stared at each other a full minute, maybe more before Brandon gave in. "Fine," he said, and stabbed his spaghetti with his fork.

Bang, bang, bang, bang, bang! Brandon raised his heavy head from his warm pillow. Had he heard something? *Bang, bang, bang, bang, bang!* It was coming from the front door. He rolled back over and buried his face in his pillow. One of his parents could see what it was. *Bang, bang, bang!* Adrenaline shot his eyes wide open as reality kicked in. His parents left a week ago. He was all alone in the house.

He threw off the covers and jumped out of bed. His breath came shallow, like a deer hiding under a pile of leaves, hoping the wolf keeps walking. Seconds passed while he thought of what to do. Whoever was out there was determined to get in, almost like they knew he was home. Hiding was no good in that case. The cops would never get here in time. That much was obvious. If he ran out the back door, they would probably see and hunt him down. His only option was to fight back.

Bang, bang, bang, bang! The pounding was getting louder. Brandon remembered his father kept the shotgun next to his parents' bed. He tiptoed towards it through the dark hallway. The dim rays of the street lights shone through the curtained windows, providing him with his only light. His fingers felt their way between his father's side of the mattress and the nightstand until they reached the cold metal of the gun's barrel and gripped hard.

"Brandon! It's me!" the voice from behind the door yelled, just loud enough for him to make out.

He released a sigh of relief. It was his uncle Gus. But that relief soon turned to anger. Could he not have at least called before coming over and almost getting shot? As the last dregs of sleep left his body, worry took over, worry as to why his uncle was pounding on his door in the middle of the night. There's no way this was good news.

Abandoning his search for defense, Brandon twirled around on one sock foot and slammed the other one into the leg of the bed. "Ouch!" He held his stubbed toe while carefully hopping to the door, trying not to let his other foot slip on the hardwood floor and hurt more than his one toe. The chain slid with ease. The bolt opened with a clean click.

"Are you OK?" Gus asked, eying the foot Brandon was still holding. An LED light remained strapped to his head.

"Yeah." Brandon let go of his toe and gingerly allowed his weight to bear down on it.

A neighbor's porch light turned on, grabbing Gus's attention. "Perhaps I should come in," he said.

Catching on, Brandon opened the door wider. "What's wrong?"

"We need to leave." Gus stepped inside. "Our plane leaves in two hours."

Brandon shut the door behind his uncle and locked it. "Two *hours*? That's not enough time to catch a flight from here! We'll barely make the drive in one. Then there's security, not to mention— Wait. *What* plane? Where are we going? What's going on?"

"Your parents need our help." Gus turned to grab a few things, but Brandon blocked his way.

"What's wrong? What could they possibly need our help for?" Worry wakened his limbs and mind as he remembered he hadn't heard from them since they left. They had said the signal would be bad, that they couldn't call every day, but this was too long. "Are they OK?" he asked.

An invisible canopy covered Gus's face. It wasn't time to tell him everything yet. "Nothing's wrong, Brandon," he told him. They needed to get going.

His uncle's words were calm and soothing, but Brandon knew differently. He could see the veil in place. His eyes turned into slits. "Uncle?" he asked in a singsong voice, ending on a higher pitch. "Tell me what has happened to my parents. Now."

The veil lifted from Gus's face as recognition of Brandon's worry entered his eyes. "Oh! Nothing's wrong with your parents! They're perfectly fine. They've just run into something they can't do on their own and need us to come and help them." He patted

Brandon on the arm before maneuvering around him, in search of a bag to pack.

Brandon sighed and followed him. "They don't need you to bail them out again, do they? I mean cause if that's the case, I can go back to bed."

Gus was bent over the hallway closet floor, rummaging through its contents. "No, no, no. They're not trespassing this time." He stopped and stood abruptly, paused for a moment in thought, then said, "At least I don't think so." Then as quickly as he had stopped, he bent back over to continue his search.

What curiosity and confusion remained in Brandon's body was quickly turning to anger. "So they're not in jail? They can talk to *you* but not *me*? I've been alone here for seven days. Why haven't they called? In fact, why didn't you call instead of pounding on the door? I almost shot you!"

With his hand clutching a large suitcase, Gus stood and faced Brandon. His face sank with apology. "You're right. I should've warned you I was coming over. I just got … excited."

"Excited?" Brandon yelled. "Don't you have a key?"

"Hmm? Oh, probably. Wait. Yes, I do have a key. Sorry. I must've forgotten it in the hurry of things." He walked around Brandon to the living room as though his statement ended the conversation.

Brandon followed him again. He hated how his uncle was so easily distracted. Getting information out of him was frustrating to the point of painful. "And my parents?"

"What about your parents?"

"Why didn't they call me?" He struggled to keep his tone respectful.

Gus scanned the area for anything he might have forgotten he needed but remember again later if he saw it. "They barely had enough power on their phones left to tell *me*. They're not in a position to be making phone calls."

His anger somewhat subsided, Brandon's concern resurfaced. "If they're so safe, then why are we leaving in the middle of the night?"

Gus stopped what he was doing and looked Brandon straight in the eye. "I promise you. Your parents are in no more danger than we are."

Something was going on, of that Brandon was sure. But his uncle's demeanor told him what he said was true. His parents weren't in trouble.

Gus stepped into the kitchen. "Is it OK if I grab a snack before we go?"

The randomness of his question caught Brandon off-guard. "Uh, Sure."

With one hand holding an open cabinet door, Gus told Brandon from over his shoulder, "You'll need to pack a few things."

Brandon gave up trying to find out anything else. He nodded and headed back to his room. "How many days am I packing for?"

"Oh, uh, two. Maybe three" The contents of the cabinet muffled Gus's voice, but Brandon could still detect his censorship.

"Yup," Brandon mumbled under his breath. "Definitely hiding something."

Once in his room, Brandon grabbed his backpack, emptied it of his books, and began filling it with clothes. When he finished, he made sure to include an extra pair of boxers. He didn't want to have another episode of what happened when he was ten at summer camp.

He turned to his desk where his laptop stared up at him. The tournament! Brandon sank onto his bed and dropped his head into his hands, letting out a long, loud groan in the process. He had been planning that tournament for weeks, months really, ever since the game had been announced. "Stupid parents!" he spit under his breath. He grabbed the nearest thing he could find, an old shoe, and threw it as hard as he could at the wall. It left a mark.

"You OK?" Gus called from the other end of the house.

"Just peachy!" Brandon retorted, making sure it was loud enough for Gus to hear. He fell back hard onto the mattress, his body bouncing in response. The minutes crept by as he lay there staring at the blank, white ceiling. It felt like his life was falling apart, that everything he had planned and hoped for was shattering cruelly before him. That scholarship was his only ticket to earn a degree in game development. His parents sure wouldn't pay for any programming classes, even if they came from the cheap community college downtown, let alone ACU, whose prices rivaled those of Harvard and Vanderbilt. They thought his choice in careers was too foolish to even talk about, and an opportunity like this probably wouldn't come along again before high school graduation.

The outside corners of his eyes prickled warningly of tears. "No!" he shouted through his teeth in a whisper and pummeled his fist down onto his bed. He sat up and forced himself to concentrate on the present situation. Thoughts ran through his brain like bees in a swarming hive. Did he have a choice in the matter? Should he ask, no demand, to stay behind and compete in the tournament?

Guilt trickled over him. His parents were in enough trouble to force Gus and himself in the middle of the night to go who-knows-where to "help" them (although no one would tell him anything about it). And they got in that trouble by studying the quakes, something everyone should be grateful for, including himself.

Still frustrated, but hating himself for being so, he pushed off the bed and marched over to his desk. With more force than was necessary, he opened his laptop case and packed his computer away. The thought of throwing everything in one bag was tempting, but he didn't want to take any chances of airport personnel getting handsy with his laptop. Next came its cord. With any luck, somewhere near the site would have wi-fi. If not, he might could use his phone as a hotspot.

"Be sure to bring your phone!" Gus yelled from the kitchen. "You can charge it in the car if you have to."

"Already got it!" Brandon grabbed his phone and tossed it in the front pocket of the backpack, threw on some jeans and a tee, then went to join Gus in the kitchen.

The sounds of Gus raiding the pantry met him on the way, then a zipper struggling to close, followed by the clinking of many cans. Brandon stepped inside where his uncle strained to carry the full suitcase.

"Why do we need all that food?"

"Huh?" Uncle Gus acted like the question was silly, as though carrying around a suitcase full of canned food to place on an airplane was a completely normal thing to do. "Oh," he said forgetfully before dropping the case with a terrible thud and turning to search through the kitchen drawers.

After several attempts, he retrieved one can opener and a few pieces of flatware. It was only then Brandon realized how this might appear to the already concerned neighbors. A crazed pounding on the door in the middle of the night followed by the sweeping circle of a flashlight in the kitchen before two people exited carrying luggage. The thought of having to explain things to the cops, especially how his parents had left him alone for nearly a week, made Brandon anxious to leave.

Gus, with the overtaxed and beginning to ravel handle of the suitcase pulling on his left hand, his right hand clutching the recently scavenged kitchen utensils, and a glaring light strapped to his forehead, motioned for Brandon to leave. "Let's go," he said and walked past him more swiftly than Brandon thought possible, given his load. He miraculously opened the door without setting anything down. "You coming?" he asked when Brandon didn't immediately follow his lead.

Brandon took one more look around, he wasn't sure why, and exited his home.

Locking every lock possible on the house behind them, they walked across the lawn to Gus's driveway. Gus popped the trunk of his car for Brandon to throw his sack into before grunting to heave the ridiculous suitcase full of canned goods in next to it. Another neighbor's light turned on when the trunk slammed shut. Brandon kept his hand on the passenger side door handle, nervously waiting for the click that told him the door had unlocked.

As soon as it did, he jumped inside, slammed the door behind him, and fumbled to get his seatbelt in place. Gus took a few seconds longer, then pulled them safely out onto the street.

His uncle drove calmly, not too slow, but not too fast either. As he drove, he hummed along to his favorite radio station. Brandon was used to his uncle's annoying taste in music and drowned it out. Once they reached the interstate though, he glanced over to Gus and saw he was still wearing his LED light. "Is there a reason you're still wearing your headlamp?"

"Oh!" Gus reached up and removed it. "Sorry." He turned it off and threw it in the back seat, where Brandon noticed several more bags of luggage.

The sight of all the packed bags demanded an answer. "When are you going to tell me what's going on?" Brandon asked.

Gus kept his face neutral. He didn't want to tell him, not now. Best wait until there's no turning back.

Brandon had seen that look on his uncle before, when his grandmother was sick in the hospital and Gus had to take him there. No more of his questions would be answered. Not now.

His grandmother died that night.

Since it was so early on a Saturday morning, traffic was clear enough they made it to the airport in forty-five minutes. Gus put the car in park, waking Brandon in the process. He then threw open his door and popped the trunk. "We need to hurry if we're going to make it," he said, not checking to see if Brandon heard him or not.

Brandon took a moment to wake up before reaching over to take the key out of the ignition for his forgetful uncle and stepping outside. After a quick survey of the parking lot, he stretched and said, "There's not a lot of people here. I'm sure we'll be fine."

Gus threw Brandon's backpack on top of the suitcase still in the trunk and heaved out an even bigger and heavier one from underneath. "Weren't you the one complaining earlier we wouldn't have enough time?"

Brandon yawned. "Yeah, but that was before I realized it was Saturday." He walked around to the back of the car.

When Gus unzipped the main suitcase, Brandon saw it contained even more food plus some mechanical gadgets his uncle always had on hand, like his ancient yellow voltmeter and wire cutters. Gus began reorganizing the case's contents, muttering to himself the whole while.

"Get the other bags, please," Gus said without looking up or pausing.

The sight of those tools frustrated Brandon further. This whole thing was getting ridiculous, and he had a right to know what was going on, but if Gus wouldn't tell him in the car or house, he for sure wouldn't in an airport parking lot while hurriedly getting them ready for their flight. Brandon squelched his desire. For now.

He opened the back doors and pulled out the smaller bags that had aroused his suspicion earlier. Meanwhile, Gus had grabbed Brandon's backpack and was going through it. After throwing a few things out and reorganizing the rest of its insides to suit his own needs, he stuffed it full with a choice selection from the rest of the luggage.

Brandon's brows drew in. "Why can't I take my toothpaste?"

"This is the carry-on. They have very strict restrictions on opened containers and sizes. I don't know all of them, so I'm not taking any chances. Anything questionable will go in the bigger case."

Brandon shook his head. "My laptop is my carry-on."

Gus paused and stared up at him. Brandon wasn't backing down on this one. "I'm not letting it leave my sight."

Gus hesitated a moment, then nodded and began switching out the luggage so Brandon could use his laptop as his carry-on.

A good ten minutes later, Brandon was carrying his laptop and one backpack, while his uncle lugged the big suitcases. Oddly, the one backpack was filled with nothing but smaller bags. Gus had explained they would not be using the suitcases once they landed and would instead pack the several smaller bags with their contents. When Brandon asked why, Gus eyed him oddly and said the path they would take required a lot of hiking, and a suitcase would be too cumbersome. Given they were going to what Brandon presumed was one of his parents' geological sites, his answer made sense.

As Brandon had hoped, the airport lines were fairly short, which was good since security made a fuss over all of Gus's tools, not to mention the exorbitant fees for his obese suitcase. Gus's nervous pacing didn't help either. Brandon kept anticipating the guards to view it as something more than it was, causing them both to be searched in ways he didn't want to think about.

By the time security decided they weren't going to blow up the place and the baggage counter had checked their luggage, they had just less than half an hour to kill. Gus handed Brandon some money and told him to grab them some food while he found a spot in their gate's waiting area. Brandon wasn't hungry but knew better than to argue. The only places open were a coffee shop and a sugary bakery. Knowing it wouldn't last, but having no alternative, he ordered them both buns whose prices matched their sugar content and two large bottles of water.

"Here." He handed his uncle's bun to him.

"Thank you," Gus responded, taking his breakfast. He balanced his bun on his knee and opened his water.

Brandon watched as his uncle guzzled nearly half the bottle down at once. "How long have you been up?" he asked, taking his first bite of his own breakfast.

Gus's eyes flitted to Brandon's face before he answered, "I haven't been to bed yet." Before Brandon could ask several angry, worry-filled questions he could no longer contain, Gus finally started to answer them of his own accord. "I got the call yesterday. I didn't want to make you get ready and spend the rest of the night waiting on me, so I didn't tell you about it until I had finished everything I needed to do first."

Brandon swallowed another bite of bun and washed it down with a swig of water. "Wait. Yesterday? What time yesterday?"

"Three."

"Three!" Brandon nearly dropped his breakfast.

Gus raised his palms and shushed him while frantically swiveling his head around in the most conspicuous way possible to see if anyone heard him.

"What do you mean three?" Brandon screamed in a whisper. "That was right before I came over after school. Wait. Were you on the phone while I was there?"

"What?" Gus did a double take. "No. No, they hung up long before you got there."

Brandon's anger rose in him like a lit firework. He couldn't believe it. Not only did they not call him, they hung up moments before he got to the phone. And everyone seemed to think he was too young or too stupid or too *something* to be told it all.

Still seething, he demanded to know more. "You still haven't told me what happened. Where are we going? What's going on?"

Gus's gaze traveled the room again, but this time it wasn't as noticeable. "We're going to the Grand Canyon," he said in an even lower whisper than before, which didn't make any sense. Since when was the Grand Canyon a secret?

"OK. And?" said Brandon expectantly.

"I'll have to tell you the rest once we get there." Gus took a sip of his water and another large bite of his bun.

"Why?"

Gus didn't answer him until after he swallowed his previous bite then filled his mouth with the remains of his sugary breakfast. Brandon shook his leg up and down, impatiently waiting for him to finish. "Trust me, Brandon. Later."

Trust me, Brandon. Trust me, Brandon. Words he had heard all his life from every adult in it. Normally, he would brush it aside. He had learned long ago not to care about adult problems. But he couldn't this time. "Are they hurt?"

"No." The answer was fast. Certain.

Brandon believed him. "Are they in trouble?" he asked in a whisper. A knowing look passed between the two of them, and Brandon knew "with the law or worse" was understood. "I mean, I know you said they weren't in jail, but that doesn't mean…"

Sometimes scientists did illegal things. A lot of times scientists did illegal things, and Brandon had learned long ago that it was entirely possible for his parents to one day get caught in something worse than trespassing. Granted, his parents didn't do the bad stuff: cruel animal experimentation, using human tissue without the subject's consent, but they did trespass more than the average person. And although no one had caught them for anything outside of trespassing yet, his parents had often dug up something that wasn't theirs during their expeditions. So the question wasn't unreasonable. Brandon did begin to wonder if they would be joining his parents in illegal activity however, considering his uncle's behavior. He wasn't sure how he felt about that.

"No." Gus shook his head. "Not yet." He raised his eyebrows with his last statement, and Brandon conceded to not asking any more questions in public.

The speaker announced their boarding. Gus wadded his wrapper, downed the last drops of his water, and threw both items in the nearest receptacle. Past those first two bites, Brandon had barely touched his bun. His uncle held his hands out in a questioning motion. Brandon shook his head no, he wasn't hungry enough to eat the rest of it, and handed it to his uncle. He then took a last drink of his water and handed the rest of that to his uncle as well. Two incomplete swallows later, Gus tossed the empty wrapper and bottle in the nearest trash can, grabbed his backpack, and fell in line, still chewing.

They boarded without incident, unless you count Brandon's embarrassment from Gus trying to thank the attendant with his mouth bursting full only to nod and offer a lumpy grin before entering the jet bridge. Brandon followed, keeping his face low and grimacing at the amused expression on the attendant's face.

After throwing their bags into the overhead compartment, they took their seats. A middle-aged businessman soon joined them, looking as happy to be on the plane as they were. Brandon frowned. Even if his uncle had been willing to talk to him in the midst of the plane noises, he wouldn't now with someone so close by. Shortly after takeoff, Gus fell asleep. Brandon wished he could, but he hadn't been awake long enough yet.

Their first layover was in Dallas. By then, Brandon's appetite had grown enough for him to want a good meal. This airport was far larger than the first one, allowing them to sit down in an actual restaurant and fill up on real food.

"Are you sure that's all you want?" Gus asked after Brandon had ordered the biggest burger the restaurant had.

Perplexed, Brandon opened his napkin and laid out his silverware. "Isn't that enough?"

Gus acted like he wanted to say something, but tapped his finger on his lips instead. Brandon rolled his eyes and sighed. "Enough. Uncle Gus, we aren't federal spies. What is going on?" He kept his voice in a whisper. "None of these people know us from their own grandmother, and I doubt they care what we're up to."

Gus twisted his head around, surveying the restaurant. His nephew was right and deserved some answers. He stretched his head across the table, looking more like a turtle reaching for a distant leaf than a person trying to keep something secret. Brandon thought his actions were more conspicuous than if he had just said it outright at normal volume. He motioned with his eyes and used his hands to gesture for his uncle to sit back.

"Your parents are in a cave at the bottom of the Grand Canyon," Gus said, catching on to his nephew's silent pleas and sitting up to a more normal position.

Brandon shrugged. He vaguely remembered something about caves in the canyon, like maybe some old Native homes or something, but that was it. "OK. And?"

"It's not a place … most people go."

"I assumed that," he interrupted. "Let me guess. It's on a reservation, and they shouldn't be there."

Gus's eyes widened, happy with his nephew's understanding. "Yes!"

"But,"—he lowered his head to meet his uncle's—"do you really think these people have any idea what we're talking about? Or care for that matter?"

Gus leaned back. The waitress was there with their food. "Thank you," they both muttered to her.

She smiled in return. "Is there anything else I can get you?" she asked while filling their drinks.

Gus shook his head. Brandon answered, "No. Thank you," and smiled.

Knowing Gus wouldn't say anything else until the waitress was far away again, Brandon dove into his meal. Several bites later, the waitress was at the other end of the restaurant. Brandon raised his eyebrows at his uncle, inviting him to continue.

Gus swallowed some water before answering, "Your parents have been monitoring certain events."

"I know that. Oh!" Brandon suddenly realized what he should have all along and felt silly for not seeing it sooner. His uncle had every reason to be cautious talking about this stuff in public. If anyone heard a single word, "quake", "geologist", "seismographic measurements", they would most certainly listen, even call the cops on them if they believed it would help stop the Earth from shaking them to an early grave. There were a lot of conspiracy theories out there, and terroristic attacks weren't immune from them. Everyone tried to play it off, but the truth was, most of the general public was terrified.

Brandon lowered his voice to match that of his uncle's. "OK. So that explains why you're being all cloak and dagger *now*, but it doesn't explain why you wouldn't tell me in the car or at home."

Gus took a deep breath and paused in contemplation before answering, "We didn't have time to go into it at the house. We were too busy getting ready to come here. And in the car..." He took off his glasses and wiped his tired eyes.

Brandon saw how exhausted he must be but didn't say anything. The answers he had been after were too close for him to stop pushing now.

"The truth is..." Gus put his glasses back on and straightened them. "I don't *want* to tell you."

Brandon's eyes shot open in surprise. "Does that mean you're not going to?"

Gus shook his head. "No," he sighed, but he didn't continue.

Brandon downed a couple of fries, waiting for his uncle to resume talking. When he didn't, Brandon urged him with, "And so…" He spoke slowly, considering each word before he spoke it so as not to say anything he shouldn't in public, yet still make his intentions clear to Gus. "They think they've found something that…" He used his hands to indicate Gus should finish the sentence for him.

"Not think," Gus said, relenting to the conversation. "Have. They presented their original theory to some coworkers, but they were disregarded. Your father believed there was even more to it than your mother, and convinced her to join him on a … vacation."

He had emphasized the word "vacation", and Brandon understood it to mean expedition. "So why do they need us?" he asked.

"Your father was right." Gus took a sip of water. "Only more right than he had ever imagined. They found more than they went looking for. Due to the way their coworkers reacted, they don't want to say anything to them. They're afraid the truth would be … covered up." Gus whispered his last words before spearing a lettuce leaf with his fork.

The waitress returned and filled their glasses. They greeted her with nothing more than weak smiles. This conversation was over for now, of that Brandon knew. He finished his meal, feeding his body in the same way his uncle had just fed his curiosity.

They paid for their meal and returned to wait in the crowded lobby until they could board again. His uncle kept nodding off, and Brandon knew he would sleep through the remaining flights, prolonging their conversation even longer. Brandon hoped he could join him this time. It would make the journey easier.

When they found their seats, the businessman had been replaced by a young woman and her baby. All thoughts of sleep were crushed when it started crying. Brandon tried not to be rude. Gus even made faces at it and cootchie cooed for a while, but the second layover was a welcomed relief. They stretched their legs by walking around the outside of the airport, still too afraid to continue their conversation. Brandon imagined before the buildings, before the smog, the Phoenix sunset would have been breathtaking.

Gus insisted they eat another full meal before departing one last time, saying they would need the energy. The last leg of their flight left Brandon waiting at the carousel for their suitcase while his uncle rented a vehicle for them. Thirty tiring minutes later, they were driving north on highway 89.

An odd combination of exhaustion mixed with anticipation came over Brandon while in the car. He forced his body out of its slouch and checked on his uncle. When they had first left town, Gus tried for several seconds to find a radio station before succumbing to the silence. His fingers now attempted to rub his eyes awake for the third time.

"Are you going to be OK?" Brandon asked.

"Huh? Oh yeah. I'll be fine. Just a couple more hours and we'll be there."

Brandon waited through another five minutes of silence before making his demand. "Look. We're alone in a car on the desert. There's no reason you can't tell me everything, and I mean everything that's going on. Now."

His uncle pursed his lips and glanced in the rearview mirror. A full minute later, he cleared his throat and took a breath. "It all started after their trip to the university last Friday."

The noon sun did little to heat the tiny capsule of a car Michael and Cynthia had rented for their journey. Cynthia had her hands buried inside the folds of her arms. She could feel the chill creeping in on her through the glass of her door's window.

Michael turned up the heat. "Still cold?"

"Thank you," she sighed, as the heated blast hit her feet and legs. "How much farther?"

As though it heard her, a metallic voice came out of Michael's phone, which he had lodged in the cup holder between them. "Turn left in one hundred feet."

"That answer your question?" Michael chuckled, amused by the coincidence. He picked up the phone and double checked their position on the map. They were in the middle of nowhere on flat terrain and hadn't seen a car in ages, so he felt safe doing it. "It looks like we have about an hour left." Putting the phone back in the cup holder, he smiled at her, trying to lighten the mood. To lighten *her* mood.

"Great," she muttered. "One more hour of snow covered, unmarked back roads." Cynthia continued to stare straight ahead, still chilly if not cold, and a little miffed with being in a car for so long, especially considering she wasn't getting what she'd hoped for. While packing, Michael had reminded her to bring heavy coats and clothing. She knew it wouldn't be warm, but she still assumed it would remain a desert. However instead of the painted sand, the red and purple lines swimming together in a beautiful desert pool she had envisioned, she got snow. The entire place was covered in a thin dusting of white. It depressed her. "Couldn't this have waited until spring at least?" she asked, not caring how bitter her tone was.

Michael's eyes flickered to her in disbelief. "The quakes aren't going to hold off because of the weather."

She pursed her lips and sighed. "True." She leaned her forehead against the pane of her door and instantly regretted it. It was freezing. The back of her head searched for a comfortable spot on the headrest, which considering its name, was far more difficult than it should have been. Several minutes later, the car's heater warmed her muscles up enough they could relax a little.

Normally she wasn't this irritable on their trips, but leaving last minute and being up for over thirty-six hours had a tendency to wear on even the happiest of people. Her eyes became unfocused as she stared out her window, wondering just how ridiculous a journey they were on. The once exciting idea turned questionable halfway through the plane ride. Michael had explained his theory in such perfect detail after the crushing meeting that she had gripped onto it with talons of hopeful desperation. But the truth was, the prospect of finding what he was searching for was minuscule in her mind. Impossible even. She allowed the past twenty-four hours to replay in her thoughts, over and over as they drove along the frozen, yet somehow still dusty back road.

It was on the way home from the failure of a conference when he told her the details of his theory. "The Hopi believe they came from beneath the earth," he said, throwing leery glances at her the whole time. "From inside of it."

She tilted her head and gawked at him, unable to believe what she just heard.

Ignoring her reaction, he continued, using one hand to demonstrate while the other stayed on the wheel. "The circle of divots is like a flower. The outer points are like its petals, and the center is the exact same spot the Hopi believe they entered from Below."

She could feel her eyebrows knit together and her jaw fall even further. "Are you serious?"

His expression remained the same, excited, like a little boy on a treasure hunt. *Is that what this was?* she wondered as she stared through her window at the ground passing quickly beside them. *Just another kid trying to dig their way to China?*

Her thoughts returned to the memory. "You *are* serious, aren't you?" she had asked. Her question hadn't been doubtful that time, it had been confirming. "This isn't one of your conspiracy videos, Michael! There is no Inner Earth with magical creatures."

He smiled. "You yourself said the divots looked like someone put them there."

"Yes, but Hopi mythology…"

"Come on, Cynthia." His patience waned. "It's been a while since our last excursion. All we're doing is looking. If it's nothing, no harm done. But if it's something…" His teeth gleamed in a mischievous smile, and his eyebrows danced like a silent movie villain.

He had won her over with that smile, from their first date to his marriage proposal. And now he had done it again.

"We're here," Michael announced, snapping Cynthia from her reverie. He threw the car into park and unlocked their doors.

Cynthia didn't move. The memories were holding her in place.

Michael exited the car and opened the back door. A frigid breeze blew in from it, grazing her neck and making her teeth grind together. Growling with frustration, she got out of the car and slipped on her heavy coat and gloves before weighing herself down with supplies from the trunk. Already suited up and loaded like a pack mule, Michael waited patiently for her.

"Here." He handed her a staff when she finished.

"What's this for?" she asked, zipping up her coat and taking the staff from him.

He hesitated before answering, "The hike takes several hours, and the snow may make it worse."

She grimaced.

A small box filled with sample phials and a small scraper remained in the trunk. Taking it, she attached it to her backpack with a carabiner and then shut the lid. The wind made her tighten her hood. "I wish you would at least have let me bring some probes or a tracer. I won't get much data from just a few phials of rock surface."

Michael frowned. "I told you. This is a sacred site to the Hopi people. We're not going to dig holes into their ground and place some instrument for someone to find while we're away."

Cynthia huffed. "We're trying to save the world, Michael. I think they'll let it go for that."

He took off towards the canyon's rim. "Not yet we're not. Right now we're just looking. It's bad enough we're here without permission, let alone a permit. If we get caught…" Refusing to finish that statement, he glanced over his shoulder and added with all sincerity, "If my theory is wrong, and we later find out that probing this area will help stop the quakes, I'll help you do it myself. OK?"

They stared at each other until she nodded in response. He then turned back towards the trailhead. Suddenly paranoid, she glanced around for anyone who might be curious of their actions before jogging to catch up to him. Aside from the tire marks their one car had made, there was no trace of the human existence as far as her vision allowed.

The corners of her mouth dug into her face as she pursed her lips in what was quickly becoming a habitual expression. The rejection by her peers made her feel inadequate, like she needed to get back into their acceptance. Hiking to the bottom of the Colorado River in search of the Hopi entrance to Below was not going to help her do that. If they found out what she was doing, it would only destroy what little respect they had left for her.

As they approached the trailhead, Cynthia was given even more reason not to do this. The hike down appeared rough, dangerous even. The snow made the trail hard to find, and she saw little evidence of markings. "Is this safe to do in the winter?" she asked.

He nodded. "It's not as bad as it looks, but we will have to be careful." His hand reached for hers.

She took it, questioning her actions as she did. If she didn't go through with this, it could harm her marriage. Michael would be more than hurt, he would feel mocked. It would be the conference room all over again only worse because this time it was her. But if she did do this, and those scientists found out... A smile crept up her cheeks. The only reason they would find out is if she and Michael found something, a big something, something they could prove beyond any doubt. As she peered over the rim of the canyon, down to the river below, her smile grew. She *wanted* to find something now, something so big it would wipe those smug, mocking smirks off their arrogant faces.

The initial descent was steep and foreboding. Once the rim obstructed their view of the outside world, Cynthia reached around for a sample phial. After carefully brushing the outer coating of dirt and snow off the rock face, she used her metal tool to scrape off a sample. She closed the phial and placed it back in the container.

"They've already sampled the Grand Canyon to death, you know," Michael called back over his shoulder.

"Yes, but I haven't," she mumbled under her breath before continuing on.

The snow thinned as the trail advanced. Michael climbed down a set of boulders dividing one level from the next and readjusted his gear. Once he was safely out of the way, Cynthia did the same, her back facing him. He stood behind her, though she rarely needed it; he wanted to be ready to catch her if she fell. Soon they reached level ground below the heavy rocks. "This way," he said, nodding his head south.

Before going, Cynthia took another sample.

They followed the snow-dusted cairns for several hours, crossing over icy patches and hugging the wall of the rim. The blue river below coupled with the snow bespeckled red rock of the canyon made for a stunning sight, and Cynthia had to pause several times just to admire it. "I'm sorry I complained about the scenery earlier," she said.

He puffed out a short laugh. "That's OK," he said, happy her mood had finally changed. He picked up his pace. Several yards later however, he noticed the lack of footsteps behind him and paused to see what the trouble was. She had stopped again, and was staring at the other side of the river where its many colors glistened in the rays of the sun.

He curved a gentle arm around her. "I know it's alluring, honey, but we need to keep moving if we're going to beat the night."

Cynthia unwillingly pulled her eyes away from the magnificent sight drawing them in. "You're right. I'm sorry."

Letting his arm fall, he continued the hike. She still caught a few glances after that, and even stumbled a time or two when she did, but she managed to keep up enough to prevent him from complaining.

As they descended, the temperature did just the opposite. Couple that with their vigorous physical activity, and Cynthia was soon sweating. "Hold up!"

she called. She didn't want him to get too far ahead, just in case. "It's at least ten degrees warmer down here!" She began to take off her backpack.

He helped her shrug out of it.

"Ah!" Her knees buckled slightly as her shoulders screamed in agony. After taking off her heavy coat and tying it around her waist, she gently pulled the neck of her shirt over the top of her right shoulder. The sight made her inhale through her teeth, causing a hiss. "Ooo. That's going to hurt."

Michael got closer to examine it. He groaned. "Oh, honey!" Her skin was already red, and blisters would certainly form without the padding of her coat. "Are you sure you don't want to leave your coat on for now? You don't usually have this problem."

With her mind on everything but the hike, it was no wonder she had neglected to keep her backpack in check. "I must not have kept my straps tight enough. Besides, I'm used to walking, not climbing, and not for so long with so much." She gingerly put her shirt back in place. "But I'd rather my shoulders hurt than sweat to death. Come on," she said, and held her arms back for him to thread the backpack on.

Michael frowned but did as she asked. It would take too long to wait for her shoulders to heal, and they were closer to the bottom than the top at this point. As his wife continued on ahead of him, he stared after her, worried if she would be alright, and purposefully keeping his own coat on.

An hour or so later, they reached the basin. A ribbon of blue ran next to the canyon's beach. A few sticks of wood littered its edges.

"OK. Now where?" She leaned onto her staff, her desire for rest overcoming the lure of the scenery at the moment.

Michael turned back and faced his wife. His hand reached up to cradle her tired face. Something about being out here, seeing her work so hard, it made him love her even more. "Not much longer. The worst is over. We just have to walk a few miles down this river, and we'll be there." He kissed her gently and rubbed her cheek with his thumb. "It'll all be worth it in the end."

She smiled, not wanting to ruin the moment for him, but wanting to ensure he realized the reality of the situation. "And if we don't find anything?"

He returned her smile. "Then we'll have at least tried."

He was right. At least they tried. Well, he had. She was just there in support.

A wave of severe guilt flowed through her like the sand in the Colorado River they now stood by. It ripped away her insides as it went. How many times had he supported her? She remembered his behavior at the conference. *But that was only because he already had this in mind,* she placated herself. The guilt was still there though. She knew the truth no matter what she tried to believe, and it made her feel terrible for not treating him the same way he had treated her. She made the decision to be more supportive and less selfish from then on.

He was already several yards ahead of her, but before she started again, she took quick samples of the sand and the rock face.

"You coming?" he called over his shoulder without stopping.

"Yeah." She hurriedly put the phials in their box and ran to catch up, wincing from the bounce of her backpack as she went.

As the sun fell behind the canyon wall, the shadows played tricks with their exhausted eyes, causing them to stumble over small rocks and jump at false nearby movements. At last, a large darkness appeared against the cliff.

"Here we are!" Michael announced. He was as tired as she was, but his excitement countered it until there was once again a spring in his step.

The opening of a small cave sat high in the canyon's wall before them. Cynthia had to tilt her head back to see it. "I hope you brought your hook."

Michael grinned. "Of course. Never leave home without it." He removed his backpack and placed it on the ground, unzipped it, and reached inside to extract a rope tied to a well-used, retractable grappling hook. He gave the top a slight twist before pushing it down, causing the fingers of the hook to spring open, and then tightened the top back into place. Cynthia took several steps back, shielding herself behind a tall boulder and allowing Michael to safely slingshot the hook onto the bottom of the cave's floor. The familiar *clink* told her it was safe to come out.

A few tugs to ensure its catch later and Cynthia was using it to pull herself into the cave. Michael attached her backpack to the rope. After she pulled both packs up separately, Michael began his climb. While waiting for him to join her, she reached into the front pocket of her pack and retrieved a head lamp. Uncle Gus may collect more than his fair share of gadgets, but they had their moments. This was one of them. Michael pulled himself onto the cave floor, dusted his clothes off, and wound up the rope before stowing it away. More of the cave lit up before them when he clicked his light into place.

She took a quick sample from inside the cave wall before donning her gear and tightening it as much as she could. Hopefully the rest of the journey would be an easy walk and not bother her shoulders so much.

"Ready?" He was standing several yards ahead of her and bouncing on his toes like a kid going to Disney.

"Ready," she said. Her smile was unstoppable.

"So the Earth isn't a planet," Brandon confirmed Gus's words back to him, still not sure he had processed them correctly.

"Yes," Gus replied.

"It's actually a giant machine that just *looks* like a planet on the outside." Brandon had his foot on the seat and was propped on his knee.

Gus glanced into his rearview mirror. "Yes."

Brandon stared at his uncle in disbelief, who despite just telling the most ridiculous story Brandon had ever heard, told it with such certainty he couldn't help but take it seriously. "And Mom and Dad—"

"Your parents didn't know what to expect, just that there might be something to the Hopi legends. So they followed the legend. That's when they discovered that our planet—"

"—is really a giant machine." His words were almost a whisper. "So why are we joining them? Why aren't they telling all the scientists who laughed at them the truth? Wait, is this going to be a cover-up conspiracy?"

Gus shrugged. "I don't know."

Brandon felt his eyes widen. That wasn't supposed to be a serious question.

"Their phone died before they could tell me much. The only way they can use their phones is to plug them into the car they rented, and they hardly had enough daylight to make the phone call to begin with."

"I don't understand," Brandon said.

Gus's phone spoke before he did. "In a quarter mile, turn right."

"Well,"—He put on his blinker and turned right onto a deserted road—"to reach the entrance, they have to take a long hike outdoors. And that hike is barely traversable both ways in one day, especially with what little sunlight we get in February. So by the time they made it to their car, got enough juice in their phone to make the cal—"

"I got it. I got it." Brandon wrapped his hands around his arms and suppressed a slight shiver. Gus responded by turning up the heat. "I thought deserts were hot," Brandon said, annoyed.

"Not in the winter. It gets cold like everywhere else, only drier."

"Glad I brought a coat," Brandon mumbled. As they bumped along the dirt road, Brandon thought he saw white on the ground. "Tell me that's sand."

"What?"

"That. That white stuff. Tell me that's not snow!"

Gus glanced around, nonchalant. "Probably."

Brandon held back a groan and let his head fall back against the seat.

>>

"In one thousand feet, your destination will be on the right," announced the emotionless voice of direction.

The car slowed as Gus peered through its windows, searching.

"You have reached your destination."

Gus's eyes squinted further, and a worried expression dominated his face. "What's wrong?" asked Brandon.

Gus shook his head unknowingly for a moment before widening his eyes and exclaiming, "Ah!"

Brandon followed his gaze to find another car, similar to theirs. "Is that them?"

As Gus parked their vehicle next to the other one, Brandon could tell it had been there for some time. Abandoned. Empty. His stomach fell. "Where are they?"

Gus turned off the car and pulled out the keys. "I told you, inside the earth."

"It doesn't look like they've driven that car in a long time. Is it broken?"

Gus shook his head and reached to open his door. "I don't guess so."

"Wait," said Brandon. "If they can't go anywhere, how are they eating? *What* are they eating?" He gasped. "Is that what all the food's for? Are they starving?"

Gus stopped what he was doing and faced his nephew. "They're perfectly fine, Brandon," he said with warm sincerity. "I just spoke with them last night, remember?"

His uncle's words were soothing, but Brandon's anxiety persisted. He knew they still had several hours ahead of them, and he didn't want to wait that long for all the details. Gus had told him he would understand when they got there and that he didn't know everything himself, but that only made Brandon more frustrated.

The sound of a popped trunk forced Brandon to grab his coat from the backseat and get out of the car. The lid of the trunk obscured Gus's torso as he unzipped the large case. He removed the small bags from the pack and filled them with items from the larger case before stuffing what tiny air pockets of backpack remained with anything else he could. "Come here," he said.

Brandon obliged.

"Turn around and hold out your arms."

As Brandon followed his order, Gus slipped a heavy backpack onto him and cinched it snug. He then began to tie the smaller bags onto the bottom, trying to keep them from dangling too low or bouncing to the point of annoyance as they hiked. Brandon stood there, facing his uncle, arms still outstretched, and wondering how in the world he could walk with what had to be the equivalent of a small elephant tied to his back.

Then Gus did the same to himself, only his bags looked heavier. Brandon started to say something but bit his tongue. His uncle obviously had this all planned out, and arguing about who carried which bag would only add to the time it took them to get to their destination. Gus made one last search of the car for anything left behind before snapping the trunk shut and remotely locking the car. "Let's go."

The moment they approached the trailhead cairns, Brandon stopped walking. The view of the canyon itself was astounding, but he was more concerned with where Gus was taking them. It didn't resemble a normal hiking trail with mostly flat terrain and a wide enough path. This trail had oversized rocks, skinny ledges, and hairpin turns that made it look like it had been rearranged by an angry titan. *Great*, thought Brandon. *Is someone going to tell me they're real too now?*

"Are you sure this is safe?" he asked.

Not having realized his nephew had stopped behind him, Gus turned around and said with a surprised expression, "Of course."

That's it? thought Brandon. *That's all the answer he's giving me?* He clinched his teeth together and grudgingly followed Gus to the depths below.

What snow lay on the ground had been brushed away before them by Cynthia and Michael along the trail, making it easier to follow, but the hike still took until the last rays of sunlight disappeared behind the canyon's rim. "Now where?" asked Brandon, panting, tired, sore, and thoroughly irritated. The hike hadn't been as bad as he'd imagined. It had been worse: climbing over boulders, clinging onto the ledge while sidestepping who-knew-how-high above ground. As far as Brandon was concerned, there better be a whole civilization where they were headed, because he had no intentions of making the trip back up.

Gus pulled out a slip of paper with a few random words scribbled on them, and mumbled:

"Hopi Trail"

"Northeast"

"fifty feet"

"food"

"climbing gear"

He then twisted his head to the northeast and squinted his eyes. Brandon stepped next to him and tried to see what he was searching for. In the depths of the shadows, higher up than he wanted to climb, was the dark outline of a small cave opening. "How are we—?"

A low, constant buzz interrupted him. It came from Gus who was now several feet away, twirling a rope with some heavy thing on the end. "Watch out," he said frivolously.

Despite his unconcerned warning, Brandon took heed and backed away several paces, splashing into the river as he did.

Clink! When the heavy object on the end of the rope hit the bottom of the cave floor, Brandon made out what it was, a grappling hook.

"Where did you get *that*?" Of all the gizmos and gadgets his uncle collected, a grappling hook was a bit on the absurd side.

"What? Oh, this?" Gus asked, tugging on the line. "Oh, my neighbor Ray dropped some Christmas lights down his chimney one year, and I used this to fish them out."

Brandon rolled his eyes. Only *he* would perform such a task in the oddest way possible.

"There." Gus pulled on the straps of his backpack, ensuring they were secure. Then he did the same to Brandon.

"Ow." Brandon winced.

Gus grimaced with concern. "Is it the straps?"

Brandon nodded, reaching for his shoulders as he did.

Gus sighed. The fact Brandon was in pain bothered him. Seeing to his comfort and safety was his job, and he obviously hadn't done it well enough. "Well, don't move your backpack any more than you have to. We've got a long way to go yet."

Brandon groaned. The thought of continuing their hike for several more hours made him want to curl up to the nearest rock and wait for his family to finish this insane quest without him. Not that he ever wanted to come in the first place. "Why couldn't my parents have been janitors?" he mumbled under his breath.

"What?" Gus asked.

"Nothing."

Gus picked up the rope and pulled it out at an angle, inviting Brandon to go first. He would keep a better eye on him from here on. Brandon grabbed it with one hand and propped himself on the rim's wall with his legs until he was horizontal with the ground. He had to bite his lip to keep from crying out in the pain the shifting weight of his backpack caused. Slowly, he made his ascent. Gus soon followed.

It was too dark to see anything inside the cave. Even if the afternoon sun were to shine its slanted rays into it, Brandon doubted he would be able see twenty feet past the entrance. Soon after rolling up the rope and stowing it away, Gus handed Brandon a headlamp and donned his own. They both flipped the ends up, resulting in narrow, but solid beams of light to shine before them.

"This way." Gus nodded toward the back of the cave.

The entryway was short, like a small hallway, with the same red color as the rock outside. It opened into a larger chamber which resembled a living room of sorts. There was recent debris scattered with the old, mainly where Natives, both now and long ago had made their pilgrimages. The rest was where others had desecrated the area with offerings of crystals and other such items.

Past it was a narrow tunnel, large enough for them to walk comfortably one behind the other. Gus stopped and grabbed the rock wall with his hand.

"What's wrong?" asked Brandon. No sooner had he spoken those words then dust fell from the ceiling. The earth shook beneath him. Fear rose from his chest into his throat, his face, his fingers. A quake at home or in a school building was one thing, but underneath the earth itself… He fell to all fours while the gentle tremor continued to vibrate the ground underneath the palms of his hands. More dust fell, onto his neck, his back, and into his clothes. He raised his head to stare at the ceiling, wondering if just enough pieces would fall on him to knock him out or break bones, or enough to kill him completely. His gaze shifted to his uncle. Gus showed no worry, only interest, like he was studying the effects of the quake.

It stopped. Relief spread through Brandon, and he slowly rose back to his feet. He blinked rapidly to clear his eyes of their excess moisture from the dust, then checked his footing, securing his belief the ground was still stable.

"Mmmm," Gus hummed in wonderment before continuing on, not even bothering to dust the tiny pebbles from his hair.

Brandon tried to swipe what he could off the back of his shorts and shake it out of his shirt. "Are you sure we're safe in here?"

"As safe as anywhere with a ceiling until these quakes stop," Gus answered morosely.

Brandon told himself his uncle was right. It didn't help much.

They followed the tunnel for about half a mile before Brandon's stomach growled, reverberating off the nearby walls.

"Oh, sorry," Gus said in response. "We should probably eat. We've got a long trek ahead of us."

"*How* long?" Brandon whined before gingerly removing his backpack and placing it on the ground next to his feet.

"Several miles." Gus set his backpack down as well and opened it up, removing a box of nut bars.

"Several *miles?*" Brandon grabbed an offered bar.

His uncle looked up at him with wide, innocent eyes. "Yes. Of course."

Brandon tried to swallow but couldn't. "What do you mean, 'Yes. Of course.'?" He forced the words around the sweet, chewy bite in his mouth.

Gus's face remained innocent. "Well, if it were close to the surface, we would know about it already, wouldn't we?"

Finally able to swallow, Brandon said, "I don't understand."

Gus sat on the ground and leaned his back against the wall. After chewing thoughtfully for a moment, he reached into the bag where he retrieved a jug of water. Instead of refilling his canteen, he chugged from the jug's mouth. He then lifted it in offering to Brandon.

Brandon shook his head. "No thanks."

Gus replaced the cap and sat the jug down. He continued to chew for several seconds before explaining, "According to your parents, the entry point appeared to be concealed prior to the quakes. Which, given everything else, makes perfect sense. You would want the façade to be complete, with no breaks to ruin the illusion, the design."

Brandon nodded like he understood, which he thought he did, then stopped. "Wait a minute. What design?"

"From the Ant People. Remember?"

Brandon felt his face twist into an extreme expression of stupor. "The what?"

"The Ant People," Gus answered, wondering why his nephew didn't remember such an important detail.

Brandon's head slowly shook from side to side. "I think you forgot to tell me that part."

A slight pink heated Gus's cheeks, but the LED made it too white to see. "I'm sorry." He hated that his memory was only getting worse with time. "The Hopi believe the Ant People came from Above, or outer space, and that man lived within the Earth while the outside was being formed. Once it was finished, they exited Below and lived on its surface."

Brandon blinked slowly. He couldn't accept what he was hearing. "So Mom and Dad believe Earth was created by alien *Ant* People?"

With a wave of his bar-filled hand, Gus said, "No, no, no. Well." He speculated a moment. "Maybe."

Brandon's eyes got wider.

Gus continued, "From what they can tell, the creators were as humanoid as we are. So if they were Ant People, Ant People greatly resemble humans."

Brandon reached out for the wall of the cave and used it to sit on the floor. His face had paled.

Gus looked him over, but figured he was OK for now. "What did you think we were doing?" he asked, taking another bite of his bar.

"I don't know." He paused. "I mean, I knew we were traveling to the center of Earth, or, really far down anyway, and that you said Earth was a machine, but alien *ants*?"

Gus pushed himself away from the wall so he could peer straight into Brandon's eyes. "Who did you think made it? The Atlantians?"

His uncle wasn't smirking, for which Brandon was grateful. His words still came out in a sputter when he answered, "I don't know. It just... I guess that part never occurred to me."

It was Gus's turn to look bewildered. "Oh," he said, then leaned back against the wall.

After several long moments, Brandon resumed his eating. With a grunt, Gus stood and reached for the water jug again. He had finished his meal.

This time Brandon took it. "Will we have enough?" he asked, holding out the jug in reference.

Gus waited for him to finish drinking before taking the jug and putting it away. "Yes. The water there is fine."

Brandon glanced down at his nut bar. Silently he calculated the amount of food they had brought with them and divided it by four. Unless they were grabbing his parents and leaving, in which case they would need half of the food they brought, what they brought wouldn't last long. "Is there food?"

"There is, and it's fine too."

Brandon nodded, wondering more now than before what to expect when they arrived. "Then why did we bring so much?"

Gus smiled. "Your parents don't like it." He stood, picked up his backpack and refastened its straps. "Ready?"

Brandon did the same, his face twisting in agony as the straps dug into his even more sore shoulders. He then picked up their wrappers and tightened his belts. "Ready."

They resumed their journey. The path sloped steeply downhill, causing their shoes to slip periodically on the dust and tiny pebbles. Every time they did, a shot of adrenaline burned the back of Brandon's throat. It wasn't just his own stability he was uneasy about, he worried about his uncle's too. Gus kept holding the walls for support, which slowed their descent. Brandon stayed far enough behind him, he hoped, that if one of them stumbled, they didn't take the other with them.

They made two more pit stops, snacking while they rested. Brandon kept his backpack on both times. "Why an illusion?" he asked during one of them. They were far too out of breath to talk much while hiking.

"What do you mean?"

"You said it would ruin the illusion of a planet instead of a machine if they didn't hide the entry point. Why did that matter?"

Gus's brow rose, and he shrugged. "Who knows? If aliens are the ones who built this, then … maybe they wanted to keep us from leaving it, like a prison."

"That's depressing. We're prisoners of long-gone aliens?"

"Well." He drew his word out. "I'm just throwing out ideas here. Maybe it was a vacation spot, a place for them to escape everything, and they didn't want to spoil the scenery with gadgets and such."

"I like that idea better," Brandon said around a large bite of nut bar. He stared mindlessly at the wall across from them, studying its knobs and dips. They ate in silence for several minutes.

Brandon asked, "So what else did they tell you?"

"Who?"

"My parents," Brandon said as though the answer were obvious, which to him it was.

"Oh." Gus shook his head. "They didn't have time to tell me much. Like I said, they were fighting daylight. You saw how long that hike took. Imagine going both ways in one day."

Brandon shuddered at the thought.

"By the time they gave me instructions and directions, it was time for them to start back. Your mother said something about the Hopi's emergence story being true, and she was gone." He snapped his fingers. "Just like that."

Brandon watched as he ate more of their food.

"I had to look up the Hopi legend for myself."

The more his uncle explained, the more confused Brandon got. He decided not to ask any more questions and just wait till they got there to see for himself. Another mile later, Brandon was ready for some real food. Nut bars and water were great and all, but he wanted meat. Salty, greasy, meat. A burger sounded nice, a real burger, not some nasty fast food imitation. As his mouth salivated and he held back a mournful groan, the tunnel opened up into another small room. This one had less debris than the first one, but still showed signs of tourists and worshippers. The trash was older and more sparce, like this place got less visitors than the areas near the entrance.

A few steps in, Gus stopped and shone his light on the room's wall. Eyes squinted, he slowly rotated his head while scanning in an up and down motion before landing on a skinny gap within the otherwise solid rock.

Brandon ran his fingers down the inside of the gap. "It looks fresh."

The beam of Gus's light bobbed as he nodded in response. "Yes, it does."

"Do you think the quakes formed it?"

His uncle turned to face him, a large grin spread across his face. "Why yes, Brandon. I believe they did." He continued to admire it for another minute or so before turning sideways and trying to squeeze himself inside. Realizing he wouldn't fit, he removed his backpack and tried again, this time with success.

After several minutes, Gus's light disappeared, so Brandon shone his own into the crevice and searched for him. "Uncle Gus? Are you there?"

There was no response.

"Uncle Gus! Are you—"

"I'm through!" Gus answered, his voice echoing in what sounded like another open area.

Brandon released a heavy breath. "Don't *do* that to me!"

Gus returned to the crack and said with his lips pressed against the rock's opening, "Do what?"

The confines of the crack magnified his voice to a deafening level and caused Brandon to jerk back in response. "Nothing," he muttered in exasperation.

"Can you make it through?" Gus asked.

Brandon glanced down at Gus's dropped backpack, then took a peek over his shoulder at his own. He loosened its belt and gingerly slid the straps off his shoulders. "Not with these bags." It landed next to him with a muffled thump.

The sounds of grunting and scraping, coupled with random flashes of Gus's light, told Brandon his uncle was nearly back through. "Sorry about that." His body still wedged in the crack, Gus reached his hand out. "Here. I'll take one."

Brandon handed the top loop of the backpack to his uncle, then grabbed hold of his own. While dragging their luggage behind them against the stubborn rocks, they squeezed their way to the other side of the crevice.

It couldn't have been over fifteen feet long, but the pressure of the rock wall on his chest and the difficult foot pattern he had to use made Brandon's anxiety rise, and the journey seem never ending. When the way ahead did become clear, and he could see his uncle's light reflecting off the walls of the new room, he lay his head back against the rock behind him and smiled with giddy relief. The last few steps felt lighter after that.

Brandon stepped out into the floor, leaving his backpack on the ground next to his uncle's. The air here smelled different, less earthy, more … sterile, clean … metallic. Gus was in front of him, perusing the area with his headlamp. The room was the size of an overly large living room, or a small, two-roomed house. Its walls, red rock where the crevice ended, diffused perfectly into metal halfway across. There was no joint, no bulge, nothing to indicate the rock and metal were two different materials. Brandon rubbed his fingers along the changing point. It felt smooth, flawless, organic.

The other end of the room was strikingly different from the end they entered into. Made entirely of metal, it contained a single small door. Excited yet cautious, the pair approached it.

"I'm guessing we need to open this," said Brandon.

Gus used his light to skim the outer edge of it. Finding nothing, he looked above it and waved his hand as though expecting there to be a motion detector or something similar.

His actions caused Brandon to stand next to him and follow his gaze. "I don't see anything," he said, his light streaking back and forth as his head moved.

"I didn't either," replied Gus. "But you never know."

While Gus continued in his attempts to get in, Brandon tried his own method. He ran his hands around the wall encompassing the door. Several feet up, and about a foot to the side, he felt a hollow spot, a small impression which his fingers fell into. He pressed it. The door slid out of their way.

Before them lay a room lined entirely in the same metal as the second half of the previous room. Large enough to hold a school bus, it was empty, barren, save for a small panel set into the wall and a large rectangle in the floor. Brandon walked to the rectangle's edge and looked down at it. As he did, the room lit up, causing him to stumble backwards onto the floor in alarm. Crabwalking himself away from the floor's indention, he twisted his head around to his uncle, whose astonished expression wasn't comforting.

"What just happened?" No sooner had he asked than he noticed Gus's hand dropping from the panel in the wall.

"Found the lights," Gus said.

Brandon picked himself up off the floor. "A little warning would have been nice."

"I wasn't sure that's what would happen," Gus responded, his tone full of innocence and happy wonder.

"So you just randomly pressed buttons even though you have no idea what they'd do?" He couldn't believe anyone could be that stupid. "What if one of them got us killed?"

"Highly unlikely. Why would anyone install a button so easily pressed in the dark, even if they knew what they were doing, that would kill themselves?"

"I don't know! A booby trap?" Brandon's shock and anger made his voice come out raspy.

Gus, no longer intrigued by the lighting, returned to the panel. "This isn't Indiana Jones, Brandon."

"Even so, you don't just press buttons without some idea as to—" but Brandon realized his words were wasted.

Gus wasn't listening. He was analyzing the panel. Each button had a tiny icon embedded into it, indicating its function. The one Brandon presumed his uncle had pressed for light had a tiny sun with rays. Two more had half arrows, one up, one down, and another had a rectangular shape for its icon.

"Old technology," noted Brandon, wondering why everything was in buttons instead of touchscreen or something more modern. The panel looked more at home in an old elevator than an underground alien bunker.

"I believe you will find that some of your 'older' technology is better than the new. For example, buttons and switches are far more easily replaced and last longer than their modern counterparts."

An image of his friend's old phone came to Brandon's mind. Its screen had stopped responding to commands, but its buttons still worked without fail. He pulled down the corners of his mouth in thought. *Maybe simpler was better sometimes*, he pondered to himself.

"Wonder what this is supposed to do." Gus was pressing the button with the up arrow repeatedly while allowing his gaze to search the room.

Nothing happened. Gus changed his testing to the down arrow. "Hmmm…" Still nothing.

"Maybe the door has to be shut first," suggested Brandon.

"Hmm?" Gus stared at him with a questioning expression.

Brandon pointed at the button with the rectangle shape. "Maybe we have to shut the door. Like you can't move an elevator with the door open kind of thing?"

"Oh!" Revelation resounded in Gus's voice. His finger hovered over the button. "We should probably get our bags first though.

"Oh, right. Sorry." Brandon retrieved the bags, excitement quickly overcoming his exhaustion and hunger.

As soon as Brandon reentered the metal room, Gus pressed the button.

A thick, heavy door slid into place. It gave Brandon an ominous feeling, like being trapped. "I'm guessing Mom didn't have time to tell you about this place."

Gus shook his head. "No. Unfortunately not." He pressed the up arrow again. It lit up this time, and stayed lit when he removed his finger. But there was still no noise or movement to suggest the button had done anything.

"Is it working?" asked Brandon.

Gus began to walk around the edge of the room, stepping over their bags when he got to them. He allowed his hands to explore the walls as he went. After he made one complete circle, he said, "I can't find anything." He brought his hand to his chin and pinched it, thinking. His other hand perched on the side of the panel and his eyes squinted into near slits, their gaze searching for anything he might have missed.

There was a small, black button on the side. Brandon hadn't seen it earlier. It had no icon. "What about this one?" he asked.

"I'm afraid to press this one till I know what it does," Gus answered.

"You pressed the light button without knowing," Brandon countered.

"Yes, but it had a symbol on it. While I wasn't *sure* that's what would happen, I had a good idea."

Brandon reached over to press the black button anyway. "We've got nothing to lose at this point," he insisted. There was a slight click, like speaker static, every time he pressed it. They both pricked their ears and listened. Nothing.

"Whew! It's hot in here!" Gus walked over to the backpacks and threw his coat onto them.

"Feels fine to me." Brandon shrugged.

Gus's gaze scanned the ceiling of the room once again. "This place must be climate controlled, but I can't tell how. The temperature's fine without my jacket."

Brandon crossed his arms and leaned against the wall, waiting for whatever would happen next.

Seconds later, a whining noise emanated from beneath the flooring, causing both of them to stare down at it. Brandon immediately wished the door was still open in case they needed to run. He would have opened it himself but was too captivated by what was happening before them.

The sound of sliding metal echoed throughout the chamber as the floor's rectangle slowly opened. Hot air, filled with a smell not unlike Gus's house, hit Brandon in the face. It was followed by the rounded nose of a metallic vehicle, a shuttle of sorts, coming straight up out of the hole like a slow, blunt-ended rocket. A single arm extended from its side and out onto the floor, reminding Brandon of a landing gear. This arm gradually lowered the vehicle until it sat horizontal on the floor before them, similar to how a subway car would sit. The vehicle lowered itself to a few inches off the floor, spun around gradually until it faced the opposite direction, then sat itself down, causing the room to go silent once more.

Brandon's wide eyes stared at the vehicle for several seconds. "What is it?" he finally asked.

Gus's face carried a big grin. "Why, our way there."

CHAPTER 8

"In *that*?" Brandon's voice hit a higher octave than he would have liked on his last word. The change from earthy caves to alien shuttles had hit him with an unexpected dose of reality.

Gus grabbed his backpack and walked towards their new ride. "It would seem so, yes."

"Didn't they tell you about this part?"

"No. They didn't have time to, I suppose."

"I guess, but—" Brandon thought a shuttle was a rather important detail that needed mentioning to someone coming to help you, time or no time. "Wait. What's this?" A symbol of a patchwork circle cradled by two hands marked the shuttle's side.

Gus leaned in to study the symbol. "It's probably a logo representing the ones who built all of this."

"The Ant People?" screeched Brandon. "Are we going to visit a bunch of aliens that live under the earth?"

Gus's eyes widened, and he bit down on what Brandon could only presume was a large grin. "No, Brandon. There are no Ant People. While your parents didn't mention any aliens over the phone, or the lack thereof, they did tell me the place was abandoned."

"So it's just us down there?"

Gus tilted his head at him in question.

"Me, you, Mom, and Dad?" Brandon clarified.

"Yes," Gus answered slowly. "Just the four of us."

Brandon breathed a little easier with that knowledge.

Gus walked over to the shuttle and began knocking on its side. "Unless of course there's something hiding somewhere, or your parents didn't search everywhere yet, and there's an entire alien civilization in the other half they didn't find." Turning to see his response, he saw Brandon standing petrified, with horror-filled eyes and a green face. Gus chuckled and went back to his knocking. "Hello?" *Knock knock knock.* "Hello?"

Brandon didn't think his joke was funny, but he couldn't come up with strong enough words to tell him that.

By the time Gus circled the shuttle twice, Brandon had forgotten about the joke and became more concerned with the present. "Where are they?" he asked. The lack of answers to Gus's "Hello's", and therefore lack of his parents' presence, made him nervous.

Gus was pensive, but unconcerned. "I don't know."

If Brandon's frustration with his uncle grew much more, he felt sure he would have what some people call "an episode". And even though he wasn't sure what "an episode" was outside of a TV series, he guessed it wouldn't be pretty.

"They may not be in it," said Gus. "If we're the ones who called the shuttle, if it wasn't them who sent it, then they *wouldn't* be in it. They would be waiting for us at …. wherever this goes to."

"Then why did you knock on it?"

Gus shrugged and hummed an "I don't know." tune. "Just seemed the right thing to do."

Despite the annoyance of his actions, Gus's explanation made sense once Brandon thought about it. It wasn't like a door popped open or anything when the shuttle surfaced, so knocking on it wasn't the most ridiculous action to take. Brandon forcibly calmed himself and started searching for an opening. Minutes later, his hand reached inside a slight bump in the otherwise smooth exterior. "Try this."

Gus joined him. Underneath the bump was a small plate, reminding Brandon of a car door handle. He squeezed it. An otherwise imperceptible door popped out and hinged open. Light illuminated the interior. Brandon stuck his head inside first. "Mom? Dad?" There was no answer. He stepped back, asking his uncle, "What do you think?"

Gus took a quick look inside then strolled around the outside to the back of the vehicle, scrutinizing it from all angles. He peered down the bottomless shaft it had emerged from, his face one of thrilled interest. His eyes soon tightened, however, as he sucked in his lips. He had found something. "I believe it is electromagnetically propulsed."

Brandon raised his eyebrows. "What, like a roller coaster?"

Gus nodded. "Yes, exactly like a roller coaster."

"Does that mean…" Brandon's stomach turned over. He wasn't in fear of roller coasters, quite the contrary, but he knew the earth was several thousand miles wide, or something like that anyway, and the vision of being shot across it at unimaginable speeds, even halfway, was more intimidating than a three-minute ride at Sam's Island.

"Mean what?" Gus righted himself and stared at his nephew.

"Won't we be going a little fast?" Brandon asked.

"We'll be going very fast," he answered with a chuckle. "Ready?" he asked, grinning like a little kid. The image didn't ease Brandon's apprehension in the least bit.

"Uh… sure." Brandon lied, then grabbed their bags and followed him into the shuttle.

The inside held a pleasant feeling in the air. One padded bench circled around the entire outer edge, leaving the middle area open. Brandon dropped their bags in the floor and sat on the dark purple cushion. There were no seatbelts, no restraints, nothing to indicate the shuttle was about to turn sideways and slingshot them thousands of miles in the blink of an eye in a safe manner. Brandon's fears returned. He wanted real answers this time. "Um, Uncle Gus?"

But before he could make his demands, the sound of the door closing grabbed him by the throat in trepidation. He jumped up from his seat. "What are you doing?"

Gus asked in worried surprise, "What's the matter?"

"You saw how this thing came up. What's to stop us from falling all over the place when it goes back down? Sideways!"

His uncle's face was sincere and devoid of any concern. "Calm down. Don't get in a panic. Something must stop us, or else blood and guts would be all over the place in here. Unless you saw another method of reaching your parents, they've taken this route, twice at least, and done just fine."

No, Brandon hadn't seen another route. He sagged onto the bench with a sigh. His uncle was going. Of that, there was no doubt. He could demand to be let out, then wait until his food and water ran out and he was forced to hike back to two rentals cars he couldn't drive. That option gave him a sense of abandonment, isolation of the worst kind. The fact his uncle was crazy was indisputable, but it was the good kind of crazy, annoying at times but not the hallucinogenic type. So, yes, his parents must have come this way. He saw the car. They told Gus how to get here. The hike down had been real. Others had been in the cave; they had seen evidence of that. This was the only path to take from where they stood, meaning, his parents must have taken the shuttle and survived or else they would not have been able to call for help. Or, as his uncle so beautifully put it, their guts would be splattered all over the inside of the shuttle.

He took a deep breath. "Do you know how to get it moving?"

Gus walked around the inside, searching for an answer to that very question. "That's what I'm looking for right now."

Accepting the fate of his decision to remain with his uncle released the anxiety and fear that had been building in his chest. The elastic bands of his headlamp squeezed into his head. He pulled it off, feeling silly for having it on all this time, especially since he caught his uncle doing the same thing in the car to the airport. A chuckle found its way out of his throat. What a day! He was hungry. His legs hurt. He needed to use the bathroom. Maybe he could curl up on the bench and take a nap. When he woke up he might get lucky and discover everything was all a dream. Perhaps it was all a dream. He pinched himself. "Ouch!"

Gus whipped his head around with that same expression of concern again. "What's the matter? Did you hurt yourself?"

"Nothing. I'm fine." He never understood why people pinched themselves to wake up anyway. It was a stupid thing to do in his opinion. Weren't people able to dream pain too?

Unable to keep himself upright any longer, he lay sideways on the bench. As soon as the side of his face hit the cool cushion, however, the vehicle moved. In which direction he wasn't able to tell, but he detected it pulsating beneath him. He rose up to see Gus standing near the rear of the shuttle, his hand hovering over a small depression at the ceiling. "What did you just do?" asked Brandon.

Gus lowered his arm, still searching for something. "I believe I told it to go. Now if only I can find — ah ha!" He pressed laterally against the wall just above the bench opposite Brandon. It slid to the side.

"A window!" Brandon jumped closer to it and watched the world literally pass by.

Gus moved out of way and slid open another panel a few feet over from that one. The outside, too dark to see any details, blurred past at a dizzying rate. Brandon grabbed the back of the bench he was kneeling on out of instinct and started to pant slightly. The combination of fast and slow had twisted his stomach. He couldn't understand how it was possible for them to be traveling at this speed when it felt like they were barely moving at all. The floor's vibration was so slight, he didn't even notice it anymore unless he tried to. He slid the panel shut and sat on the bench, facing the door they had entered from. Swallowing several times, he tried to get the queasiness to settle.

"Wow! Look at that!" Gus whispered hoarsely.

"I already did." Brandon rested his elbows on his thighs and held his head in his hands.

Gus rapped the window with his knuckles. A low thud sounded, like he had hit wood instead of glass. He placed his palm on it. "Warm. This should be cold…" He glanced at Brandon. "Are you OK?"

Brandon swallowed, keeping his eyes directed at the floor and deliberately out of focus. He tried closing them, but that made it worse. "Yeah. As long as this doesn't take too long."

Gus sat down beside him. "I don't think the windows are made of glass. They sound too muffled when I knock on them, and they're too warm to the touch. Real glass would be—"

"Uncle Gus?" Brandon had to swallow the extra saliva about to drip from his lips.

"Sorry." Gus kept the rest of his astonishments to himself. "You didn't have any trouble on the plane or in the car. What's wrong now?"

"I don't know," Brandon groaned, wishing the shuttle would stop and his uncle would shut up.

Gus gasped. "You know, you might be experiencing the effects of the inertia dampeners."

Brandon knew he would regret doing it, but he asked anyway, "The what?"

"The inertia dampeners. It's like a ballast on a sailboat. See, the large mast of the ballast prevents the wind from tipping over the boat. Whatever technology this shuttle is using to prevent us from slamming into the back as it accelerates may be related to its artificial gravity, or the reason we're being pulled to the floor even though we're currently perpendicular to the Earth's gravity. The combination of forces could be acting on your body in such a way as to…"

Brandon tuned out his uncle's voice, allowing it to become background noise. It was almost soothing enough to take his mind off the nausea.

As they neared the other end of the tunnel, light seeped in through the windows. "We're slowing down," Gus said.

"Good." Brandon readjusted his feet, bracing for what he could only assume was to come.

However, the stopping of the vehicle was as unnoticeable as the takeoff. His only clue was the end of the floor pulsating under his feet. Brandon took several deep breaths before allowing his head to rise. He stood, shakily at first but soon regaining his strength. After grabbing one of the backpacks, he didn't care which, he pressed the indented button over the door. It popped open, allowing him to push it the rest of the way.

The room they entered was identical to the one they had left, except the same cradled planet symbol from the shuttle was also on the door. He walked over to the panel and pressed the button labeled with the door opening icon. Instead of the half metal, half rock room like in the caverns, the door opened to an empty chamber with metal walls and a mesh floor. "What do we do now?" asked Brandon.

Gus crossed the chamber to the closed door on the opposite side, dragging his backpack behind him. There was no obvious way to open it. He felt around its edge, his nose practically rubbing against the wall in his search. "I don't know."

The door behind them suddenly shut. Brandon dropped his pack and ran to it, pressing his palms against it in a vain attempt to slide it back open. After several tries, he screamed at his uncle, "Help me!"

Gus joined him, and although he did help, it wasn't with the same urgency as Brandon. He had no fears, no worries. This was an adventure to him, not a trap.

A melodic, guttural voice came over invisible speakers. Gus stopped what he was doing, his ears perked. Brandon also strained to understand what was being said, but it was no use. He barely knew two complete sentences in Spanish, let alone whatever language this was.

First a click sounded, then a hiss. The air began to smell like a cross between a pungent acid and how it does after a good rain. Brandon's hands grasped for the wall, and he fell into them. "What's going on?" he gasped between pants.

Gus's penetrating gaze shifted across the room studiously as he sniffed the air. A second later, the light changed colors, raising the temperature in the room. It was not uncomfortable, but Brandon jumped away from the metallic wall in case it would get too hot.

"Are they gassing us?" he screamed. His breaths became short and quick until he was hyperventilating.

Careful not to touch his sore shoulders, Gus held Brandon by the upper arms in an attempt to calm him. "I believe," he said quietly, stroking Brandon's arms with his thumbs as he did so, "that we are being sterilized."

"What?" Brandon shot out between gasps.

The second door opened before Gus could explain any further. Two arms wrapped around Gus's neck and pulled him through the doorway. "Uncle Gus!" Cynthia shouted.

"Mom?" Brandon recognized her voice.

"Brandon!" The sight of her son after everything they had been through the past week, after being without him the entire time, made her dive and throw her arms around him in severe relief.

"Ah!" He cried out in pain when her arms grazed his shoulders.

She backed away immediately. "What's wrong? Are you hurt?"

He gingerly pulled the neck of his shirt over to show his injuries. "It's just my shoulders, from hiking all that way with the backpack."

Cynthia grimaced and nodded in understanding. "We'll take you to the hospital in just a minute."

Brandon met his mother's gaze with a shocked expression. "The *what?* How?"

"There's one in the center of the Hub," explained Michael.

Cynthia lovingly held her son's hands. "We'll show you." She smiled. She hadn't touched him like this since … he didn't remember the last time. He awkwardly tried to mirror her smile, giving her hands a light squeeze in return.

Brandon's eyes met his father's. He hoped there weren't any cameras in that sterilization room — gas chamber as far as he was concerned. He felt silly for his overreaction now it was over.

Cynthia released Brandon's hands. Michael reached up to pat him on the back in his usual manner but decided it might hurt him further, so he let his arm hang there clumsily before putting it in his pocket. "Good to see you. Did you keep the dishes done like your mother asked?"

"Seriously? Now?" Were these really the first words his father would ask him?

Michael gave him the demanding father face.

Giving in, Brandon answered, "Fine. No. I didn't do the dishes."

"What about the dusting and the bathroom and everything else that needed doing?" his mother added.

"I did do some of that."

"*Some* of that?" Cynthia eyed him, waiting for further explanation.

Gus deliberately placed himself between them. "We didn't get a chance to talk much on the phone. What have you found so far?"

Taking the hint, Michael turned his attention to Gus as pink climbed up Cynthia's neck. Brandon thought more fondly of Gus after that.

Michael placed his arm around Gus in a friendly fashion and led him down the hall. "Let's get you settled in. Did you bring the food we asked for?"

"I brought as much as I thought we could carry," he answered.

Brandon's shoulders were proof of that. Michael smiled broadly. He was getting sick of what he and his wife had dubbed "alien food" and was looking forward to something familiar, even if it was canned meat and beans.

"Uncle Gus said the food here was OK, that you just didn't like it." Brandon countered while falling in line with his mother behind the other two.

Cynthia grabbed his bag for him and answered, "It's … not what we're used to. You'll see. It's not bad; it's just … different."

Somehow her answer worried him more than the thought of going hungry.

Michael led them down the curved hallway to another doorway on the left.

Once there, Cynthia stepped in front. "This can be your room, Brandon," she said. She placed her palm onto the door and waited. A minute, orange-yellow glow emanated from beneath her palm, and the door disappeared.

"Whoa!" yelled Brandon.

Michael chuckled at Gus's expression, which was nothing less than flabbergasted. "You'll find a great deal of interesting technology here," he said.

Brandon stepped inside his "bedroom". What looked like a very soft and comfortable bed stood against the opposite wall. Its covers lay neatly across it.

"I made your bed for you," Cynthia said.

"Thanks," Brandon said habitually. Not that he cared. To him making a bed was pretty pointless since you were just going to mess it up again later.

She plopped his backpack onto the only desk in the room. "There are lights in here." She pointed to several areas around the room, some in the ceiling, the floor, the wall. "But we don't know how to use them."

"We're hoping you can help us with that," Michael told Gus.

Gus was patting his chin with his fingers, his face hovering one inch from the wall as he inspected every inch of its plain surface. "Hmm?" he hummed. "What do you mean?"

"I need my laptop up and running to understand some things around here, and I'm hoping you can do that."

When Gus gave him a quizzical stare, he explained further, "We think the lights are voice activated, and I need my computer to help figure out what words to use." He quickly held his hands up when Gus started to interrupt him. "I'll explain it all later."

Cynthia sat on the bed and smoothed out the covers. "Some of the beds were already made, others not. This room even had some trash in it, a couple of dirty glasses and bits of food. It's like they just got up and left one day."

"Um, that's really cool and all," said Brandon, and it was really cool, but right now his bladder was more pressing than his astonishment and curiosity. "But is there a bathroom I can use?"

"This way!" Cynthia jumped up with a smile and led Brandon to a side room. Its door disappeared beneath her palm in the same manner.

"Cynthia really likes what they use for a toilet here," Michael quietly told Gus. "I think she just likes not having to clean it. It *is* more hygienic. I have to say that."

In the center of the room was a seat shaped similarly to a saddle and much cleaner than any toilet Brandon had ever seen.

"When you're done," instructed Cynthia, "press this button here." She pointed to a round button on the wall.

Brandon assumed that would flush it, but he would soon come to find out it was the sonic cleaner. For him.

While Brandon took care of business, and screamed out in shock when the sonic cleaner did its job, Michael and Cynthia took Gus to his room next door.

After they settled the newcomers, Michael said, "Me and Cynthia took the room across the hall if you ever need us."

Brandon tried to nod but swayed on his feet instead.

"I realize you're tired," Cynthia said. "But you need to eat first."

Brandon shrugged in response, flinching from the pain as he did.

"Actually, you can eat second. First, I want to take care of those shoulders."

"You might want to come, too," Michael told Gus, grinning broad enough to show several teeth. "It's a sight to behold."

Gus grunted with pronounced curiosity.

Cynthia led them down the hallway, continuing in their previous direction.

They walked for several minutes. Gus paused to run his hand across the back wall then placed his cheek up against it, using his line of vision as a level as if to see if the wall were straight enough. "Is this curved?"

"Yes," said Michael with a grin. "We're in a sphere."

Gus continued to stroke and eye the wall as they walked. Brandon tilted his head and squinted his tired eyes. The slight arch of the wall was barely visible, if he tried hard enough. Cynthia and Michael stopped in front of a door and opened it to a small room with no furniture and led them inside.

When Brandon turned around, he noticed a column of buttons next to the door they just walked through. Each was labeled with an odd, hieroglyphic symbol. "Is this an elevator?" he asked.

"Yes, it is." Cynthia pushed a button near the middle, shutting the door. Brandon thought he felt the floor vibrate like the shuttle's had.

As she did so, Gus gasped. "Hieroglyphs!"

"Cuneiform." Cynthia corrected. "So far everything has been written in it, but we can't translate most of it."

Brandon didn't understand at all what his mother was talking about. He looked to his father for more information. Gus's expression, on the other hand, remained fixated on Cynthia, as though waiting for her to clarify just exactly how she knew this. Once Brandon thought about it, he wanted an explanation too; his mother was a geologist, not a linguist.

Taking in their reactions, Michael explained, "During one of my summers in college, I worked for a professor of anthropology. He introduced me to Assyrian studies, and I became intrigued." He shrugged. "I kept it up as a hobby of sorts ever since. I was never fluent, of course, but my laptop has several dictionaries on it."

The floor stopped vibrating the same moment the door reopened.

Another hallway identical to the first lay before them.

"This is the main floor of the Hub, the sphere we're in now," Michael explained after seeing their confused faces. "This level contains more than just the hospital, but we can save the rest for tomorrow."

Cynthia was way ahead of them now, walking too briskly for them to easily catch up to her. Gus and Brandon shared a look before turning to Michael for clarification.

Michael wiped away his grin with a hand. "Cynthia's … really taken to this place. It's become almost a home to her."

Gus's eyebrows rose. Brandon grimaced. He knew how his mother could get when she fixated on something. Michael led them in Cynthia's wake to the opposite side of the Hub where her palm was pressed against a dark grey door in the same manner as with the bedrooms. The door disappeared.

"This is the hospital," said Michael.

Through the grey door was an enormous room with beds, unidentifiable machinery, upright chambers, chambers encasing beds, hoses and gizmos coming out of the ceiling, and a plethora of other stuff Brandon didn't have names for.

"Up on the table." Cynthia told Brandon, patting an examining table in line with several others against one side of the room.

Michael led Gus on a tour of the hospital where they pondered over all the technology and what the purposes of items might be.

Brandon eyed his mother cautiously as he pushed himself up onto the table. Whenever she played doctor, he got hurt, especially when it involved pimples. And he didn't put pimples in too far off a category from raw blisters. "What are you going to do to me?"

She had gone off to the center of the room where a wide, octagonal podium sat. The podium contained several tools, shelves full of supplies, buttons to press, and lots of counter space. She took one of the tools and approached him with it.

"What is that?!" His body retreated from her in alarm until he was nearly lying on his back.

Her brows drew together in thought. "We don't know exactly, but it grows the skin back. We call it the rejuvenator."

"You don't know?" His voice cracked on the end.

She bit back a smile at his reaction. "It's perfectly fine. I used it on myself when we first got here."

That calmed him slightly. "For what?"

She pulled the neck of her shirt over the top of her right shoulder. The skin once blistered and sore looked brand new, better than her older, freckled skin that surrounded it. "I had the same problem as you did coming down. Worse than a sunburn."

He leaned forward and grazed the top of her shoulder with is fingers. "Does it hurt?"

She released her shirt and shook her head. "No. Its beam tickles a little though." Her nose scrunched up from the memory.

"Beam! Wait, like a laser beam?"

Cynthia rolled her eyes. and reached up to pull his shirt off his shoulders.

He pulled away again. "Are you sure?"

"Yes, Brandon," she assuaged. "I promise you'll be just fine."

He let her put her fingers under the rim of the shirt's neck, cringing uncontrollably as she did so. When she pulled it back, it was her turn to cringe.

"Oh, honey!" The raw area spanned from the edge of his shoulder to the top of his back.

He grimaced. "Yeah, it's no paper cut."

"Maybe it would be better if you took your shirt off." She carefully replaced his neckline. "I'll have more room that way."

He crossed his arms and started to take his shirt off the normal way. As his skin doubled onto itself, he cried out in pain and dropped the hem of his shirt. Cautiously, he pulled one sleeve off one arm, then the other. Then with both arms inside his shirt, he pushed the neck up and over his head, allowing the rest to slip off naturally.

Cynthia gasped. Even knowing she was about to remove all injury and pain from her son, the sight still bothered her. She blinked away the excess moisture from her eyes and held the rejuvenator in place.

A cool, blue beam emanated from the side of it, causing Brandon to inadvertently jump. "You're right. It does tickle."

Cynthia smiled.

She held the tool over one spot, only moving on to the next one once the first had healed. Brandon peered over his shoulder and watched as his raw, blistered skin turned white and sloughed off, like an old sunburn.

"How does it do that?" he asked, after his mother brushed away the discarded skin cells.

She shook her head. "We don't know. Due to the method in which the damaged skin is released, we can only assume it penetrates deep into the underlayers, causing an accelerated growth of new skin cells."

After finishing the first side, she progressed to the other. This time Brandon didn't watch. Instead, he reached up to brush his fingers against his healed shoulder.

"Don't move," she said. "You'll mess me up."

The temptation to touch his new skin was overwhelming. He faced forward and fixated on the examination beds beside them so the sight of her working didn't tempt him.

"All done." She smiled and patted him on his newly repaired shoulder.

He wiped his hand over it, brushing away any remaining dead cells before taking the time to really explore it. It was smooth, perfect, not a single flaw. "My mole's gone!" A tiny brown mole, one that had been with him his whole life as far as he knew, had disappeared without so much as a pink spot to mark its place.

Cynthia returned from putting the rejuvenator back in its place and surveyed the spot he was referring to. "Hmmm." She hummed thoughtfully and lightly rubbed her fingertips across it. Not a single bump. "We wondered what all it would heal. Interesting."

The others joined them. Gus's fingers replaced Cynthia's. "Does it get rid of wrinkles, too?"

Michael answered with a grin, "Not now, Gus. Maybe tomorrow. We need to eat first."

Gus nodded, but appeared sad and wistful.

"Come on." Cynthia smiled. "We'll show you the cafeteria."

CHAPTER 9

As Gus's eyebrows rose with interest, Brandon's fell. Cafeteria? Images of fold-up, multi-colored rectangular tables surrounded by attached circular seats filled his head.

They returned to the elevator where Brandon noticed his mother pressing the first button on the panel this time. "Are we going to the top floor?" he asked.

She nodded in response.

Brandon perceived no movement as the elevator sped past the floors, gliding by the one the shuttle and their bedrooms resided on. They only realized it reached its destination and stopped because the door opened.

A well-lit communal area spread before them. Its ceiling was domed by the slightest degree, signifying they were at the top of the sphere. Clusters of comfortable looking seats outlined the room, while tables and odd devices were scattered throughout its center. Brandon took one cautious step forward.

"It's OK, honey." His mother smiled at him. "No one's here but us."

But people had been here. Whoever built this place, whoever had lived in the center of the earth had been human. There was no other alternative. Giant fungal spores or intelligent jellyfish would not build a cafeteria, this Brandon knew. They all knew. But the overwhelming concept of it all had to remain a mystery, for now, if they were to function, to remain sane.

Cynthia walked up to the nearest apparatus, leisurely explaining its function as she went. "These are the food dispensers. You can get as much of whatever you like. The food comes in small squares. There are green squares, blue squares, red squares… Pretty much any color you want, although to be honest, the colors are dull, like they're made from real food instead of synthetic. There's also water and a couple of other drinks. We haven't tested them all, so we can only guess what's in some of them, but we haven't died yet." She chortled.

Gus asked, his eyes wide with intrigue as he took in the marvelous alien vending machine, "I'm assuming this is the food you've been living off of since your arrival?"

"Yeah," Michael sighed. "It's OK, and I'm sure it's nutritious. I haven't been hungry or sick or anything, but it's practically tasteless."

"Give it a day or two, and you'll be fighting us for those canned beans you brought," Cynthia said sardonically.

The whole idea of eating "alien" food brought an excited smile to Brandon's face. It reminded him of the old point-and-click adventure games from the nineties he had played for a while in middle school on an ancient OS emulator he used to use. He approached the machine. "Can I try a blue one?"

"You can," said Cynthia. "But I recommend the red. I think it's supposed to be meat, though what type I couldn't tell you."

"Oh, and *don't* eat the black ones," cautioned Michael. "They're a type of drug or something. I'm guessing even ancient aliens had bad recreational habits."

"Be sure to include some green for vitamins," Cynthia added.

Brandon searched his mother's face for any sign she might be joking. She wasn't. "Great," he muttered under his breath too low for anyone else to hear. "My first chance at alien food, and it has to be balanced." He raised his voice back to an audible level. "What should I drink? Is the stuff other than water nasty, or…?"

"There are a few sweet ones." His father grabbed an odd-shaped glass from the side of the vending machine. "I prefer the yellow one. It's bitter, but only just."

Brandon held the glass in his hand. One side of it came out in a dip, like it was ergonomically shaped for a human mouth to drink from efficiently. He chose to play it safe with the drink, one experiment at a time. "I'll just have the water for now."

Michael pointed where to place the cup and pushed a button above it. Pure water poured into the cup; not a single drop missed its target. Brandon took his food and sat at the nearest table. As soon as his uncle got his too, they all sat together as a family.

Gus picked up his yellow and white cubes and compared their sizes, sniffed them, and otherwise analyzed their structure and composition. "You said you were having trouble translating their language?"

"Yes," said Michael. "What small time I had with my laptop before the battery died I used to translate what I could, but that's not the problem. The problem is, these symbols don't match anything I've witnessed before." He pushed his chair back and leaned onto his knees with his elbows. "See, the earliest known cuneiform didn't contain a vast vocabulary. It gradually changed to where symbols represented syllables instead of words. But what we're seeing here, I can't explain." His face held a mixture of awe and confusion. He shook his head with his next words, uncertain. "Maybe … maybe a linguist could but… but I can't." He sat back up, falling against the back of his chair. "It's like the language here is more complete than anything found in ancient Assyria."

Secretly, Michael wanted to take his findings to that old professor, providing he was still alive. He had an open mind and would probably believe their story, keep it secret even, thrilled with the opportunity to study something so enlightening. Perhaps when they returned to the surface…

Seeing her husband was lost in his own thoughts, Cynthia finished what she presumed he was going to say. "In other words," she directed at Gus, "we need your expertise in charging our equipment. We barely had enough juice to call *you*, if you remember, and our laptops would certainly come in handy."

"So that's why you needed me to bring my tools," Gus said.

"Yes and no," she responded. "That's the easy part."

Gus's eyes widened in curiosity.

"We'll go over the hard part tomorrow." She glanced at Brandon, who was sagging over his plate like limp asparagus. "You have to be tired, and you'll think better on a full night's sleep."

Gus followed her gaze and nodded. "Probably so."

Brandon supported his heavy head with his elbow on the table and sniffed at his green cube, curling up his nose in response. It smelled of grass and pollen. The red one smelled more appetizing. He decided to try it first. His teeth went through it easily enough. Chewing wasn't difficult. It tasted salty, with a slight memory of meat, kind of like how a peanut or a mushroom tastes meaty, or even a fish, but he had to search for the flavor. He tried the green one next. It was harder to bite through, but less chewy. The back of his throat held an old memory of grass he chewed on as a curious, gullible kid. After forcing himself to swallow, he chugged some of his water before making an involuntary disgusted noise and face.

He glanced over at his parents and didn't blame them one bit for chowing down on a cold can of beans like it was a fudge brownie. It probably tasted like one compared to this.

His vision blurred as his tired eyes drooped lower … lower. He jerked his head up after nodding off again and realized everyone was staring. "What?" A half-eaten green cube detached itself from his forehead and fell to his plate with a muffled *clank*.

CHAPTER 10

The next morning, Brandon lay in bed, aching from head to toe, and trying to remember how he got there. Thankfully, the bed had surpassed its appearances. It was the most comfortable bed he had ever slept in, and he was confident his body wasn't as sore as it would have been otherwise. A slight vibration emanated from pivotal areas as he moved, making him wonder if the bed had a type of massaging technology responsible for his muscles not hurting as much as he expected.

He sat up, his bare feet touching the soft floor after he swung them off the mattress, and reached for his phone. The lack of signal made their phones almost useless down here, but not completely. Until they figure out how to work the lights, he was using his as a flashlight. He turned it on and used its glow to guide him to the wooden table where the water he didn't remember placing there stood, and took a swig.

His laptop lay next to where his water had sat. The tournament seemed eons away, as did school, his friends, even his home, but he still couldn't keep from fixating on it. He sat his glass down and rubbed his face in his hands, trying to remember what day it was now. Sunday. It was Sunday. The tournament was over. His dreams of a scholarship, of becoming a game designer, popped like a cartoon bubble in front of his face.

He blamed his parents. They never did have his best interests in mind, he thought. He couldn't think of a single good reason for them to want him here, unless it was to destroy his life, which it was doing. Not that visiting an alien underworld wasn't amazing and all that, but couldn't it have waited twenty-four hours? Just twenty-four measly little 'ol hours?

The glow of his phone disappeared as it turned itself off. When he turned it back on, he noticed a handwritten note from his mother propped against the wall. "We're in the cafeteria. Top floor. If you can't remember how to get there, stay in your room, and we'll come get you when we're done."

The imagined voice of his mother reading the note fed his anger. Why *did* they need him here? He threw on a clean set of clothes and walked to the elevator, determined to speak his mind and get some answers.

As soon as the elevator doors opened to reveal the cafeteria, his father's jovial voice called, "There you are, sleepyhead!"

Cynthia smiled affectionately at him. They were making it awfully difficult to start yelling straight away. He ignored them and went to the vending machine instead.

"Brandon?" Michael called.

Brandon remained silent.

"Is everything alright?"

No, he thought. *Nothing is alright. I'm stuck in an alien underworld in the center of the friggin' Earth, and my life's dream just ended!* Treating the food dispensing device with more force than was necessary, he got a random set of cubes and a glass of blue liquid. He hoped it was a sweet one.

"Your father asked you a question, young man." Cynthia glared at him with crossed arms.

He ignored her. He owed them nothing from his perspective. They had brought him along on a needless joyride, and he wasn't about to be cordial to them.

He placed his plate and cup on the table and sat next to them. "Why am I here?" He popped a cube in his mouth, not bothering to look at the colors.

"Excuse me?" Cynthia asked, still perturbed and demanding the respect her son owed her.

"Why am I here? From what I can tell, you just needed Uncle Gus to plug up your laptop. You don't need *me*! And even if you did, it could have waited a day so I could finish my tournament!" He threw another cube in his mouth and chewed it roughly.

Cynthia stared at him. Never a good sign, but he remained determined to hold his own. He took a sip of the blue stuff. Thankfully, it was sweet, almost too sweet, especially with whatever cube that was he just ate.

"Fine," she said, and grabbed him by the arm.

He was old enough and strong enough now to stop her from leading him away, but he didn't. As angry as he was, there was still a core respect for his parents he wouldn't break.

"Where are we going?" he asked.

"We *needed* you, Brandon, because what we're having to do will take several more days." She led him into the elevator. Gus and Michael barely made it in before the door shut. "*And*, I couldn't leave you home alone while Gus was down here, especially if something happened to any of us to where we weren't able to make it back."

His anger only slightly assuaged, he quit stiffening his arm in protest. She let go of it.

When the door opened, Cynthia lead the way down the hallway Brandon recognized as the one with the hospital. "Are we going back to the hospital?" he asked.

She ignored him. They would be there soon enough. She led them to an inside door with that same sewn together sphere cradled by two hands, and opened it. A long hall stood before Brandon, who was now watching Cynthia march down it alone and surrounded by a faint glow, like from a television set.

Gus cleared his throat to get Brandon moving again. Brandon took the hint.

The hallway took them to a circular room covered with screens and control panels with chairs placed in strategic places. "Welcome to the control room." Michael said to Gus while opening his arms out in a grand gesture as though his wife's frenzied behavior was just a fantasy.

Brandon didn't want to be in awe, but he was powerless against it. "Is this a spaceship?" he asked, hoping the earlier tiff with his parents was forgotten, or at least put off until a later time.

"Actually," said Cynthia, "yeah." Her voice still carried an edge to it as she stood on the opposite side of the room, facing Brandon with crossed arms.

Brandon turned to his father, hoping he wasn't as angry. "What?"

"Technically," said Gus, "wouldn't a spaceship have some sort of propulsion. Surely you aren't suggesting that—"

"Oh, no no no." Michael waved his hands in protest. "The Earth rotates around the sun of its own accord in an orbit, but it's not a *planet*."

"What do you mean?" asked Brandon.

"Oh, you're *interested* now?" sneered Cynthia, clearly not ready to let her anger go.

"Not now, Cynthia," said Michael. He gestured to Gus. "Let me show you."

Michael led Gus to the center of the room where a grand pedestal held an illuminated map of a sphere. Brandon could only assume it was Earth.

"We're here." Michael pointed at its center, a small sphere with arms radiating out from equidistant points along its exterior. As the arms neared the surface of the Earth, smaller branches split off, extending so they uniformly touched the entire earth's surface.

"Wait a minute," said Brandon. "This is the Earth? But I thought—" All his related lessons from school passed in front of him. Mantle, core, magma, solid nickel. Even as he stood in what was undeniably the Earth's center, rode a shuttle to get there, he still couldn't accept what he was hearing. Or seeing.

Michael saw the doubt in his son's face. "Most of what you're taught in school is theories. Very little has been proven."

This confused Brandon more. "Then why do they teach it if it isn't fact? Isn't that lying? Isn't that like telling us the French Revolution didn't happen or something?"

Michael overlooked his questions for now, hoping they would answer themselves as he continued. "When an earthquake occurs, it releases two measurable types of waves, S-waves and P-waves. While P-waves can travel through both solids and liquids, S-waves can only travel through solids. By measuring the two different waves from the same quake, scientists hypothesize what composes the inside of Earth based on presumptions of its formation and what they assume causes the earth's magnetic field."

"Right," interrupted Cynthia, visibly calmed. "If scientists are wrong on anything they found a hypothesis on, the entire theoretical complex collapses."

Michael leaned onto the pedestal. "Like what's happening right now. Perfectly round equidistant divots do not form on the generally accepted scientific Earth."

Cynthia added, "Unfortunately, the majority of the scientific community treats their theories as doctrine, and will therefore ignore anything that threatens them."

"Which is why they're ignoring this." Michael signified the map.

Gus stood back and pulled on an imaginary beard, his brow furrowed in contemplation.

What they were saying made sense to Brandon, but he still felt lied to and confused. He stared at Earth's map before them. Tentatively, he reached his hand out to touch it.

Cynthia grabbed the projected model before he could and rotated it so a particular area displayed directly in front of his face. Her finger traced one of the main arms. "You entered through this tunnel here."

Most of the diagram was a uniform blue, but a few of the supporting structures, including the tunnel they had traveled through, were glowing orange, or red in some instances. "Why are they different colors?" asked Brandon.

Gus glanced up at them, still in his thoughtful stance, waiting for an answer.

Michael and Cynthia shared a worried look. Michael's expression was grim when he answered, "We've speculated the red and orange ones to be damaged."

Gus's eyes returned to the model. He repeated their words back to them, verifying he understood everything they had said correctly. "The earth is a machine…"

Cynthia bobbed her head in confirmation.

"…we're living on it…"

Another bob.

"And it's broken." He raised his eyes back to the pair of them, hoping he was wrong.

Cynthia clarified, "It's not broken yet. But it is break*ing*."

"I know you mentioned your peers didn't believe you, but now you have proof, why do you need me? Why haven't you contacted them to help you find a solution? This isn't exactly a one-man job."

Michael and Cynthia shared a glance. Brandon searched their faces for an answer. "Even if there were any scientists we trusted—" began Michael.

"That would listen," Cynthia mumbled under her breath, her arms crossed again and her mood visibly darker.

"—they wouldn't be able to help."

"I don't understand," said Brandon. "Why couldn't they help?"

"We don't need a team of scientists," said Cynthia. "We need an engineer."

"From what we can tell," explained Michael, "the damaged tunnels are collapsing."

"What?" Brandon screamed.

Gus leaned in further so he could examine the map more closely.

Cynthia explained, "The damaged tunnels are directly under the divots forming on the surface. We surmise if we can fix the tunnels, we can stop the quakes. And the earth from collapsing in on itself."

His brow creased with concern, Gus said, "I don't think I can repair Earth on my own, Cynthia."

"We don't have a choice, Gus." Michael stared at him with sympathy. He was probably right, but they had to hope otherwise. "By the time we convince people to take the journey here—"

"—and form a team to organize the repairs—" interrupted Cynthia.

"—and *got* that team here, it would be months from now."

There was a pause as they let Gus absorb it all.

"Earth doesn't have months," said Cynthia. Her voice was gentle but sincere.

Brandon stood to the side in silence, his eyes glued to the floating map, his face contorted in horror.

A long moment passed. Then Gus took a deep breath, clapped his hands together, and rubbed his palms with an excited expression on his face. "Right! I'm guessing it's up to us to fix it then!"

CHAPTER 11

The three adults spent the rest of the day in the control room, discussing their options for repairing Earth before it collapsed in on itself. Brandon listened to enough of their conversation to obtain the gist of it. Only a few areas concerned them for now. The rest, they believed, could wait for repairs.

Brandon thought about returning to his room then and playing on his laptop, anything to take his mind off the enormous responsibility that lay before them, not to mention the consequences of it if they failed, which he was pretty sure they would. But the instant he pictured the game he would play in his mind, he realized the futility of the idea. His laptop couldn't have much of a charge left. Besides, playing a game right now would only be pouring salt on his still fresh wound. So, he settled for wandering around the edges of the control room, exploring a little alien tech. As he did, he came across a notebook labeled, "Journey to the Center of the Earth." *Coy*, he thought. The date on it started just over a week ago. He opened it.

Someone had torn out the first page and folded in half before placing it back in its spot. He unfolded it to reveal a map he recognized as Michael's work. It represented the Hub.

IT IS NOW SUNDAY EVENING. ALL OUR BATTERIES ARE DEAD, FORCING US TO WRITE OUT OUR NOTES INSTEAD OF RECORDING OR TYPING THEM. WE HAVE BEGUN MAPPING THE HUB BUT ONLY MANAGED THREE FLOORS TODAY. ONE OF THOSE FLOORS IS THE CAFETERIA. I DETAILED IT ALREADY, ALONG WITH THE SECOND FLOOR, ON MY COMPUTER. EACH OF THE FLOORS IS MARKED BY A SYMBOL. I HAVE REPLICATED EACH SYMBOL ON THE MAP.

MONDAY—WE MAPPED OUT A FEW MORE FLOORS. SEVERAL DOORS WE HAVE COME ACROSS ARE LOCKED, WITH NO KNOWLEDGE OF WHAT'S BEHIND THEM. HOWEVER, WE DID MANAGE TO DISCOVER SEVERAL ROOMS OF INTEREST. ONE IS A ROBOTICS CHAMBER. THE ROBOTS THERE APPEAR TO PROVIDE A VARIETY OF SERVICES FOR THE HUB, BUT WE ARE UNSURE AS TO WHAT THAT LIST OF SERVICES COMPRISES, MAKING THEM POTENTIALLY DANGEROUS TO ACTIVATE. WE ARE THEREFORE HESITANT TO POWER ANY OF THEM ON, ESPECIALLY SINCE WE DON'T KNOW HOW TO SHUT THEM DOWN. ANOTHER ROOM OF INTEREST WE FOUND TODAY APPEARS TO BE A RESEARCH FACILITY. THERE ARE SEVERAL WORKING HOLOGRAPHIC DISPLAYS WE CAN OPERATE. SOME OF THEM APPEAR TO PORTRAY A MICROBIAL LIVING ORGANISM OF SOME SORT. I'M SURE GREG IN MICRO WOULD LOVE TO GET HIS HANDS ON THOSE! THE RESEARCH FACILITY FEELS MORE THAN ABANDONED. UNLIKE THE BEDROOMS AND CAFETERIA, WHICH LOOKED LIKE SOMEONE JUST GOT UP AND LEFT UNTIL CYNTHIA STRAIGHTENED THEM UP, THE RESEARCH LABS APPEAR CLEANED OUT. IT HAS BECOME CLEAR WE ARE IN A SPHERE, WHICH IS ONLY TO BE EXPECTED SINCE WE ARE IN THE CENTER OF A GIANT SPHERE. I

Brandon glanced at the finished map for a second. Then he quickly flipped to the end of the book. Several earlier attempted sketches with haphazard notes filled a few of the pages there. After studying them for a moment, he returned where he had left off and resumed his reading.

CONVINCED HER TO WAIT UNTIL WE FINISH MAPPING THE HUB AND LEARN A FEW MORE THINGS.

WEDNESDAY- IT WAS EXHAUSTING, BUT WE FINISHED MAPPING THE REST OF THE HUB TODAY. THE LOWER HALF APPEARS TO BE CLOSE TO A MIRROR IMAGE OF THE UPPER ONE, ALL THE WAY DOWN TO THE CAFETERIA ON THE BOTTOM FLOOR.

THURSDAY-WE RETURNED TO THE CONTROL ROOM FOR FURTHER STUDY. SEVERAL OF THE TUNNELS SEEM DAMAGED, AND WE BELIEVE THAT DAMAGE IS THE CAUSE OF THE CURRENT QUAKES. WE TRIED TO GET MORE INFORMATION, BUT WITHOUT MY LAPTOP TO GUIDE ME IN MY TRANSLATION, IT'S USELESS. WE BOTH AGREE IT'S TIME TO RETURN TO THE SURFACE AND CALL FOR HELP. WE ALSO AGREE OUR FELLOW SCIENTISTS—

Brandon quit reading. The rest was just about their plans to return and draft Gus and himself to help them save the planet, or, whatever this was.

"Hey, Brandon," Michael called. "You ready for supper?"

It sure didn't feel late enough to eat. Brandon's stomach growled in opposition to his thought. "Sure."

CHAPTER 12

After supper, they returned to the control room, where Gus spent several hours rigging together couplings for modern American tech and ancient inner Earth tech, and Brandon's head repeatedly drooped from exhaustion.

His thoughts drifted back to the tournament. He was no longer mad at his parents. He understood why they did what they did now, but he was still mad at the situation. He didn't even get the chance to tell his friends he couldn't participate. It would be a long time before anyone would invite him to play on their team again.

"It's running!" Michael called from across the room, rousing Brandon from his pity party.

"What's running?" he asked.

"The laptop," Cynthia answered.

Michael was already behind it, tapping his foot like mad while he waited for the screen to load. "Come on come on come on come on. There!"

Many long minutes later, he was walking excitedly around the room, attempting to translate any symbol he came across. Brandon got up to leave.

"Where are you going?" Cynthia asked.

"To bed. I'm falling asleep." He continued walking towards the door.

"Wait!" his father called. "I want to try something." He picked up his laptop and brushed past

Brandon and out the control room. "I just started charging this," he called over his shoulder as he speed-walked his way to the elevator. "So I don't have a lot of time before the battery dies again."

The door opened, and Michael hopped inside. Brandon had to jog the last few steps to make it before the door closed. Michael swayed impatiently from foot to foot as the elevator ascended to the level their bedrooms were on. Once it stopped, and the door opened once again, he flew out into the hallway, not waiting for Brandon, and ran to the first bedroom he came to, his own.

Curious with his father's actions, but not curious enough to go at more than a sleepily stumble, Brandon followed.

"OOahd." "Uuudd." "Ahhhd." Michael formed his mouth awkwardly around the foreign word. He was standing just inside his and Cynthia's bedroom with the door open.

"What … on earth … are you doing?" Brandon asked sardonically while leaning against the doorjamb.

"I think I know the word for lights now." Michael kept scanning various areas of the room, checking for any light activity.

He had Brandon's attention. "That would be nice."

"Owd" "Yuud" "Ud." The room filled with a soft, natural light. Michael laughed giddily. "That's it! Ud!" The room went dark again.

"You try it," he told Brandon.

"Try what?" Cynthia called out, startling them both.

She and Gus were standing in the hallway peering in.

Michael ran and pulled Cynthia into the room. "Watch this! Ud!"

The lights came back on. Cynthia raised her eyebrows as her head jerked back in surprise. "Wow. Nice job, honey."

Gus walked over and pressed his face against one of the illuminated areas. "Remarkable!"

Yes, having lights was really nice, but the last twenty-four hours had all been a little too much for Brandon. "Can I go to bed now?" he asked. "I'm glad you got the lights working, but I'm still exhausted from yesterday."

"Sure, honey. Go ahead." Cynthia waved him away without looking.

Michael's eyes never left his monitor when he said, "Night, son."

Brandon didn't wait for a reply from Gus. He would remain engrossed by their new discovery for quite a while still, even if it was just a light bulb.

He placed his hand on his bedroom door and allowed it to disappear. "Ud." The room lit up on his command. Nice. But not nice enough to keep him awake. He shuffled his feet across the floor before falling into a seated position on the bed. He kicked off his shoes, allowing him, in the light, to appreciate the floor for the first time. It was soft and khaki, like the color of sand. It held a supportive quality yet somehow managed to cushion his steps, like Earth's natural ground. He rubbed his naked toes into its surface, reveling in its caressing attributes. Wondering what else he might have missed in the dark, he scanned the rest of his room. The walls, a pale blue undertone, bore speckles of red and orange. Not too bold, it felt … natural. Gazing at it instantly put him at ease. A lot of work must have been required to create a room this serene.

But as beautiful as it was, it wasn't enough to keep him conscious. After nodding off to the point he nearly fell onto the floor, he pulled back the covers and crawled inside.

CHAPTER 13

"Ud." Brandon's room instantly illuminated. Saying the word felt weird, foreign, silly even, but at least it worked. He stared up at the ceiling, his thoughts drifting to how it all got here; who built this room, who built the Hub, who built Earth?

There was no way he would learn the answer to those questions here. Throwing off his blanket, he sat up and reached for his phone to check the time. They all agreed to keep with the same time zone they left home with. Three A.M. He must have gone to bed earlier than he realized. He was completely rested.

Not wanting to wake the others, and not hungry, he decided to play a bit on his laptop. Last night's sleep had done a world of good in his acceptance of what had happened. A nice hack and slash was just what he needed right now, providing his battery lasted long enough.

But his laptop wasn't on his table. He searched the room, his backpack, even the toilet area, but it was nowhere to be found. "Oh, Dad!" he groaned. Believing Michael must have taken it to the control room to aide in his translating, he threw on his socks and shoes and set out for it.

The hallway was too silent for his comfort. He thought there should be noises of machines or something, the inner workings of Earth or whatever took place down here, but the only sound he could hear was the echo of his footsteps against the hard floor. Outside the individual bedrooms was not as comforting as the insides. It wasn't unpleasant, just more like walking around in a large retail store instead of a nice small market. As the elevator came into view, he glanced at the symbol on its top and hoped he remembered the one for the main floor where the control room was located. He stepped inside and searched for it. Many of the markings shared the same features: three lines with a wavy line, three lines with a slanted line, two lines with a hat. He pressed the circle with the dot in the middle. It was the only logical choice and vaguely familiar. The door closed.

The moment it reopened, he stepped into the hallway. Right, left, the choice became silly after a moment. The hallway was a circle, after all, so even if he did make the wrong decision, it would only add a bit of time to his journey, not lead him away from his goal. He chose left. All the doors looked the same. Nothing struck him as familiar or incorrect. They gave him no hint as to whether he was on the wrong floor or not. But, he knew all he had to do was keep walking and the elevator would appear once more, allowing him to return to his bedroom, or the cafeteria at the very least.

The idea of wandering around in exploration was not daunting. In fact, it was a pleasurable thought. The center of Earth was unique but not so massive as to be intimidating. He felt free to walk its hallways undeterred, much like his parents had when they mapped it out. The thought of what other areas he might discover within the Hub was just crossing his mind when the door to the control room came into view.

He traveled down its straight hallway and stepped inside the room. The glowing blue globe in its center illuminated everything in a pale blue light. The darkness of the surrounding surfaces made its features stand out even more. They consumed him, making his original objective of retrieving his laptop forgotten. As though in a trance, he found himself walking towards the hologram. Tunnels for shuttles to transport people to and from the Hub and surface of the planet filled the luminous structure.

Planet. He huffed derisively. Were all the planets ships, or was Earth just special? He studied the map, wondering if after they figured Earth out, they would figure the others out too. Maybe this place had a secret library with answers to all his questions. Maybe it answered even more, questions he didn't know to ask, questions he couldn't imagine.

As he stared at the tunnels, one of those unthought-of queries came to mind. There were so many tunnels leading to so many places on Earth's surface, how could no one have known about this before now? Obviously someone in Earth's history had to have known at some point in time. Hopi religion proved that. But how far back did it go?

The map rotated as he watched it, the red paths twisting his stomach with worry. He broke himself from the hologram, took a step back, and slowly scanned the rest of the room before him. "All these control panels," he mumbled aloud to himself. "What do they do?"

"Ud." The room lit up. "Huh. Guess that works in here too." He was glad for that. Due to all the illumination from the maps and panels they didn't truly need lights in the room, but it made things easier nonetheless.

Starting on the left, he worked his way around all the panels, examining them as he went. His parents may have had several days start on him, but they were more into rocks than computers. This was his world. Granted, it was alien tech, but he still thought he could get more out of it than anyone else had already.

Each of the panels seemed to correlate with their own section of the earth model. They also seemed to be set up for a single person to man each one. There were a few, however, that were different. He assumed they were for internal functions or something similar.

He browsed the panels for similarities, trying to match each one with its Earth-section. The red ones were easy to match up. After that, it was just following a pattern, like longitudinal pie pieces.

Wanting to label the sections so he could reference their match-ups in the future, he returned to the central globe.

A plethora of controls lay beneath it. Surely his parents had pressed all of them, but he hadn't. His finger hesitated over the first one, the one with a symbol of two concentric circles. It had to be safe, right? Silently chastising himself for his own ridiculous lack of bravery he pressed hard on the button.

As he did so, a second layer appeared over the first on the holographic map. The new layer showed the entire topical Earth: continents, oceans, everything. He released the button; the layer vanished. He pressed the second button. All but the damaged sections disappeared. The map again went back to normal when he released it. The third button zoomed in on the Hub. Releasing it did nothing. The fourth button returned the map to normal.

He continued the sequence until he had pressed every button. In the process, the map turned off, back on, changed colors, shape, size, and held still from rotating. While the benefits of many of these functions were obvious, some remained baffling. He pressed the button that held the earth still again and released it. A second press would resume the rotation. With gradual deliberation, Brandon raised his hands to touch the map's surface. It felt almost solid. There was something beneath his fingertips, not a hard ball or a soft pillow, but something. The hologram had mass.

He gripped the hologram with both hands and removed it from its pedestal. It worked! He decided to test the boundaries of how far he could venture away from the pedestal. About halfway to the sectioned panels, it disappeared, only to reappear in the center. "Must've taken it too far," he murmured.

He revisited the pedestal and held the glowing earth in his hands again, peering deeply into its structure. His thumbs brushed its surface. In response, the underlying tunnels moved out of the way, giving him a clear picture of the Hub. Answering his mind's question, his hand reached in and grabbed the tiny Hub. "I can touch it!" he whispered in astonishment. His words would have been inaudible had anyone else been with him.

His other hand dropped the earth and joined the first in cradling the Hub. He wanted to get closer. His fingers instinctively tried to pull the image apart like they would on a tablet to zoom in. It worked! A delighted grin spread across his face.

He moved the Hub around in his fingers, zooming in and out, studying the intricate details of each individual room. He found his own, or at least the one he believed to be his, the cafeteria, the control room, the hatches to the tunnels.

He dropped the ball and let the map reform itself. Pressing the appropriate button, he caused it to rotate again then stopped it, this time wanting to examine the damaged areas. "What is wrong with you? How can we fix you?" The way he talked to the map reminded him of Gus talking to his machines. He pretended not to notice the similarity.

The red tunnels were just that however, red tunnels. They told him nothing more, no specifics, no instructions, just blue tunnels painted red. He flung the map from his hands in frustration.

"Wait. What was that?" Something had caught his attention when he tossed it aside. His hands reached for the map again. A tiny white light glowed amidst one of the blue, hopefully undamaged, tunnels. "Three left of the second red…" he told himself. His voice trailed off as he scanned for the corresponding control panel. "There!"

He threw the globe to the side and rushed to the panel. A tiny white light, exactly as the one in the map, flashed rhythmically. He sat at the panel and tried to read the screen. *Maybe Dad could…* he began to ponder. "No," he said, shaking his head to quell the thought before he finished it. His dad was no closer to fully translating this language than when he had started.

So used to modern surface tech, his fingers instinctively reached out to touch the screen before him. The moment one of his fingers grazed the screen, a map, much like the one in the center, jumped out of the panel, causing him to throw himself and his chair backward and tip onto the floor. Glad no one was around to see what he had just done, he picked himself and the chair up and began to study what he still termed a hologram, because he didn't have another word for it. As far as he knew, holograms weren't capable of being touched and manipulated like these were. These went beyond simple light projections, even complex light projections.

This map contained only the tunnel assigned to that specific control panel, but it was far more detailed than the main one. Using his fingers, he zoomed in to the flashing light. It formed a trail all the way to the surface, which he squinted his eyes to follow. "Why is it…?" he whispered to himself.

Jumping from his chair, he ran back to the main map, excited with the notion of finding something new on his own. He zoomed in on this map like he had the other one. The trail was faint, but still there.

This threw gas on his fire. "It's coming out of the top. But where is it going?"

With a thrilling rush, and a grin to match, he pushed the button which added the topical layer. His eyes narrowed in concentration as he matched the two layers together. "Africa," he whispered. "Italy is there…" He held the globe in his hand, stopping its movement and zooming in on the land above the flashing tunnel. "What's— Is that India?" Geography never was his best subject.

He snorted in frustration and threw the map aside. The mystery tore at him, pulling his brain into a hundred different pieces as he tried to figure out what the little flashing light could possibly be. As he stood there, bouncing his leg impatiently, he wondered if this was what his parents had felt like this whole time. It was as if the reality of what was happening finally hit him, and he wanted to be a part of it.

He stood up to pace and thought what his next move should be, how he could learn what the flashing light meant without a translator. "Wait a minute." There was a brief pause while the solution clicked into place. "Duh!" he shouted, and hit his head with his palm.

The journey back in the elevator was agonizing, like knowing about an upcoming vacation and having to wait for it. The moment its door opened, he flew down the hall to his room. The sensation he now had made him feel more alive than any game or any win ever had. He felt like Indiana Jones, on the verge of a new discovery that would change the world. Or put him in danger.

The door to his room disappeared. Ignoring that last thought about danger lest it stop him from what he was about to do, he quickly grabbed his flashlight and headlamp and took off for the tunnel's hatch. A momentary thought of waking his parents did flash across his mind; maybe he should ask to borrow his uncle's grappling hook, just in case, but he knew what their reactions would be. And there was no way he was going to sit this one out while they explored his discovery. They had their chance already. Besides, they were the ones that brought him down here and wanted him to be interested in their work. They asked for this.

The elevator opened, presenting him with the challenge of picking the right floor and the eventual realization of being a complete moron. A growl of frustration followed by, "Idiot! Idiot! Idiot!" later, and he was pushing the main floor's button like a raving woodpecker so he could sprint back to the control room. Before he could enter the tunnel with the signal, he had to know where its entrance was.

He bobbed on the balls of his feet while waiting on the control room door to open. The map was still there, casting its brilliant blue glow on the room while slowly spinning in place. He rotated it with his hands until the flashing tunnel was directly in front of him. Using his finger, he followed the tunnel back to its hatch and pulled up the corresponding Hub's floor.

As he started counting how many floors down he needed to go, followed by how far around the Hub the hatch would be, he noticed something he hadn't before, something that made his immediate life enormously easier. "Labels!"

Each floor had a tiny label on it. So did each hatch. "Square with three dots. Four lines…" There was a pad and several pens lying on one of the control panels. He quickly scribbled down everything he needed to remember, hoped it was enough, and tore the paper off the pad. After putting the pen and pad back where he had gotten them from, he gripped his flashlight in one hand, the wadded symbols in the other, and sprinted once more for the elevator.

Its door opened, far more slowly than he would have liked. As soon as he got inside, he spun around and bent over to look at the buttons. "Four lines… Four lines…" He opened up the wadded paper with his scribbled notes for comparison. Back and forth, his eyes went from paper to buttons until "There!". Four lines and a squiggly dot. He had found it. Using his thumb, he held down the button until well after the door shut. "Come on come on come on," he said as he commenced to bouncing on his toes again.

His impatience caused him to exit the elevator before its door had opened completely, which resulted in a painful thud and a shouted expression of frustration. Once clear, he sprinted down the hall to the left, consulting his notes as he went. "Square… square… Ah!" His pace slowed to a jog. "One… Two…" He skidded to a halt. "Three!" A square with three dots marked the wall where he stood. Next to the mark was the hatch door.

CHAPTER 14

He raised his finger to press the button that would open the door to the tunnel's hatch. Bile suddenly worked its way into his throat. He wasn't expecting that. Until this moment, this had been the preamble to a thrilling adventure, like waiting in line at Sam's Island. He had never been afraid then. No roller coaster or haunted house had ever induced fear, just exhilaration. And while most people had trouble sleeping at least a couple of nights when the quakes started, and then continued, he didn't.

"But I wasn't alone then." The realization came out in a whisper, his index finger hovering a millimeter away from its destination. "No. Wait," he thought aloud. "I've been alone all week, so that can't be it." His hand fell. "Oh. Uncle Gus." Uncle Gus had been next door the whole time. Someone had always been with him during every quake, sometimes many someones. He had never been alone, not truly. As understanding crept its way into his conscious thoughts, the bile returned.

He was about to do something new and dangerous for the very first time all by himself. And it terrified him. It also angered him. He was *fifteen*, and in the center of the friggin' Earth! The fact he was afraid over an opportunity most people would kill for made him feel like a coward, like a little kid wanting his mommy. He clenched his hand into a fist and gritted his teeth. The fear remained, but it wasn't going to stop him.

A hiss sounded as the door opened. He stepped inside, his heart pounding through his ears like a river. The door shut behind him, and Brandon braced himself for the sterilization procedure. But nothing happened. He opened his eyes, not realizing he had squeezed them shut, and glanced around.

"Hmm." His brow furrowed. He didn't know if the lack of sterilization was because he already had been or because the room was broken. Or, maybe the Hub only sterilized people coming in and not going out. That idea didn't make sense to him though. Wouldn't "they" be more concerned about the larger surface population instead of the few dozen or hundred within its control room? *Well, no*, he thought. *The control room was probably more important than—* Wait. Was he actually deciding which long dead presumably human lives were more important than others?

He shook the ridiculous conversation from his mind and concentrated on what was before him. Holding his flashlight with a death grip, and checking to make sure his headlamp was still firmly attached, he walked across the mesh floor to the shuttle room door. It opened on its own when he neared it.

The adjoining shuttle room was identical to the one he and Gus had arrived at the Hub in. A shuttle sat waiting for him. After a few more studious glances around the area and over his shoulder, he squeezed the handle to the vehicle's door and stepped inside.

Brandon had seen how his uncle got the first shuttle moving, so he had no trouble finding the right spot to push, but nothing happened. "Why is it not…?" He swiveled his head around, searching for something he missed or any other explanation for the shuttle's lack of response. "Oh! Duh! Come on, Brandon. Think!" He had forgotten to shut the door.

With the door shut, he tried again. The floor vibrated, the only signal it was now moving. He walked over to the side and placed his knee onto the bench. Reaching up, he once more followed his uncle's example and removed the covering to the vehicle's window.

He watched the room turn sideways and disappear. Then the wall of the tunnel passed by, faster and faster until it was flying. This journey was smoother than their arriving one. He didn't feel as sick. Maybe the adrenaline was helping him in that area, he wondered.

Not that he expected to at this speed, but he couldn't tell any difference between this rock and the canyon rock they had entered through. It all looked the same to him. He sat on the bench and faced the interior of the shuttle. The nausea finally returned, and staring out the window at the moving scenery wasn't helping.

After a minute or so, he noticed the piece of paper with his hurried notes was still scrunched up in his hand. He shoved it down into his front pocket. When he thought he could stomach it, he chanced periodic glances out the window until the scenery began to slow. Then he resumed his previous position and watched the opening of the earth slide past, and the surrounding room of his destination tilt into the upright position.

This room was dark, its only light coming from what shone from the shuttle's exterior. Brandon turned on his flashlight and entered a room identical to the one they entered in the caves of the Grand Canyon, barren and metallic. He found the control panel and turned on the lights. He knew he wouldn't stay in this room long, but still, the lights made it more comfy, not as spooky.

He pressed the button to open the door and walked through. Once again, he found a place similar to the halfway room under the Grand Canyon. This room did have two differences though. The first difference was the rock. Unlike the red and orange walls of Arizona, this rock was … almost white. The second difference, and the most interesting, was the way out.

When they entered the first halfway room, they had to sidestep through a crevice that appeared to have been opened by the recent quakes, as though it were meant to stay hidden and not accessed from the surface. This room held no such crevice. Instead, an arched tunnel led straight off into the unknown ahead. It appeared natural, but Brandon was beginning to question just what was and was not natural anymore.

Keeping his flashlight on, he flipped down his headlamp, allowing its beam to add to the inadequate existing one. Once again he chastised himself for not thinking as he realized how far he would more than likely be walking, and therefore how much water and food he would want, maybe even need. But he continued.

Along the way, the tunnel widened before abruptly dropping about five feet. He placed one hand on the floor of the tunnel and hopped down to the next level. The path continued from there, eventually leading into caverns, pits, and narrow corridors, much like any expected cave system, which differed from the first tunnel beneath the canyon. That tunnel's only distinguishing features had been graffiti and a change in slope. There had been no caverns, no change in the width or ceiling height. It had felt more like a hallway than a tunnel, like it was made for traveling instead of just a natural phenomenon you happened to be able to travel through.

One more thing differed here too, the bugs. In addition to the occasional crunchy squish he felt beneath his step, webs frequently got in his way, forcing him to push them to the side. Thankfully, their creators didn't seem to be home at the time.

Brandon kept following the uneven path, but when it opened into a spacious intersection of sorts, things got a little more interesting. First, he slipped and fell, with a splat. He had become too engrossed with what lay ahead and hadn't been paying attention to what lay below, which landed him in a rather thick collection of guano.

After scraping as much as possible off onto the rock face, he pointed his light to the ceiling. There, he hoped hibernating, hung a vast colony of bats. He knew these, like most bats, were not aggressive, more likely to carry disease than attack or otherwise hurt a person, but still. Peering up to the ceiling only to see more live creature than rock was disturbing. He stepped back into the tunnel he had exited from.

Five tunnels met at this intersection. He didn't know which one to take, and he didn't want his path to take him under the bats. It didn't matter why he was afraid, not that he understood the reason anyway, but making his body move forward was still more difficult than not.

"This is ridiculous," he muttered, angry with his body's reaction. He wasn't going to come this far only to be thwarted by sleeping bats. He scanned the other tunnels for any sign or symbol which might hint which one to take. Nothing.

Realizing his only choice, he groaned, curled his lips in a cringe, and grabbed a handful of guano. He used it to mark his way by swiping it down the right-hand side of the tunnel he was standing in, forming a "1".

"Ick." His hand shook the guano off without his order, like it was more disgusted than he was. He grabbed another handful and whispered under his breath, "I better get a medal for this, or something." This time he smeared a "2" next to the neighboring tunnel. "Gah!" He shuddered, emitting more noises of disgust. A few steps into the tunnel, he wiped his hand on its walls before proceeding down its path.

What felt like half an hour later, it opened up into a deep, wide cavern. As he surveyed the gaping hole before him, he realized it was too ample to cross. There was no way around it on either the left or the right. He pursed his lips and sighed. A dead end. Reversing his path, he returned to the intersection and repeated the guano process with the next tunnel, labeling it number "3".

This tunnel had more variance, and even branched off into some impassible offshoots, but about a full hour in, it ended with a cave-in. If it was the correct path, he wasn't taking the time to find out.

The next tunnel continued far longer than the previous two. Its path was direct and shot upward, much like at the canyon. As he heaved labored breaths in his attempt to climb the steep slope, he knew it had to be the correct trail.

Although he could travel faster alone than he had with his uncle, it still took over two hours of nonstop marching to reach the top. By then, he was panting heavily and craving water like an oyster in the Australian desert.

The top did not lead to daylight. It lead to stairs. These stairs were not made of the metal or smooth ceramic Brandon had come to expect from those who built the Hub. They were stone with a worn groove up their center that must have taken centuries of constant use to form. With one hand on the wall, and another still holding his flashlight, he climbed the stairs, counting as he went if for no other reason than to keep from thinking about food, water, and a nice, soft bed. Four hundred and fifty-seven steps later, he entered a square room, its walls completely covered in gold.

Two round dishes with charcoaled remains sat on short, rectangular pedestals placed on either side of a golden, square throne. Around the throne, and on every visible surface for that matter, were the unmistakable vertical symbols of ancient Egyptian hieroglyphs.

"Mmmmm," Michael groaned before rolling over and draping his arm over his wife. "Morning."

"Morning," she answered, sleepily and unwillingly. The past week had been anything but boring, but now her family was with her and safe, and they had more answers, the drain was finally taking its toll on her body.

Michael could tell how tired she was from the way she still wasn't moving. "Want to sleep in?" he asked.

Not wanting to expend the energy to answer him verbally, she thought about nodding instead. That wouldn't be any easier, she decided, so she nuzzled her head under his and answered with a faint, "Hmm mmm."

He sighed, smiling. *Poor thing*, he thought. She was probably exhausted. They all were. The catch in his back wasn't going to let him get any more sleep though. None of the beds they found were larger than a twin, but he wasn't comfortable sleeping in a separate bed from his wife, let alone a separate room inside an alien … whatever this was. (Machine? Test tube? He didn't know.) So, he squeezed in next to her every night, and suffered the consequences of it every morning.

He kissed the top of her head. "Is it OK if I get up?"

"Hmm mmm," she hummed back, silently glad to have the entire bed to herself for a while. Maybe she would sleep better that way.

Michael rose from the bed, being careful not to disturb her too much. He shook out his clothes and got dressed before opening the door. One more look over his shoulder assured him it was OK to leave her alone for a while.

Even though the hallway had been light enough to seem like daytime, the cafeteria's white glow hurt his eyes, forcing him to take a step back and squeeze them shut until the pain subsided. After several blinks and a good eye rub, he dragged his still sleepy feet to the drink machine and ordered the bitter yellow liquid. It was too early to stomach canned goods, so he also ordered two blue cubes and a white.

The sound of the door opening made Michael spin around in surprise.

"Morning," Gus said, smiling with unmistakable excitement to start another day working in the Hub.

Michael lifted his glass in response. "Morning." He walked over to a table and sat down, giving Gus room to order his own food.

"What's the white stuff?" Gus had taken one of Michael's cubes and was rolling it between his fingers. His face was screwed up in a half disgusted, half curious expression.

"I don't know," said Michael. "Eggs?"

Gus gave a low chuckle. "Square eggs." He looked over at Michael. "We could sell this you know." He dropped the cube back onto Michael's plate.

Michael grimaced and sipped his drink. Gus was always coming up with new ideas, nearly all of which would require more time to get off the ground than he had left. Michael had learned to ignore most of them.

Gus filled his plate with a variety of cubes and brought it over to sit across from Michael. "Where's Cynthia?"

"Still in bed." Michael swallowed his food and took a drink. "Have you seen Brandon?"

Gus shook his head. "Not since last night. Do I need to go check on him?"

"Naw. I'm sure he's just sleeping. How'd he do on the hike in, by the way?"

"He did well. He's not as out of shape as Cynthia likes to think he is. I realize he's into his games, but he did better than *me* half the time."

Michael wanted to say, "That's not saying much since you're well over seventy," but didn't.

Gus took in his expression. He raised one eyebrow and said, "I know what you're thinking. I'm not dead yet. I think I've proven myself pretty well over the years."

A half grimace, half smile worked its way onto Michael's face. "I didn't say a word."

Gus's eyes twinkled. "But you thought it."

Michael's smile deepened.

CHAPTER 16

Brandon's breath clung to the inside of his throat, refusing to shift either in or out of his body. In his mind, there was only one location he could be, underneath the pyramids of Egypt. He paused, remembering one of his father's crazy videos. Those video didn't seem so crazy anymore. This particular one had said something about multiple places sharing the same culture as Egypt. So which one was he in?

He shook his head and called himself stupid for not thinking. The Hub had a map; he had just looked at it. His position in the world should be obvious. Scouring his brain, he tried to remember it and compare it to his dismal knowledge of geography. The tunnel had exited somewhere in Africa, of that he was sure. And he was also sure that Egypt had the Nile River. *Wait.* He paused a moment. The Nile was in Africa, wasn't it? He closed his eyes and tried to remember one of the countless maps from all his Social Studies lessons. *Yes!* His eyes popped open. *The Nile was in Africa, so chances are...* he thought. "I'm under Egypt."

As the realization of where he was standing hit him, he stared at the throne. The light of his flashlight reflected off it, producing within him an intense urge to sit on it while simultaneously making him wonder if it might be cursed. Or trapped. White spiders scurried out of his way as his feet scraped the sandy stone, his legs periodically halting with hesitation. Powerful. Inviting. Intimidating. The throne sat before him like an actual monarch, able to let him live or kill him where he stood.

"Who used to sit in you?" He approached it, slowly and with respect. "What powerful Pharaoh ruled from where you stand?"

He stared at it for several seconds before deciding it was worth the risk to share the same seat as an ancient Egyptian Pharaoh. The very idea of such a momentous task warmed his entire body. As he got closer however, the invitation waned. Webs draped across the golden chair as thick as an old sheet. Not wanting to get them all over himself or his flashlight, the only thing he was carrying with him, he scanned the room for something else to clean them off with. When his light left the shine of the metal throne for the dull, lackluster floor, he saw that it seemed to have dimmed.

"Wait." He returned the beam to the throne. It was shiny, but not like it had been a moment ago. No, it was definitely dimmer.

His chest quickly burned with fear as his face went numb. His hand flew to his head to turn off the headlamp. What small amount of glow remaining from his flashlight flickered. "Crap crap crap crap crap!"

He turned back and sprinted to the stairs, his feet slipping on the loose sand all the way. Once he saw the stairs, with their hard surface and lack of modern safety railings, he grabbed the wall with his free hand and slowed to a safer pace, yet still faster than he would have liked to.

"Comeon comeon comeon comeon," he urged himself, his feet meeting each step with an echoing slap. More than once the sand between the soles of his shoes and the step rolled, causing his foot to slide and his adrenaline to fly.

"Come on... Come on..." This time he was begging his flashlight to keep working, at least until he reached the bottom step. Its light had faded to less than half of what it had been, and its flickering worsened.

And then it went out.

Brandon stopped on the step his feet were on and pushed his back against the wall. The darkness was so encompassing, he could feel it pressing in on him and sucking the air out of his lungs. He shut his eyes and leaned his head back. Somehow this darkness was quieter, less consuming than when he had his eyes open. It allowed him to think. For his mind to pretend the area outside his eyes was lighter than it was.

He took a deep breath, then another, and then another. *If I turn the other light on now,* he thought, *I'll use up what juice I have left.* He turned his head and opened his eyes, instinctively aiming them down the steps without first thinking of the ridiculousness of his action.

He could always take the batteries out and put them back in. That usually worked for a little while at least. But he'd undoubtedly lose them in the dark and wind up stepping on one. It would roll underneath his foot and he would fall the rest of the way down, breaking his neck during his graceless descent. No, he sighed, the best course of action would be to keep going. In the dark.

His thumb pressed the flashlight's off button, and he prepared himself for the task ahead. The stairway was straight with no openings or deviations, so he knew he wouldn't get lost at least until he reached the bottom of them. His fingers groped the wall with a death grip, much like the one his other hand had on the now useless flashlight, and he lowered his right foot down from his left.

It hit solid stone. He had known the step was there. He had known what would happen when he hit it, but somehow the support of it under his foot gave him great relief.

He moved his left foot to join it and proceeded to slide his way sideways, one step at a time and with his back hugging the wall, down the black stairwell.

"One hundred thirty-six, one hundred thirty-seven…" When he began his return journey down the steps, he hadn't counted them, but for whatever reason the action comforted him now, much like when he climbed them.

"Two hundred seventy-five." His hand reached ahead as always, and his body followed along behind it, but when his toe reached out to feel for the other step, it hit floor a lot higher than he expected. His eyes widened uselessly. With great caution, he probed around with his toes, and then the soles of his feet, trying to confirm he had hit bottom.

A relieved smile spread across his face when he did. Giving his flashlight a good shake, he flicked the switch to ensure he was indeed at the bottom of the steps and could now continue safely along the path ahead. Nothing.

"Stupid… blasted… *work*!" he screamed at the lifeless instrument and shook it again. And again. And again.

He didn't want to use his head lamp. He knew he would need that for the guano section or maybe another area he hadn't thought of yet. It was difficult to be logical while panicking.

"OK." Taking a deep breath, he unscrewed the back with a shaking hand. "I can do this."

A tilt of the flashlight let both batteries slide into his hand. With his eyes squeezed shut and his teeth clamped hard on his lips, he switched their positions one at a time by feel before putting them back. "That one in, then…"

As the second one slid into place, he released a breath he didn't realized he had been holding, then screwed the cap back on … tight.

He aimed the flashlight forward, held his breath (purposefully this time), and pushed the button. It shone! The tunnel stretched down and out before him as he'd hoped.

After allowing himself a few steps, he switched the light back off. The tunnel leading to the stairs had been steep but undivided, and he knew he could travel through it quickly, certainly more quickly than the stairs. "I won't need my light again until the intersection with the guano…" he thought aloud. But the echo served only to make him feel more alone and vulnerable than he already did.

With his hand brushing the wall to guide him, he half slid, half jogged his way down the sloping trail until it began to level out. He realized that meant he was close to the intersection with the bats, but how close exactly he couldn't remember. Since the sidewall of the tunnel would end when he reached the guano area, he decided it wasn't worth using the last of his light to check on his progress and simply continued on at a slower pace.

Another two hours had passed, this time in complete darkness. It no longer consumed him as it once did. As useless as it was, keeping his eyes open while he walked seemed natural by this point.

His fingers found an edge. He stopped. The smell of guano was strong. He was where the tunnels met.

He clicked the power button to his flashlight with no result. Flinging it several times in an attempt to jar the batteries, he tried once more. He even switched the batteries again. No. The flashlight was completely dead now. Fighting the urge to throw it to the ground, he instead followed the edge around the rim to the bat cave and in the direction he knew the identifying numbers he had written were.

His face scrunched up involuntarily as his fingers touched something slimy. Against his inner desires, he forced his fingers to trace the outline of the guano-drawn number. Round at both the top and bottom, like a half-drawn number "8". "Yes!" He beamed. He had found the third tunnel.

The lack of a guiding wall as he crossed the tunnel's opening was unsettling to say the least. His feet dragged slowly along the floor while his outstretched hands searched wildly for the next edge. He let out a sigh and grinned when they made contact.

The new wall led him to a new number, round at the top and slanted to the bottom, the number "2". His grinned changed into a smile. "One more," he whispered to the darkness.

Once again he crossed the empty space of the tunnel's opening. Confidence from his last success caused him to do it more quickly than before. He felt a wall. His fingers groped along its surface until he found the straight line he was looking for, the number "1". His way home.

He stepped inside the tunnel and waited. This was going to be tricky. Unlike the path to the stairs, this part of the cave was wrought with caverns and deep pits, not to mention the creepy crawlies he had so far managed to avoid. Not that he was particularly bothered by them, but he had no idea of knowing whether they were poisonous or not.

The time had come for him to use what precious juice remained in his headlamp. He didn't know what the battery configuration was on it, so he couldn't even try his earlier trick of switching them around.

Tired, thirsty, and kicking himself for being a complete idiot, he stepped away from the wall, shook out his hands and blew several noisy breaths through puffed cheeks. "You've got this. You know what's there. You can make it." His pep talk was very similar to what he told himself before a difficult level in one of his games. The anxiety that filled him much the same as well. It gave him confidence.

He crouched down, bracing for a sprint, and flipped down his headlamp. Its dying light gave him his path. His shoes slapped the floor as he raced down the tunnel before him. He could have flashed the lamp, seen what was ahead, travel as far as he able and then repeat the process over and over, but he was afraid that would cause the light to wear out faster, at least he *thought* turning stuff on and off again did that. He wasn't sure.

He jumped a small pit and pushed off the wall ahead of him to turn the next corner without slowing down.

Maybe he could ask Gus about the turning on and off thing when he got home. Or his parents. They might know. But Gus would probably know better.

He skidded to a halt at the sight of a cavern and quickly pivoted to go around it.

Ohhhh, his parents. He would be dead meat after this. It had all seemed so innocent before. Granted, he knew they would've told him no. They would've considered it too dangerous to do on his own. He wasn't responsible enough, didn't think things through. *Huh*, he thought, realizing the irony of that concept. *Maybe they were right about that part.*

His light flickered, interrupting his thoughts. He quickened his pace. It flickered again.

Then it went out.

He stopped. His feet didn't slip, they didn't skid. It was like his body instantly froze in place. The darkness was less terrifying this time. He had survived the stairs by finding his own way. He could do it here too. But how?

His eyes squeezed shut as his face pulled together in thought. "Think think think," he whispered inaudibly to himself. "There was the archway, then the tunnel. It got wider. It fell a few feet." His eyes shot wide open. "All of that came before the first cavern."

He started walking again. The caverns were behind him. All that lay in front of him now was the drop, and not even that. It would be a climb from this direction, then a wider hall, and then the arch, the arch that connected to the halfway room. "Almost home." He smiled.

Keeping his hand in constant contact with the wall, he used the echoes of his feet as they scraped the floor to help guide him. If the sound traveled into the distance, he knew the way was open and clear. If it bounced back quickly, something was getting nearer, and if the sound snuffed out with no return, a wall or other obstruction lay ahead of him.

His confidence in his system grew too high, however. Several minutes into the not-so-straight path ended with him running toe-first into the climb.

"Ow!" He shook out his foot, wondering why his system had failed him. That idea scared him. If he had forgotten even the smallest of falls, a dip or even a hole, it could have been catastrophic for him. In the worst case, he would have fallen to his death. In the best, he would have twisted his ankle and had to hop or crawl the rest of the way, never knowing if another unremembered trap lay in wait for him in the blackness.

But for now, he was grateful it was just a stubbed toe. He gropped around the rock wall in front of him, all the while wondering, hoping, praying it was the last of the obstacles, that his memory would prove more accurate than his echo system. Although knowing better, he couldn't resist the urge to try his lights one more time to check if he was right. They didn't work. Disappointment told him he had actually held onto hope one of them would, if only for a second.

It wasn't a tall ledge. He was able to run his hands across the floor at its top, meaning it was shorter than he was, but there was still no way he would be able to climb it one-handed. So the first thing he did was shove the handle of the flashlight into his pants. Then he grasped the top of the ledge with his fingertips, probed for a good hold with the toes of his right foot, and tested his weight on it.

His foot slid off with a scratching noise, causing his knee to bang into the rockface. He searched again for a foothold. And again. Deciding it might be better to give the other side a go before he got hurt too much, he switched his body weight over and lifted his other foot.

The first hold was successful. He used it to push himself up enough to throw his elbows over the ledge where he panted for a few seconds to catch his breath. When he surmised he was in a good position to, he brought his right leg up. Leaving his supporting foot in its hold, he used his right leg and both arms to push himself higher. More than half his body was now over the ledge. He collapsed onto the rock, panting.

With the side of his face flattened against the ledge floor, he could feel the dust move with the breath escaping his open lips. The handle of the flashlight dug into his pelvis, and his right leg still dangled against the side of the rock. He was so tired, he could have lain there and slept for hours, but he placed his hands beneath his shoulders and pushed himself up.

Standing at the top of the path, he leaned against the wall and rested a minute. When he wiped the dirt off his face, he noticed that he had stopped sweating. It may have been cooler than a summer's day in here, but he had been working hard enough to know that meant he was dehydrated. He owed his parents a big apology. It was stupid of him to try this alone. They would have known that, and now he did too.

Almost home, he thought. The only thing before the archway was the widening, or so said his memory. He returned to his sliding-hand-against-the-wall technique for what he hoped was the rest of the way.

Keeping track of time was hardly an easy task for him underground, but what he speculated to be half an hour later, he saw—

"Light!" The surprise caused him to stay put, one hand still clutching his dead flashlight while the other gripped the wall of the tunnel. Then it hit. He started running, laughing and tripping all the way. The moment he passed under the archway into the halfway room, he fell back against the wall and let himself slide to the floor.

Maybe it was entering it or the relief of being safe, but a few precious beads of sweat formed, churning more laughter and causing him to wipe them away with his hand. The thought of lying against the cool floor and sleeping did cross his mind, but he knew he needed to get back, not just to keep his family from worrying, but to share with them what he found.

CHAPTER 18

"What on Earth?" Michael exclaimed upon entering the control room. When they went to bed last night, they switched everything off but the map. But now, the lights were on, and most of the side panels too.

"Cynthia?" The only explanation was his wife woke up while he and Gus were eating and started work without them, but a quick glance around the room told him that wasn't the case. Her telltale scattering of notes and writing utensils were missing. Still, he couldn't help but cover his bases. "Cynthia!"

There was no answer. Unless she was hiding somewhere, she wasn't in this room, and she wasn't one to play those kinds of games.

"What's the matter?" Gus entered from the hallway.

"Did you come back here last night and mess with this?" Michael used his thumb to gesture at the panels behind him.

Gus shook his head. "No. Why?"

"Because we turned it off when we left," he said.

Gus shrugged. "Maybe someone came in here since then. There's no reason to get upset about it. They didn't harm anything, did they?"

"No. That's not the point." Michael steadied his patience. Sometimes his wife's uncle could be so… so… "There are only four people here, Gus. I didn't do it. You just said you didn't do it. Cynthia's still in bed. So is Brandon, probably. So if none of *us* did it…"

Gus nonchalantly walked over to one of the chairs and sat down. "There's nothing to get excited about, Michael," he said while giving more attention to a button on the nearest panel than his nephew-in-law. "Cynthia may have came here in the middle of the night or while we ate breakfast to work on some stuff alone. Brandon likes computers. Maybe he came in here and played with them. You've been down here for a week, right?"

"About, yes."

Gus reached one hand under the panel, searching. "You haven't seen anyone else so far, so I doubt they just all of a sudden appeared now. I'm sure there's nothing to worry about."

Michael wasn't convinced, and his patience with Gus had ended. "I'll go check on Cynthia." He swiftly walked to the door and turned towards the elevator.

As he entered their shared bedroom, he called out, "Cynthia? Cynthia!"

"Mmm? What?" she groaned angrily. *Can't I get one lousy good night's sleep?* she thought.

Michael sat next to her on the edge of the bed and placed one hand on her shoulder. He gave it a tiny shake to ensure she was awake. "Did you mess with the control room last night?"

She rolled over just enough to give him a death stare. "You mean other than with you?" Her voice cracked from exhaustion when she spoke.

"Yeah. Did you go back and turn anything on after we left?"

His concern bled onto her. She wiped the sleep from her eyes, blinked several times, and rolled over more to see him better. "No. Why?"

"Is Brandon still in bed?"

"How should I know?" She propped herself up on one elbow. "I've been in bed all night." She was still irritated at being disturbed, but that was quickly changing into worry.

Michael jumped off the bed and left the room without a response.

"Michael? What's going on?" She threw the covers off and sat up. "Michael!"

Michael ran to his son's room. There was only one option left, and if it wasn't him— "Then we have a problem," he muttered to himself.

The door to Brandon's room disappeared when Michael pressed his palm against it. Bracing himself with both hands against the frame, he poked his head inside and quickly scanned the place. The bed showed signs of being slept in, but now lay empty. The floor was clean too, meaning his clothes and shoes were gone.

He could hear Cynthia's running footsteps behind him. "Michael! What is going on?" Her eyes were wild as she spoke each word separately and with deliberation.

Rage and terror fought within him. His next words came out like daggers. "Our son has taken a field trip."

"Where is he?" screamed Cynthia with a sharpened edge of anger. She twisted her body around as she exited the elevator and marched ahead of Michael for the control room. "Where did he go, Michael?"

"I don't know exactly." His voice was serious, grim. He pursed his lips. The confirmation of his son missing shot a flash of panic through his system, but logic soon overpowered that feeling, causing him to concentrate more on solving the mystery of where Brandon was than fretting over any potential danger he met while there.

"What do you mean, 'exactly'?" Cynthia glanced to where she thought Michael was walking next to her, but he had fallen behind. She stared straight ahead, her stride unfaltering.

Michael answered anyway, "I found the main map and several of the panels already on this morning and Brandon missing. I can only assume he's gone exploring."

Cynthia quickened her pace. Any faster and she would have been running. "I'll kill him! He knows not to go off alone like that in a place like this! If he-"

Michael had to jog to keep up with her now, causing his voice to shake. "I know, dear. I know. He's probably fine. He's just—"

"He won't be by the time I'm done with him! I will *kill* him!"

"Calm down." Gus was walking slowly towards them from the other end of the hallway with his palms up. "I'm sure he just went to look around or something."

His actions had their intended effect. She slowed her pace, but only so as not to run into him. "I told him *not* to!" she spat back at her uncle.

He shrugged. "Boys will be bo—"

She rolled her eyes and strode past him into the control room. When she saw it, she froze. The main map was up and zoomed in onto a specific tunnel. Another, more defined map was hovering over one of the panels. It was also zoomed in on a tunnel. Panic replaced anger within Cynthia as understanding came. "He's gone to the surface." Her voice was barely a whisper.

"What?" Michael didn't hear what she said, but her tone worried him. She sounded terrified.

"He's gone through one of the other tunnels," she repeated.

"No!" He couldn't believe his son was *that* stupid. "We should search the Hub first, just in case."

"No, Michael," she said. "I'm telling you—"

The main map suddenly reverted to its normal appearance, zoomed out and without the topical layer. At the same time, a beeping noise emitted from it.

Relief ran down Cynthia's back and arms like ice water when she recognized it. "He's back." Her voice still shook as it had yet to regain its strength.

Gus's brow furrowed, and his lips pursed in confusion. "I don't understand. What do you mean, he's back?"

At the juncture of where the tunnel Brandon had searched met the Hub, a light flashed repeatedly.

Michael, still worried about his wife and son, answered Gus quietly. "It's how we knew you were here. The map signals when the shuttles and decontamination rooms are being used.

"How do we know it's him?" asked Gus.

"It better be." Cynthia's arms were crossed in front of her chest.

Michael and Gus pitied whoever it was.

CHAPTER 20

The ride back in the shuttle proved more tiring than the hike, or perhaps it was just more relaxing. Either way, Brandon jerked awake when it stopped at the Hub. As the door opened, he rubbed his eyes, trying to force himself alert enough to keep going. His feet dragged across the floor, and he almost dropped his flashlight more than once. He had to brace himself with one of the walls to keep from collapsing during the decontamination cycle.

When it completed, he hobbled his way to the door with a slap-happy smile on his face. He may have been exhausted and dehydrated, maybe even hungry—it was hard to tell, but he didn't care. The only thing he wanted now was his bed, which he envisioned waiting for him with an open blanket.

"Brandon!"

Cynthia's voice caused his eyes to nearly fall from their sockets. He stumbled backwards with his arms raised in front of his face for protection.

"Where have you been?" Each word commanded its own moment in time.

He glanced over his father's tense, angry face and registered the disappointment on his uncle's. All the joy from looking forward to sharing his discovery with his family had elated him to where he forgot about the yelling and the screaming he was sure to endure first. And the disappointment. That was the worst part.

"I shouldn't have done this," he told them, his throat dry to the point of pain.

"Ya think?" his mother retorted. She then grabbed his arm and marched him to the elevator. The two men followed.

Being yelled at and dragged through a hallway like a naughty toddler woke Brandon up a bit. He no longer had to fight the urge to lie on the floor and sleep. Although that action was preferable to what he knew was coming.

The moment the elevator's door shut behind them, Cynthia snapped, "Start talking. Now."

Despite most of his sleepiness vanishing the second he set eyes on his mother's livid face, his muscles remained fatigued. This not only caused him to sway like a drunken man but his words to slur periodically when he spoke. "I couldn't sleep."

Their expressions told him he was off to a bad start. But as stupid and terrible as admitting the truth made him feel, he accepted if he were ever to gain their trust again, if that's still possible after this, he would have to be honest from the beginning.

"When I couldn't sleep…" He had to think a minute to remember exactly what happened next. It all seemed so far away now. "Yeah!" He remembered. "When I couldn't sleep, I went to the control room to search for my laptop, but I found something on one of the maps, a path or a signal or something in one of the tunnels. Anyway, I wanted to figure out what it was, but I couldn't do that unless I followed it to the top." He glanced quickly at their faces, which hadn't changed. "I didn't plan this! Like I said, I couldn't sleep. I admit I shouldn't have gone without you, but I was afraid you wouldn't let me go at all. And, I don't know, I just … It was just something I *really* wanted to do, and I didn't want to chance you making me stay in the Hub while you did it instead."

The door to the elevator opened, and Cynthia grabbed his arm again to lead him to the cafeteria.

His drunken stupor had not left him, and he stumbled all the way there. He conceded he was in trouble, but he also knew what he found was important, or at least he thought it was.

"Mom."

She didn't stop.

"Mom!" He stopped moving, refusing to let her drag him another step. "I found Egypt."

His actions caused Cynthia to falter, and her anger to multiply. "Of course you found Egypt, Brandon," she snipped. "The tunnels go all over the world."

"No, you don't understand." He jerked his arm away and faced them all. "It wasn't like in the Grand Canyon. This one had been *used*. There were steps and a throne and…"

"Wait a minute," said Michael.

Cynthia's eyes widened incredulously at her husband's response. Yes. It was all very interesting. And yes. She wanted to learn more. But as far as she was concerned, that could all wait until her son learned not to do anything like this again. Ever.

Brandon, grateful for his father's reaction, turned to him and explained further, "This tunnel wasn't hidden like the Grand Canyon one. There wasn't a wall with a crack in it or anything. I mean, it was like, like the Egyptians *knew* about it or something." As he spoke, Brandon's gaze soon included Gus. Cynthia narrowed her eyes at them in annoyance. She was being ignored.

"You mean," Gus began, his face plastered with disbelief. "You went to the surface? All the way through and broke ground?"

Brandon shook his head. "Not the surface, no, but... It was just different! I can't explain it; you'd have to see it."

"You're not going anywhere, young man." Cynthia had had enough.

Michael, seeing his wife's fury, stopped himself from saying anything else. And, even though somewhere in the forgotten deeps of his conscience he realized he shouldn't be, he found himself on his son's side.

Gus took a step back and lowered his head. "Your mother's right, Brandon. You shouldn't have gone alone." His eyes however, peering up from under his brow, told Brandon he would've done the same thing in his shoes, and he wanted to hear more about it when this was over.

Brandon chanced a peek at his father before forcing his eyes back onto his mother's. Michael gave him an encouraging hint of a smile. "I'm sorry, Mom. I … I wasn't thinking."

Cynthia knew Brandon was a good kid. He wasn't perfect. He was still young and needed to learn more responsibility, but she understood he meant it when he apologized. "You will stay exactly where we tell you to at all times."

"Yes, ma'am."

"One of us will always be with you."

"Yes, ma'am."

She crept towards him, making each step a statement, until their noses were inches from each other and she had to tilt her head back to look at him. "And if you ever…"

He swallowed.

"I *will* kill you."

Brandon nodded slowly at her words. He loved his mother very much, and it pained him to hurt her like this. "I'm sorry, Mom. It won't happen again."

You better know it won't, she thought to herself. She backed away. Feeling foolish for losing her temper like that but knowing she was in the right. She kept her head high, refusing to be the first to sever the gaze between them. If he was going to go traipsing about some alien world without even telling them where he was going, he needed a good scare. Maybe more.

Michael cleared his throat, allowing everyone to turn their attention to him. "What did you find, Brandon?"

With the last drops of his adrenaline consumed from facing his mother's wrath, Brandon's eyelids drooped uncontrollably, and his words slurred even more heavily. He leaned against the wall as he spoke. When he had finished telling them all he had seen, Michael caught him from falling over and said, "You need to go to bed."

Brandon nodded in response. He wasn't going to argue with that one. There was one thing he needed to warn them about though, despite the repercussions of doing so. "Oh … um … the flashlights need charging." He removed the headlamp from his head and handed it with the flashlight to his uncle Gus, purposefully avoiding his parents' gazes.

Gus took the lights, trying not to touch whatever was all over them that stank so much. "Do I want to know what happened to them?"

"No," answered Brandon. "I'd wash my hands after cleaning them off though."

Gus pulled one closer and sniffed it, instantly regretting his actions as his nose wrinkled and his head turned to the side uncontrollably. He held the lights as far away from himself as possible.

Cynthia's eyes widened with the comprehension Brandon was hoping so much wouldn't come, of what the flashlights being dead meant. "You mean you came back in the dark?" she nearly screamed.

Not wanting to listen to another lecture, Brandon turned away from her and headed for one of the food vending machines. "Is it OK if I take some food to my room?" He may be practically sleepwalking, but he was also famished. A gallon of water would be nice, too.

Michael held out his arm to stop Cynthia from advancing towards their son. "Sure," Michael answered him. He could tell Brandon wasn't going anywhere other than his bed from the way he was acting.

Brandon wobbled his way along. Cynthia pushed slightly on her husband's arm as if to follow him. Michael turned to his wife and said, "He'll be fine, Cynthia. Look at him. He's exhausted. He won't do anything stupid, for a while at least." He smirked on his last statement.

Cynthia didn't find him amusing. She grimaced heavily but then relaxed her stance.

Michael's eyes smiled as he asked Gus, "Did you bring any extra batteries?"

"Not for the headlamps. They have to be charged. I'll have to connect them to the Hub like I did your laptops."

"Is that something you think you can do?" asked Michael.

Gus shrugged. "I don't see why not. It won't be quick. Even after coupling the two technologies, we'll have to wait for it to charge."

"That's OK," said Michael. "I want to make a more intense inspection of the maps in the control room anyway."

CHAPTER 21

"What is it?" Michael had been staring at the Egyptian tunnel map for nearly an hour, trying to understand what made it different from the rest. "Brandon was right. It is different. But why?"

Cynthia sat at the main map, twiddling it with her finger, her anger long forgotten. "The light is pulsing in perfect time. There has to be a reason for that."

Michael watched the pulse travel the entire tunnel's length. "And it goes all the way to the surface. Why?"

Cynthia pressed the topography button and zoomed in on the tunnel's exit. Her eyes tightened as she attempted to spot any details that might explain what they were witnessing. "That is Egypt," she muttered in confirmation to herself. "But what—" A tiny detail of the map caught her attention. Three miniscule pyramids. Lined up exactly as they were today. She gasped.

"What did you find?" Michael ran to her side; Gus was still busy trying to connect the headlamp with the Hub's power.

"It's the Giza pyramids," she answered.

"Ow!" Gus jerked his head up with her announcement and banged his head on a panel.

"You OK?" shouted Michael.

"Yeah," Gus grunted, pushing himself off the floor. "Did you say the signal goes to the Giza pyramids?"

Cynthia backed away, opening up the map area for them to get a better view. "See for yourself."

Both men peered at the glowing orb, tilting their heads and looking at it from different angles.

"Hmph," Gus grunted and then walked away from the map.

"What?" Michael recognized that grunt. Gus was pondering something.

Gus went back to his coupling work. "Nothing."

Cynthia and Michael exchanged a glance. "I know what that sound means," said Michael. "Spit it out."

Gus sighed, deliberating for a few seconds. Then he shook his head and busied himself again. "Don't worry about it. It's a silly idea. You wouldn't believe me anyway."

Michael retorted, "We're sitting in an ancient Hub in the center of Earth after discovering it's more machine than rock. What could you possibly be thinking that we won't believe at this point?"

Gus let his voltmeter plop into his lap. "There is a theory that the ancient Egyptians placed the Giza pyramids so they lined up with the Orion constellation. Orion became associated with the Egyptian underworld god Osiris, due to … the Nile or something like that. Anyway,"—he resumed his work, giving the impression he gave little credence to the argument—"they built the pyramids because of the underworld and all, and … well, there's also a theory they used them as transmitters or something."

Cynthia didn't move. She knew her husband would eat up a theory such as this. In retrospect, she was surprised he wasn't the one to think of it to begin with, given he had probably watched over two hundred YouTube videos on just such a theory already. But, as ridiculous as it was, everything Gus just said made sense. The flashing signal, the pyramids. It all connected in a logical way.

She and Michael slowly turned their heads to face each other, each wearing similar faces. "He's right," Cynthia said, refusing to believe it but having to.

Michael's brow furrowed, but only slightly. His expression was still mostly one of grand stupor. "What do you suppose it's transmitting?"

The question shook Cynthia from her shock. "Oh! Um…"

"It's an S.O.S." Gus said from under his panel, still working on the coupling.

"What?" asked Michael.

Gus glanced up without pausing his work. "The Hub is calling for help."

Cynthia blinked several times. "Are you sure? I mean, could it be something else? Besides, who is it transmitting to?"

At this point Gus stopped what he was doing and came out from underneath the panel he had been working on. "No, I'm not positive." He leaned against the top of the panel. "It could be anything: a monthly status report, visual analysis on the current inhabitants… But if that were the case, where are the scientists?"

Michael crossed his arms, seriously contemplating this new theory. "What do you mean by, 'the scientists'?"

"If the Hub's purpose is to send up reports, then someone would have to be here observing Earth and creating those reports." He shrugged. "This place would have to be occupied most, if not all the time by researchers for it to be useful, and we haven't seen any sign of that.

"The seriousness of the damage to Earth also tells me that whoever or whatever built this place left a very long time ago. The only thing that makes sense, to me anyway, is an automated S.O.S."

"But to whom?" asked Cynthia.

Gus shrugged. "I'm going to go check on Brandon." He motioned to the coupling. "The lights are charging now. They need to be left alone for several hours at least."

"OK," Cynthia said weakly. "Th-thank you," she managed to shout out just before the door shut behind him.

Neither she nor Michael spoke for several minutes until, with her hands holding her elbows across her chest and her face remaining slack, Cynthia finally said, "He's lost his mind."

Michael remained unable to pull his gaze from the floor. "He's right, you know."

"Of course he's right." She rubbed her face with her hands and took a deep breath, trying to swallow everything they just realized.

Cynthia's reaction only solidified the reality of the situation for Michael. *Give her time*, he thought to himself. *She just needs to let it sink in.* Deciding a change of subject would be best, he said, "As soon as the lights finish charging, we need to start on the repairs."

Cynthia nodded her agreement.

"We should probably take naps until then, so we're fully rested."

She nodded again.

Another glance to make sure she was OK, and Michael headed for the door.

"Michael." Her voice shook slightly.

He paused and faced her.

Her eyes glistened in the map's light. "Who is it transmitting to?"

CHAPTER 22

Several hours later, what he could only assign as early evening, Brandon groggily rolled onto his back and groaned. After wiping away as much sleep from his eyes as he could, he took a deep breath and forced himself to sit up.

It took a while to get his bearings straight. In those last few moments before reality took over, he had gone from the weird dream state to the "Where am I? This isn't home!" thought process. He was currently in the "Discovering Earth is a machine and living in its center isn't nearly as much fun as I would have thought," mood.

Another face wipe and two grumbles later, he had his clothes on, two food cubes in one hand, and a glass of water in the other. He satisfied his painfully dry throat, cringing with each swallow until it quit hurting. Then he popped a cube in his mouth, he didn't care which, and chewed. The taste was irrelevant to him at the moment. After washing the pieces down with another gulp of water, he did the same with the other cube. Still not fully rested, but desperately wanting to know if they learned anything more, he set out to find someone with answers.

A hushed sound like sleet in the wind told him his bedroom door had reappeared behind him. He glanced down both directions of the hallway. There were only two places his family would be without telling him, the cafeteria or the control room. That realization made his guilt ten times heavier for not notifying his parents where he was going when he took off. They would have told him. He could trust them.

Assuming they were probably in the control room rather than eating, that's where he set out for. He arrived to find each of them bent over a different panel, studying their individual maps. They didn't notice him come in.

"It isn't giving me any information, just that it's broken!" Cynthia slapped her panel in frustration.

Michael was studying a red tunnel from halfway across the room. "Mine either."

Uncle Gus had left his panel and was flitting about the room examining anything he hadn't already for a hint. "Have you tried searching the Hub yet?"

"Not all of it," replied Michael. "I was hoping this would be quicker."

"Brandon!" Gus had nearly run into him on his way to the door.

Cynthia turned around to face him. "I'm glad you're here. You can help us search for whatever we're supposed to use to repair the tunnels."

Apologizing didn't seem appropriate anymore. "Have you tried asking the computer?"

They stared at him in disbelief. He didn't understand why. The question seemed logical to him.

The lights were voice activated, why not other things? "Where's your laptop, Dad?"

Michael pointed. "Over there, why?"

"I want to try something."

"It's not hooked up to the Hub, if that's what you're trying."

Brandon opened the computer and sat it on his lap. "Is that possible?"

"What, hooking it with the Hub?" asked Michael.

"Yeah."

Michael's words stretched out with apprehension. "I … don't … know about that. What will the laptop enable you to do that the controls won't?"

Understand English, for one, Brandon thought. "Nothing really. Not in the time span we're dealing with at least. I mean, I could set up a translator that would allow us to communicate via the keyboard instead of trying to figure out how each word is pronounced, but that would take too long."

"You can do that?" asked Cynthia.

Brandon peeked up from the lit screen. "Yeah, Mom. I don't just play video games all day. I write them too, you know."

She could feel her eyebrows rising up her forehead. She recalled his talking about his game making in past conversations, but she never took it seriously. The gaming industry wasn't something she considered a legitimate career field. Besides, her own ambitions had always taken precedence over his, which currently made her feel too awful to respond.

Assuming his mother's silence meant she didn't want to argue with him, for which he was grateful, Brandon dropped the subject and searched the Desktop for a Cuneiform dictionary. A few minutes later he found the Cuneiform word for "repair". "Nonnniituu." He strung the syllables out, trying to pronounce them correctly. "Nonitu," he said with more confidence.

"Maybe you have to say, 'computer' first or something," Michael suggested.

Brandon flashed him a sardonic grimace. "This isn't Star Trek, Dad."

"No," Michael said with pure sincerity. "But how else is it going to distinguish the difference between commands and generic conversation?"

Brandon sighed. "Good point." His dad was right, which meant this was impossible. The time it would take to figure out the prompt word wouldn't be worth it. He sat the laptop aside and stared at it unfocused.

After several seconds, he said, "Wait a minute. Wouldn't anything used for repairing the tunnels be *in* the tunnels?"

An approving smile slowly stretched across Gus's face. "Why yes, Brandon, I do believe it would."

They started with the tunnel that led from the canyon, mainly because they were the most familiar with it, but it also served the purpose of being marked as slightly damaged by the maps and therefore giving them something to work with.

When they reached the shuttle's room, Gus planted himself in front of the control panel so he could study it. He dropped his bag of tools he had insisted on bringing next to it. Brandon scanned the walls and ceiling. Cynthia went inside the vehicle to search, and Michael got down on all fours and crawled across in the floor in the hopes of finding another hatch.

"That does the door..." Gus mumbled to himself. He pressed one of the panel's buttons, and the room's door obeyed.

Watching it close reminded Brandon of their journey here from the surface. "Why does the door have to be closed for the shuttle to run?" he asked no one in particular.

While maintaining his crawling position, Michael raised his head and stared at the door with a puzzled expression on his face. "I don't know. I guess the same reason the shuttles always come back to the Hub after they're used."

Brandon swiveled his head around to look at his father, who had returned to his investigating. "Yeah. I noticed that when—" He was about to say, "when I returned from Egypt," but didn't want to open that can of worms again.

The atmosphere of the room changed when he stopped, like they sensed what he had stopped himself from saying. The air felt sharp now, and heavy. Gus cleared his throat to avert the subject away from one that made everyone uncomfortable. "Yes. I did notice that when we made our way from the canyon."

Brandon knew Gus was only saying that to help him out of the hole he just dug for himself. He almost wished his uncle would quit saving him from his parents' wrath. At this rate he would never be able to repay him.

"How did they get this so smooth?" Michael's hands slid effortlessly over the seamless sheet of metal which made up the floor. He inched forward. "And what keeps us from slipping on it when it *is* this smooth?"

Brandon ignored his father's musings. It was clear he was asking himself more than anyone else. Brandon returned to scanning the walls and ceiling, which was proving just as fruitless as the floor. "I'm not finding anything," he told the others.

Gus placed one eye inches from the edge of the panel to peer into its sides and behind it. He then tried to wedge his fingers between it and the wall, probably trying to tear it apart from what Brandon could tell. When nothing came of it, he abandoned his efforts. Brandon returned to his scanning, with no hope or expectations this time.

Several minutes of silence later, everyone but Cynthia stared at the shuttle in apprehensive wonder as its underneath emanated the sound of whirring gears. "Did anything happen?" Cynthia's voice sounded muffled from inside the vehicle, like she had her head under something.

"Yes," answered Michael, still on all fours and looking ridiculous from where he had contorted his body to learn what that noise was. He stood up and slapped his hands clean, although there was really no reason for it. The floor was cleaner than he was.

Several metal arms with differing tools on the ends now extended from the front end of the shuttle. "What did you do?" he asked.

Everyone waited for her to answer. When she finally exited the vehicle, it was to three pairs of eager eyes. She laughed at the image. "There's a control panel behind one area of the seats." Unable to stop smiling at their goofy expressions, she waved her hand and added, "Come on. I'll show you."

The three men followed her into the shuttle and spread out inside its spacious cavity. On the end with the mechanical arms sat a podium that appeared to have sprouted from behind the seat cushion.

Cynthia demonstrated as she spoke. "This backrest pulled out, and I found a handle. When I pulled it, this"—she gestured to the podium—"*thing* popped up."

The "thing" as she called it was similar to the pedestal beneath the main map in the control room of the Hub, but smaller. Several buttons lined the bottom, and a holographic image of the room directly in front of the shuttle shone above the middle of the panel. Brandon reached out to touch the image, curious if that was how they would control the arms. It didn't respond.

"Wait a minute." Gus exited the shuttle and threw his bag of tools in front of the arms. As he did, a holographic bag appeared in the image. Everyone inside the shuttle gasped.

Brandon reached out again, this time aiming for the bag. But still nothing happened. "I don't understand."

"Let me see something." Gus pushed his way in front of the others.

Each of the buttons bore a symbol presumably corresponding to a tool. He pressed the first one. As it lowered, it slid back under the panel, revealing a hole. His eyes widened in response. A hand-sized tool replica poked its way up through the hole. After waiting a brief moment, he pinched the tool with his fingers and pulled it out completely.

A cable connected it to the podium. "Hmm." Gus rotated the tool in his hands, examining it from all angles.

Brandon peeked over Gus's shoulder. The tool was like nothing he had ever seen before. It didn't appear to have any moving parts, just a long rod with a fine point. Gus lowered it back in.

"Try this one," Brandon said, pointing to a button that looked like a tool made for grabbing might be hiding underneath it.

Gus pressed it. A set of "pliers" appeared. With wide, excited eyes, Gus reached out to take them. "Extraordinary!" He grinned childishly while everyone gave him a few minutes to play with it.

When the others started shifting their stances and sighing with impatience, Michael cleared his throat to signal it was time to get back to work.

"Oh, yes," agreed Gus. A bit of a blush filled his face. He took the miniature set of pliers and tried to grab the holographic bag with them. As he did so, an image of the corresponding tool appeared in the hologram and moved with his motions.

The sounds of the real tool outside drifted into the shuttle. Brandon stuck his head out the door to watch. The giant pliers headed smoothly for the bag but suddenly jerked and fell. With a furrowed brow, he pulled his head back in to see what was wrong.

Gus had dropped the miniature pliers. He picked them back up and tried again, but his grip was too weak. They fell from his hands a second time. Sad frustration swept over his face. Pity took control of

Cynthia's, but she soon hid it well. It was age that had done this, but no one would dare acknowledge it.

"Here." Brandon, after glancing at his father to make sure it was alright, stepped next to his uncle. "My fingers are smaller."

Michael nodded his approval of the pretext, and Brandon took over. Everyone knew it wasn't the size of Gus's fingers, and everyone knew Brandon was giving his uncle a graceful excuse. They said nothing.

The strangest perception of a surreal video game filled Brandon's mind, making it difficult to concentrate. While the pliers in his hand were real, and he undersood the image before him was merely a representation of the outside world, he could feel the items within that representation. When he lifted the bag with the pliers, the weight of it came through to his hand. Not the same amount, more like a scale replica of the weight, much as the tool he held was a replica of the actual one.

An uncontrollable grin filled his face. His ears lifted when it did. "This is so cool!"

Michael and Gus went outside to watch. Cynthia stood on tiptoe and peered over her son's shoulder. The real tool overlaid with the image confused her, like she was seeing double. "How are you doing that? How can you tell which is real and which isn't?"

He shrugged. "It's just like a VR. It doesn't take long to get the hang of it."

Cynthia admitted to herself she should be familiar with what a "VR" was, and was consequently too ashamed to ask.

Michael was listening to their conversation from outside and yelled loud enough for them to hear, "Are the updated headsets any better?"

Michael's knowledge of her son's interests only deepened her shame.

Brandon shrugged, not realizing Michael couldn't see it. "I guess so," he yelled back. "I can't really think about that right now, Dad."

Cynthia wanted to say or do something to close the gaps in her and Brandon's relationship, to make it what it should be, but she couldn't discern what that something was. She allowed the passing seconds to go by in silence. Then, after making an inner vow to change their relationship, to change herself, she joined the others outside.

The tools moved smoothly, like living appendages to the shuttle. It made her wonder, what if her son could be a highly skilled surgeon, one of those that used robots to do the surgeries online? She bit her lip. She was doing it again, not accepting her son for who he was and what he wanted to do. Plotting his life course must be a personal objective of her job as a mother.

Her torturing thoughts were thankfully interrupted when what resembled a thick orange laser beam shot from one of the tools, hitting the bag and catching it on fire. All three jumped away from the bag in fear.

"What did you do?" yelled Michael.

"I tried out one of the other tools," replied Brandon. "Sorry."

The bag continued to burn in silence. Michael approached it with the intentions of stomping it out. A holographic likeness of him came into Brandon's view.

"No no no!" Brandon yelled from inside the shuttle. The tools continued to move flowingly as he spoke. "I want to try and put it out."

"I rather liked that bag," Gus mumbled to himself.

Tilting his head sideways so he could look at Gus askance, Michael said, "We do need to know how they work, and if this helps him figure it out…" He trailed off, suggesting anything was fair game as long as it aided in achieving the final goal.

"Then use *your* bag," countered Gus.

Before the situation escalated, a burst of pale green foam shot out of a different tool, encasing the bag in a quickly hardening shell.

The outside tools froze in place. They had become lifeless. The three adults approached the bag cautiously.

"What'd it do?" Brandon ran outside to join them.

Gus knelt beside it and hit the shell with the side of his fist. It resonated like dense polystyrene would. He wedged his fingers between the coating and the floor. Although he had to strain at first, the coating with the bag eventually pulled from the floor like a separated tip of an iceberg. He lifted it up for all to witness.

Michael moved in for a closer examination. A few droplets of the coating remained on the floor, which he knelt next to and touched.

"Is that wise?" asked Cynthia.

"Probably not," he answered, and promptly stood again. "It looks like it didn't finish."

"What do you mean?" she asked.

Michael used one hand to point out gooey spots on the bottom side of the hardened mound and his other to point at similar places on the floor. "See where those spots on the floor match up with these?"

She tightened her eyes and angled her head to observe the area more clearly. "Yeah."

"It reminds me of melted plastic. I believe if this had been on the floor any longer, we wouldn't have been able to prise it up. The shell and the floor would've been welded together."

Brandon felt the blood drain from his face. What if he had hit one of them? He glanced at their expressions to see if anyone was angry. No one seemed to be.

Gus continued to hold the shell, which contained his bag and resembled a miniature mountain, at a tilt. "If it's not too much trouble, could someone retrieve my bag?"

"Oh! Sorry." Michael grabbed hold of the bottom of Gus's bag and pulled, hard.

Gus braced himself and held the green rock of a shell with both hands. A loud ripping sound echoed through the room as the bag tore from its captor.

Holding it at arm's length, Michael grimaced with disappointment. "Sorry, Gus." He offered the torn shreds to his uncle-in-law.

Gus dropped the foam mound with a loud thud and walked slowly over to Michael. He took the bag and held it with a wistful expression. "I loved this bag," he said.

Michael cleared his throat. "Sorry about that." He gestured to Brandon. "Why don't you show us which tools do what?"

"I really loved this bag." Gus muttered to himself. He threw the ruined bag into the room's corner and joined his family in the shuttle.

Brandon picked up each tool he had used and explained their attributes to them. Afterwards, everyone had a general understanding of the pliers and the fire extinguisher.

"How do we discover what the rest of them do?" asked Cynthia.

They all three stared at her.

"What?"

Gus said, "Don't look at me. That's the only bag you're getting from me," and left the shuttle.

Cynthia rolled her eyes in exasperation and stared at Michael, waiting for a response. Brandon's gaze shifted uncomfortably between the two of them.

"Don't worry, Cynthia," said Michael. "I'll figure it out."

"But what if you don't?" she asked.

Brandon backed away from the conversation and inched his way towards the door.

Michael used his hand to gesture towards the buttons on the panel. "I'm sure it's obvious. This one probably … um … moves things, and this one—"

"Ugh! Men!" Cynthia threw her hands up in the air in frustration and marched back to the control room.

After a few weary glances between themselves, the others followed.

Several minutes later in the control room, they spotted Cynthia holding the main map in her hands, adjusting it to survey the damaged areas more clearly. She spoke without looking up. "Brandon, you and Uncle Gus can stay here—"

"What?" screamed Brandon in protest. "Why do I have to stay here?"

Cynthia gave him her usual mother's face for when he argued with her, stern and in control. Her voice dared him to protest more. "Because we don't know what's out there. You're not going anywhere unless we're sure it's safe."

He objected anyway. "The entire world is collapsing! Where could it possibly be safe? The inner core? You know, that part the rest of the earth is collapsing in on?"

Cynthia squared her shoulders, bracing for a fight she had to win. She took a deep breath. "I—"

The floor of the Hub shook beneath them. All four of them grabbed the nearest structure to brace themselves with. Their faces searched their surroundings as a piercing sound wailed through the air.

"What's that?" gasped Cynthia.

"I'm guessing an alarm of sorts," answered Michael. The quaking had stopped, and he used the opportunity to search the map for answers.

One holographic tunnel had turned not just red, but flashing red. Michael brought up the topical layer to get a better understanding of what they were dealing with. Another quake shifted them sideways as he did, throwing him to the floor.

"What's going on?" Brandon could feel his eyes bulging and his breath hitch. Being on top of the earth where the quakes were a weekly or more occurrence was one thing, but having them happen in what he considered the quake control room was an entirely new type of fright.

Gus's eyes were wide as he held onto the railing behind him. His reaction only added to Brandon's fear.

Michael readjusted the map. The top of the newly damaged area, inflamed compared to the others, flashed ominously. The moment each of them realized what was happening was evident on their faces.

"The ocean," whispered Michael.

The newly damaged area was directly beneath the Pacific Ocean.

CHAPTER 23

Brandon took a step back. "What do you mean, 'the ocean'?" His voice was weak. He'd deduced exactly what his father meant by it, but he wanted to be wrong.

The corners of Cynthia's eyes and mouth fell with despair. Michael looked to her, worried. He swallowed. Neither of them could force themselves to answer his question.

Gus, his eyes glazed with thought and focused on the distant nowhere, answered for them. "It means that somewhere on the surface of the Pacific Ocean, a giant whirlpool is forming as the waters get sucked into the crust. And that hole in the crust is now growing, breaking away at the edges with the increasing flow of the ocean's waters. Ships as large as towns will be sucked into it, breaking in half as they go."

Michael, seeing the expression on his son's face, shouted, "Gus! That's enough."

Gus turned his head towards them, his eyes coming into focus. "Oh." He blinked rapidly. "I'm so sorry." Blush rose up his neck. A forced smile pushed his cheeks up. "I'm sure we can fix it. Right?" He turned to Michael and Cynthia now.

Their emotions guarded, they spared the slightest of glances at their son before answering, "Yes."

"We better get going though." Cynthia took a step toward the door.

"Michael." Gus motioned for Michael to join him away from the others. Michael's brow furrowed with concerned curiosity. Gus kept his voice low for Cynthia's sake. "You have to take Brandon to the ocean."

"What? I don't understand."

"He's faster. His coordination is better than the rest of us put together."

Michael turned to his wife. She had heard.

Panic strangled Cynthia, and tears burned in her eyes. She shook her head, whispering, "No. No."

Gus was right. They did need Brandon. Michael knew it, and he could tell by the way she was acting Cynthia knew it too. Cynthia didn't want to admit the truth. She wasn't ready to put her baby in danger like this. Her head shook unsteadily in defiance. No. She wasn't ready.

Michael placed his arm around her shoulders. "We have to, sweetheart."

Another shake threw them to the ground, as if to prove his point. No longer able to hold it back, sobs broke through Cynthia's façade.

Brandon crawled over to her. "I have to do this, Mom." He tried his best to be comforting yet sincere, and he wasn't at all sure he was getting it right. "Mom." He pulled her chin up with his fingers. "Look at me."

She kept her eyes closed and swallowed, gathering her strength. When she opened them, it took everything she had not to lose it again at the sight of him. Fresh tears welled up despite her efforts. "I know," she whispered.

"Michael," Gus called, an edge of alarm in his voice. "We have a problem."

A second inflamed area had appeared on the map. "We're out of time." Gus strode to the door. "Brandon, you're with me."

Michael almost objected, but stopped himself. Cynthia jumped up from the floor. "What do you mean, 'he's with you.'?" When Gus didn't respond, she spun her head around and asked, "Michael?"

Michael had a hard time lifting his eyes to meet her gaze. "You and I need to repair this other tunnel. It's on dry land and not as dangerous. The ocean could destroy all of us in seconds. Brandon's the fastest. He needs to go to the ocean." Another tremor shot through the Hub. "And he needs to do it now."

Emotions fought each other in Cynthia's chest until her mind became too fuzzy to concentrate. She glanced up at the men in her life and realized her inability to focus meant their judgment was probably more sound than hers at the moment. Unable to say the words, she silently nodded instead.

Brandon ran to her, giving her a tight hug. "I love you." He pulled away. It was time to go.

"I love you too," she managed to whisper.

One shared smile with his father later, and he and Gus were running down the hall to the elevator.

Brandon knew he had faster reflexes than his parents. Years of gaming had given them to him. He was also more inclined to pick up on how things worked, although Gus was probably better in that category than any of them were. A career in machining tends to do that.

They hopped into the elevator. "Did you catch which floor we're going to?" Gus asked.

"No. I didn't get a chance to look at the map." His parents had been in the way.

"I think it was this one." Gus pushed the button with a triangular symbol. He sounded certain enough.

The elevator jerked to the side but kept moving. Brandon braced himself against the wall just in case. "Do you think it's safe in here?"

Gus grimaced. "No less safe than out there."

His voice was grave. Brandon saw the charade was over. "How bad is it?" he asked.

The door opened. Gus pretended he never heard Brandon's question and began searching the hallway for labels. "Help me find the right door."

Brandon didn't press for an answer to his previous question. If Gus didn't want to tell him, he probably didn't want to know. "Which one are we looking for?" he asked.

Gus twisted his mouth in thought. "Uh… A square with two dots and a line."

Brandon jogged in the other direction. Time passed immeasurably. It could have been seconds; it could have been hours. There was no way for him to tell.

"Brandon!" His uncle's voice sounded from the other end of the hallway.

Brandon spun on the ball of his foot and twirled around to run in the opposite direction. Gus was standing at the shuttle room door, waiting for him.

"D'you find it?" Brandon asked him.

"Yes. Let's hurry."

The shuttle sat there waiting for them. When Gus opened the door, Brandon ran inside and threw the seat cushion aside. He readied the tools on the podium.

"It might be best to leave those put away until we need them," Gus said.

Brandon lowered his brow, puzzled. "Why? Don't we need to have them ready ahead of time?"

With his fingers poised over the launch button, Gus said, "That's good thinking, but they're probably not made for the journey. They may break off on the way or slow us down or…" He shrugged.

Brandon nodded. "Good point." He quickly put the podium back in place and sat on the bench, waiting.

CHAPTER 24

The soft cushion of the shuttle's bench did little to calm Cynthia. Her fingers had formed a death grip over the front of it, and her breaths came hesitant and shallow as she stared into the imaginary nothing before her.

"You OK?" Michael asked. He was waiting to press the launch button. When she gasped and jumped in response to his speaking to her, he left the button for now and sat next to her, his hands stroking her arm reassuringly. "It will be OK."

"You don't know that." Her voice shook as she fought to keep control.

"No," he said. "I don't." He stopped his hands for a moment. "But thinking otherwise, no matter how truthful, won't help you right now. I know we may all die, or just some of us will, but I'm OK with that."

Her head jerked around so fast, Michael had to pull his away.

He shot his hands up in surrender. "No, not OK like *that*. I mean…" A tired, yet thoughtful sigh escaped him before he said his next words. "I'm able to accept it as a possibility and still function."

She returned her head to its previous position and allowed her gaze to go out of focus again.

He laid his head against her shoulder and stroked her arm with his hands. "You can't do that. If you're going to get through this, you'll have to live in denial for a while."

His words gave her the excuse she was looking for. She shifted her eyes to the floor, took a deep breath, and swallowed. Her chin rose jutted and determined. It reminded Michael of their meeting with the other scientists just before he convinced her to come here. The memory made him smile. He liked his wife when she was strong like this.

Her tears blinked away more easily this time, but her voice still shook when she spoke. "I'm ready now." Wiping what remained of her fear from her cheeks, she stood up, her voice now firm. "Who's doing the virtual work, you or me?"

"It might be best if I do," he answered businesslike. "I have a steadier hand at the moment."

She agreed, then took the two steps over to the launch button, and pressed it.

The shuttle slowed prematurely. Brandon watched through the window to learn why. A terrible screeching sound of metal scratching rock vibrated through the walls of the craft, forcing them to cover their ears in pain. It stuttered to a stop, throwing them forward when it did.

"The inertia dampeners must not work here," Gus said from the floor.

Brandon propped himself up on one arm. "The what?"

"The inertia dampeners. That thing I told you about that keeps us from turning into Jell-O in here?" He gestured to the inside of the shuttle.

The memory was distant, like it had happened four years ago, not two days. So as not to sound rude, Brandon answered, "Oh right," though he really didn't care anymore. His biggest concern was fixing their current problem.

Gus muttered aloud to himself, "If the inertia dampeners aren't working now, then they're probably tied to the track, not the shuttle, which means… Oh dear."

Brandon didn't ask. He didn't want to know.

The shuttle lurched backward. Brandon peered out the window to see a gush of water run past them. He ran to the cushion to set up the podium. "What's keeping us in place?" he asked as he hurried.

"I can only imagine, but my guess is a magnetic field of sorts, the same force allowing us to travel as quickly as we do when going back and forth." He used his finger to mimic the motion.

Brandon pulled the podium into place and waited for the holograms to come into view. "How long have we got?"

"What? You mean till the water breaks us free?"

"Yeah." The tools' images still hadn't produced themselves. Brandon drummed his fingers impatiently.

"Oh, I have no idea. There's no way for me to tell really."

Brandon didn't like that answer. In hindsight, he might find that he preferred it to the truth, but not now.

An image came into view. It looked like a metal wall. "Uncle Gus? Can you come look at this?"

So much holographic water spewed from the image, Brandon couldn't make anything out. Gus leaned in closer and pursed his lips, focusing his sight on the hologram. "Looks like a bulkhead."

"What? Are you serious?"

Gus nodded. "Yes. I would say the tunnels have built in safety measures in case something like this happens. A bulkhead would at least prevent the ocean from pouring down the tunnel and therefore drowning out the Hub." He pointed at the mess of water in the image. "The water has formed a fissure, a crack in the bulkhead, or the bulkhead was unable to close all the way in time. Either way, we'll need to repair it."

The shuttle jerked backward again, shooting adrenaline into Brandon's chest. He wiped his palms onto his pants and grabbed the narrow hosed tool, the one which had put the fire out back at the Hub. Since the pressure of the water was so high, and it seemed to be shooting from every direction, he didn't know where to start. So he shot it straight ahead.

The result was a backsplash of green foam. He immediately released the tool's trigger, but a hard coating was already beginning to form on the outside of the shuttle. The holographic images before him became muddled, staticky.

A loud, low rumble originating from the back of the tunnel vibrated around the shuttle. Brandon gasped; his eyes flew open in fear. "What's happening?" He turned around to face his uncle.

Gus was calmly tinkering with a smaller podium on the other end. "I'm closing the bulkhead behind us."

Brandon's fingers wrapped around the tools' podium behind him, his knuckles turning white. "What?!"

His hands still working, Gus glanced over his shoulder. "That way if anything goes wrong, it protects the Hub."

"What about us?" Brandon's voice was frantic, out of his control.

Gus faced him, his voice quiet and serious. "We need to worry about your parents." His eyes bore into Brandon's until they watered. "If we don't place that bulkhead there, the Hub will drown if we are unsuccessful, and the ocean will drain even more than it already has."

He turned back around. As he did, Bradon caught a glimpse of his immensely sad eyes.

The shuttle moved again, but not with a jerk or a loud noise. It was with a wave, like riding on a boat. "Are we floating?" Brandon jumped to the nearest window to look out. Water surrounded the entire shuttle.

He reeled his head around to check the door for leaks. "Is this thing waterproof?" The sound of his own voice shamed him. It sounded like a scared child's.

Gus peeked at the door seams nonchalantly. "I believe so."

Brandon opened his mouth to ask if Gus had known they would be safe beforehand or if he had just hoped they would be, but then decided he really didn't want to hear the answer to that question. He made his way back to the tool podium.

The image in front of him swirled with bits of debris but was otherwise much clearer than before. Without the constant stream of gushing water, he could see the problem easily now. The corner of the bulkhead pointed towards them, as though it hadn't fully closed before the water pressure had risen enough to bend it in.

Brandon searched the tools before him, pulling each one briefly from their spot before deciding it wasn't the right one and dropping it back down again. "No. No. No," he muttered to himself between them.

"Try that one."

Gus's voice startled him. Cylindrical in shape, the tool he pointed to resembled a pistol with a rounded head. Brandon picked it up and aimed it at the bulkhead. He couldn't find a trigger. He moved the tool forward until the top of it touched the bent corner.

As the resistance of the bulkhead pushed against him and made his job harder, Brandon leaned into the motion, forcing the corner into place. Several minutes of hard pushing later, the door snapped back into its groove.

Brandon released the tool. "I don't understand. How was I able to do that?"

Gus, whose attentive eyes were filled with speculative interest, answered, "I don't know." He leaned back away from the podium. "My only guess is that it's using a gravitational force, probably the same thing it uses to keep us upright in the shuttle. Come to think of it…" His gaze traveled across the ceiling in a lost path while his fingers scratched his chin out of reflex. "It's probably the same thing they're using to create *Earth's* gravity."

"They?" repeated Brandon.

"Huh?" Gus still acted lost in thought.

"Hey!" Brandon yelled to snap him out of his daze.

Gus started. "Oh! Sorry. Yes, the Architects. The ones who built this." He walked back over to the podium he had earlier.

They had all come to accept that someone or something had built the Hub, had built Earth for that matter, but they never talked about them. Not much at least, and certainly not enough to agree on a name. If they survived this, Brandon thought, *whoever* they were had a lot of questions to answer.

The shuttle swayed slightly. Gus had opened the repaired bulkhead.

"What are you doing?" Brandon screeched.

Gus calmly explained, "With the pressures equalized, we can open this bulkhead now and travel to where the real damage is."

It took a moment for that to sink in. "You mean the ocean?" Brandon's voice rose two octaves on "ocean".

"That's why we came."

Gus's voice gave Brandon the distinct impression his coddling time was over. Brandon swallowed, and braced himself for traveling forward.

CHAPTER 26

Michael and Cynthia's journey through their tunnel was well underway when the temperature started rising. "Doesn't this thing have an air conditioner?" Cynthia fanned her shirt, now sticky with sweat.

Michael knew the answer, but he didn't want to tell her. The shuttle was nearing something it wasn't designed to. It only made sense. If it were designed to travel through temperatures this bad, it would be keeping them cool. "Maybe it's broken," he said, hoping she would buy it, for now at least.

Cynthia's mind flashed to Brandon. What was he facing right now? Was he OK? At first she had wished for a radio between them so they could talk. Now she realized it would only make her more anxious and was therefore grateful they didn't have one. Besides, her constant worry would have probably gotten in the way so bad they would have eventually taken it from her anyway.

Cynthia's eyes involuntarily shot to an open window. An orange spark flew past the same window, causing her heart to falter. "We're not equipped to be here."

Michael grimaced. He had hoped his façade would last longer. "Probably," he admitted.

"You knew," she said, turning to face him.

His eyes flickered across hers. "I had a hunch."

Random small objects tapped the outside of the shuttle. Michael ran to the tool podium and readied it for use. Tiny holographic dots darted by the images of the tools. Cynthia's heart raced as she realized what they must be.

"Burning metal." The confirming words brushed by her lips without her consent a second before she was thrown to the floor by a sudden lurch of the shuttle. Michael reached to help her up.

"What happened?" she asked, all thoughts of her son forgotten.

"Something flew by the right of the image station just before we moved, so I'm guessing whatever it was hit us." He returned to the podium.

The shuttle was stopped. From the window, Cynthia could tell the shuttle had wedged itself at an angle. When she looked out the other side, she noticed black with flecks of orange, the telltale sign of cooling magma. The sight made her back away instinctively. "Michael." She swallowed. "We're in trouble."

"I know." His voice was full of tension. The image before him was growing and although he was unable to discern its color, the shape was unmistakably that of flowing magma.

A long moment passed where he could do nothing. He couldn't breathe. He couldn't move.

Then, the image of Brandon putting out the fire back at the Hub crossed his mind. With a short gasp, he took control of his body and realized what to do.

He searched for the extinguishing tool, frantic yet still in control. But just. He felt the panic rising, realized if he didn't solve this soon, they would both be too distressed to do anything. With his teeth gritted against the swelling fear, he grabbed the extinguisher and aimed it at the magma.

The blast forced him back a step to brace himself from falling, but it worked. Cynthia watched the green foam through the window as it covered the magma with zero obstructions or problems. It made her breathe a little easier. She glanced at her husband. He wore a huge grin on his face like he was a teenager again, shooting aliens at the arcade. She followed his gaze to the holographic display. The movement within its imagery had changed from a slow moving blob to an engorged growth. He had succeeded.

Cynthia wiped the sweat from her forehead and sat down with a relieved sigh.

Michael let out the fearful breath he had been hiding from his wife and soon joined her where they sat, holding hands and basking in their shared relief for several minutes.

A wet trickle running down Cynthia's neck caught her attention. It was still just as stiffling in the shuttle as it was before they made the repairs. "Why hasn't the temperature changed?"

Michael thought for a moment. "You're right. With the heat of the magma blocked by the hardened foam, it should have."

He rose from the bench and assessed their recent repairs. The newly formed shell completely contained the magma with no signs of leakage. He checked the front window. The tiniest speck of orange shown in the distance. "There's more?"

Cynthia jumped up to join him. "What do you mean, there's more?"

He pointed at the speck. "See that?"

She pushed his arm aside and peered into the far distance. Then her head drew back as her eyes swelled with fear. "I see it."

Michael grabbed the shuttle's throttle and jerked it in reverse. The shuttle creaked and popped as it eased out of its angled position. Cynthia crouched instinctively.

He threw the lever forward. It moved the shuttle a few inches and jolted them slightly. He pushed it backward; the shuttle moved a small amount in the opposite direction. Back and forth he continued to move the throttle, roughly jerking them along with the shuttle until it finally got back on track. At that point, the dampeners came back into play, for which Cynthia was very grateful.

Not wanting to accelerate too quickly, Michael eased them closer to the orange glow ahead.

The temperature inside the shuttle grew as they neared it. Cynthia found herself dizzy. "I think … I think I need to sit down." Her voice was breathless. She grabbed the wall with her hand and used it to lower herself onto the bench.

"Cynthia!" Michael let go of the throttle and ran to her. He patted her cheeks with his hand. "Cynthia! Wake up!"

Her lids fluttered from the strain of trying to stay conscious. Michael blew on the sweat which was pouring down her face. It helped. Determined, she opened her eyes and, with a grunt, pushed herself up. She wiped her face with her hands and shook her head. Reality crept back into her consciousness. She glanced at the window ahead.

When Michael had let go of the throttle to attend to Cynthia, the shuttle was several yards from the magma ahead. Now it was inches.

"Michael!" Cynthia screamed out in warning.

Michael's head swung around to face the windshield. He jumped to the controls and threw the shuttle in reverse. Once at a safer distance, he stopped it. Before the molten rock could get close again, he grabbed the fire extinguishing tool and aimed it at the flow.

It took several minutes. As he worked, magma would break through the fresh, still not hardened shell. Areas had to be reworked continuously. Once completed finished, the temperature inside the tunnel stopped rising.

Before them stood a solid wall of the sprayed foam. "We can't fix this," he said. "There's no way we'll ever be able to bypass this and repair the real damage. Do you think the earth's crust will last this way?"

There was no answer.

"Cynthia?" He turned around to see why she wasn't answering.

His wife lay on the floor, crumpled, and no longer sweating.

CHAPTER 27

The flow of the water around the shuttle caused it to wobble through the tunnel instead of glide, making Brandon nauseous. He bent over, holding his stomach while gripping the shuttle wall for support.

"You OK?" Gus asked.

"Just car sick," Brandon moaned.

Gus's mouth twisted in thought. The last several sections they went through had been filled with as much water as this one, but they contained no current, at least none that he observed. Travel had been slow, but smooth. As they neared the surface however, a current appeared. And the shuttle's wobble was becoming a lurch. Gus was beginning to wonder how much worse the current would get.

"I thought we equalized the pressure," Brandon shouted over the bangs of the shuttle against the inner surface of the tunnel. "How can there be a current if there's not any flow?"

Gus peered through the windshield. He pulled on a lever behind him, stopping the shuttle.

The jolt threw Brandon forward, but he stopped himself before falling over. "How are you able to drive through this mess anyway?" His nausea prevented him from paying attention to his uncle's actions.

"Oh, this vehicle is extraordinary!" Gus's voice was empty of the worry and fear that filled Brandon's head. It even had a bounce of excitement in its tone. "While you were playing with your tools, I found this control panel which allows me to steer it. I can even open the windows remotely."

Several of the windows' shutters opened and closed via his command. Brandon closed his eyes to keep from puking. He forced a swallow. "Stop!"

Gus glanced at his green face. "Oh. Sorry. Do you want me to leave them open or closed?"

Brandon took several breaths, his eyes tightly shut. "I don't care. Just stop messing with them."

The shuttle, although paused in its current location, shunted to the side every few seconds. "That must be coming from another leak somewhere," Gus said.

Brandon chanced a peek. His stomach was starting to settle. "Any idea where?"

Gus studied the outside view for several seconds. "I believe it's coming from behind us. The water must be rushing out of the tunnel and into the depths of the earth itself."

"S'at mean we have to go back?" Brandon knew the answer to that question, but he also had the tiniest bit of hope he was wrong.

"I'm afraid so," Gus answered. "Do you need a minute?"

"Do we have a minute?" he asked rhetorically.

Gus shook his head, but Brandon still had his eyes shut. "Probably not."

"Then no, I don't need a minute." He took a deep breath and blew it between puckered lips. Twice more he did this while Gus drove the shuttle in reverse.

"We're here. The water's quit moving."

Gus was right. Brandon felt the stillness of the shuttle, and it made his nausea subside almost immediately. One more huff through his lips, and he was ready. He walked to the holographic tool podium. A representation of the outside was still there. He studied the view out the window.

Water had blown out the side of the tunnel. Its metallic surface, now torn with ripped, jagged edges, bent outward from their side and into the earth, or whatever was between the Hub and the surface. Brandon tried to peer into the hole, to see what was really there, but it was too dark and the water too rough.

"You'll probably want to weld it," Gus said over Brandon's shoulder. "I don't think that green stuff does very well in water."

Brandon replied, "I thought underwater welding was dangerous."

"It is. But it's less dangerous than the earth drowning itself. Besides, I doubt this has what we call a "welder". It more than likely utilizes a different way of repairing the damage. I'm not even sure this is metal." He indicated the tunnel as he spoke.

Brandon studied the tools before him. "Which one should I use?"

Gus dipped one eyebrow in thought. "That one?" He pointed at a hologram most resembling a blowtorch on the end.

Brandon turned his head around to meet his uncle's face. "What do I do if you're wrong?"

"Quit using it." He shrugged, a jovial expression on his face.

Brandon bit back a retort, knowing his uncle was after one and refusing to give him that satisfaction. All playfulness aside, he gave the leak his full concentration now. The outside tool followed his lead as he aimed it at the heart of the fissure and pulled its trigger.

A thick, white jet flew out of the real tool, a holographic representation mimicked it. The kickback tested Brandon's grip, surprising him. "I knew these holograms were realistic, but good grief!"

The outside water turned to steam, blocking his view. "I can't see anything!" He didn't need to shout, and his voice echoed painfully within the shuttle.

"Try doing it in short bursts," Gus shouted back, though not as loud.

Brandon let go of the trigger. The water continued to gush into the hole in the tunnel's wall, clearing the smoke and bubbles quickly. A large glob of material now sat attached to the left of the hole. He had missed the fissure's edge entirely. "I don't know what I'm doing!" Anxious anger filled his chest, jumbling his thoughts into a foggy mess.

Gus's hand lightly touched Brandon's wrist. "It's OK. Missing won't cause any damage to the tunnel. The track's pull on the shuttle is well equipped to escape being sucked in with the current."

As Gus said that, Brandon noticed the shuttle still swayed, though it wasn't as noticeable as earlier. The track's pull must be keeping them in place.

Gus continued, "We are as safe as we can be."

Brandon blew out his cheeks as he exhaled loudly. From what he could tell, *no* place on Earth was safe at the moment.

"Take your time," Gus said.

Anxiety constricted Brandon's throat again. He opened his eyes and said through clenched teeth, "We don't *have* time."

Gus rocked back a moment to think. After a pause, he said, "This isn't real, Brandon."

Brandon whipped his head around, his face contorted in confusion. "What?"

"Think of it as a game."

"But this isn't a game. This is real. And if I mess up—"

"If you mess up, you mess up, but at least you tried! The world is caving in on itself, boy!" Gus had lost all patience now. "There's no time to get anyone else for the job, and you know what to do! Grab your joystick and weld the hole shut!"

Gus's words stung, but Brandon had no choice but to concede. There was no time for self doubt. Win or die, he had to keep trying. Brandon closed his eyes and took a breath. *It's just a game*, he told himself. *It's just a game*.

When he opened them again, he held the weight of the hologram of the welder in his hand. His controller. His eyes locked on the hole ahead. His breath became invisible. His entire body tensed, ready to spring on command. He braced his legs firmly to the floor, and pulled the trigger.

Giant billows of steam filled with dancing bubbles, making it impossible to see anything. He released the trigger.

Another miss.

Adjusting his weapon, he tried again. The bubbling smoke turned into an ignorable blur, allowing his other senses to take control. The welding went smooth for a while, then hit a snag.

Immediately, he released the trigger to see what caused it. The globs of metal formed messy lines which inched their way closer to the leak. The last line, the one he just made, fell into the hole. They both watched as a tiny fragment of newly formed metal, forced into a dance by the strong current, fluttered until it lost its grip, and disappeared into the void.

He smiled. He understood what to look for now. Keeping his controller exactly where it was when he last released the trigger, he started again.

The rough edges of the gap vibrated his hands, catching them with hitches, while the undamaged metal felt smooth. Slowly, far more slowly than any surface welder, he dragged his tool from the outside of one of the fissures to the center of the hole, making sure he hit resistance all the way. After several minutes, he checked on his work.

The ripped line had sealed with nothing more than a smooth scar. He wanted to touch it, to reach out and run his fingers along its surface. It looked like it was part of the metal, like it belonged there.

"This isn't welding," he marveled.

"No. It's not." Gus's voice was in equal awe.

Brandon jerked himself back into the moment. He had to move fast, repair the damage before the current could do more. The repaired crack of the fissure formed the first point of a warped star that bent in at the center. He started on the edge of the second star point, once again working his way towards the middle. This time was easier, though he still made a mess at the beginning.

Another smooth scar. He grinned, unable to control his relief and pride. The rest of the work took every bit of his concentration. He couldn't remember the last time he had breathed, though he must have or he would be on the floor, possibly dead. His legs no longer existed, their feeling long forgotten. It was just him, and the challenge ahead.

When he believed himself finished, he stepped back, his hands clammy and his lungs empty. He shook out his hands and legs before catching his breath. "There! How's that?"

The shuttle swayed one more weak wobble before going completely still, a good sign. Gus eyed the repair work. A light colored uneven star marked the tunnel wall, nothing more. If they hadn't stopped to examine it, they would have never known the hole once existed.

Gus pushed the throttle, inching the shuttle forward until the repair work lined up with a side window. He pressed his face against the window, searching for any mishaps, any leaks that might still be there. "Perfect! This is amazing." His voice was a whisper. His fingers hung off the edge of his bottom lip. "How on Earth…"

"Uncle Gus?" Brandon didn't want to say it. The last thing he needed right now was another bout of nausea, but he knew he had to. "We need to keep going."

"Oh yes, yes. Of course." Gus pulled himself away from the window, still muttering under his breath, "Remarkable!" as he did.

He moved the shuttle forward to continue their mission. One by one they traveled through the different sections, closing each bulkhead as they passed. A few bulkheads in, Brandon's nausea subsided enough for him to walk around. He joined Gus at the console and studied the controls.

Another hologram was currently floating above a string of buttons. "I don't remember a hologram there. What's it for?"

Without breaking his concentration, Gus answered, "It's the tunnel. If you poke it certain places, it'll do things."

Typical Uncle Gus response, Brandon chortled to himself. "What's this do?" he asked aloud, while pointing at a holographic blue square hanging on the side of the map of the tunnel.

Gus glanced at what he was pointing at before turning his attention back to the path ahead. "I don't know."

Brandon pushed it. In hindsight he realized that was a very stupid thing to do, but it wound up being a productive action.

At first there was no cue his momentary lack in judgement had caused anything. Then Brandon noticed that the part of the tunnel nearest the blue square he had pressed was slowly turning white from the top down, like a glass of water being emptied by a straw.

"What's that mean?" He pointed at the phenomenon.

Gus studied the area intently a moment, then yelled with surprised delight, "What did you do?"

"I just pressed the button I asked you about. Why?"

"I think it's pumping out the water from that section of the tunnel!"

Brandon's expression mimicked his uncle's now. "Oh! Should I do that to the others?"

"I would," Gus said, then added, "But make sure to only do it to the sections already secured by bulkheads." He returned to his driving.

One by one, Brandon pressed the button next to each section as they checked it for leaks. He tried not to think about where they were going.

CHAPTER 28

"Cynthia." Michael's soothing voice sang his wife's name aloud. "Cynthia."

Her eyes began to flutter.

Tears of relief fell from the tip of Michael's nose as a smile stretched from one end of his face to the other. "There's my girl."

The shuttle was cooler now. After stopping the magma, he had set the shuttle on a course back to the Hub. As they traveled, the air conditioning had worked its magic until it was almost comfortable again.

"Michael?" Her voice cracked. Her neck dampened with sweat, a good signal she was returning to normal.

"You scared me," he said.

"What happened?" She tried to sit up.

He didn't let her. "Stay down. You need to stay like you are until I'm sure you're alright."

"Ow." Her hand reached for her head. "My head hurts."

"Probably," he sighed. "You suffered heat stroke and fainted. You're probably dehydrated. Don't worry, we'll be back at the Hub soon enough, and you can—"

"The Hub?" She sat up, forcing his firm hand out of the way. "That's all? We're just going back to the Hub?"

Michael frowned, concerned she might be hallucinating or something. "Of course, honey. Where else would we go?"

"The surface, Michael." She said it as though it should have been obvious. "There must be damage to the surface. We can't simply plug the hole and call it fixed."

He sat on the cushioned bench across from her. A remnant drop of sweat tickled his forehead. He wiped it away. "Even if we could get to the surface from here, I don't know how to stop a volcano. This shuttle is not equipped to drill through hardened rock, and as you saw, it's not made for these extreme temperatures. Besides, it's not like the surface hasn't had lava before. They're probably fine."

She opened her mouth to argue.

He held up his hand with understanding patience. "We stopped it from entering the Hub and causing the crust to collapse. That's what matters. But when we get back, I'll try to find a way to diagnose the surface's damage and repair as much as possible."

"Thank you." She lay back down, allowing herself to relax a little and for him to continue his explanations.

"Whoever built this obviously used something to drill these tunnels out, and place the magma, and… and…" He shook his head and rubbed his eyes hard with his fingers. The concept, the very idea of building such an entity, a *planet*, was beyond his comprehension. He had long accepted the possibility of modern scientific Earth models being incorrect. The hours he spent watching conspiracy videos attested to that. But daydreaming science fiction and coming to terms with it in real life were two immensely far apart actions.

Cynthia propped herself on her elbow. "Does that mean there's an entryway within a volcano somewhere?"

"I doubt it," he said. "Just because the tunnel's here doesn't mean it leads all the way to the surface. Look at where Gus and Brandon are going. I doubt their tunnel leads to an opening for humans at the bottom of the ocean. Unless…" He stared off into dreamy space.

She tilted her head and pressed her lips into an accommodating grin. "Michael. They went to the Pacific Ocean not the Atlantic. I don't think they'll find Atlantis."

He let out a disappointed sound.

Several seconds passed in silence as the shuttle quietly continued its journey. Michael raised his arm to once again wipe sweat from his face and recoiled in disgust when he got a good whiff of his own armpit.

"That bad, huh?" Cynthia asked with an upcurled lip.

"Yeah." He was still making a face. "What I would give for a good, hot shower."

"You don't like the steam baths here then?"

He shook his head. "No. I want something I can *feel*. I want water running down my body and the harshness of a shower sponge scraping the dirt off my skin."

She smiled. "It's called a bath pouf."

"Not the one I use, it isn't. It's a shower sponge."

"Yeah, I'll remember that the next time I buy you one. You wanted pink, right?"

His glare held the hint of a smile. "Very funny."

She peeked out the window. They had reached the port. They waited for the shuttle to right itself before exiting. Michael jumped out first, wanting to survey the damage.

The fresh air from the Hub woke Cynthia further. She felt good enough to stand and joined him outside. "What are you doing?" she asked.

Cautiously, he moved his fingers towards the damaged tip of the shuttle. It was still too hot to touch. Its heat radiated enough to warm the room.

Cynthia gasped when she saw it. The tip of the shuttle had turned a solid black with charcoal streaks running up its side. It had the appearance of a space shuttle after surviving re-entry. She instinctively reached out to it. Michael slapped her hand down and away, hard. "I wasn't going to touch it!" she snapped.

"Sorry. I just didn't want you to get burned."

She ignored him and reached her hand out again, palm forward. The shuttle felt like a campfire on a cold fall's night and warmed her palm from several feet away.

Meanwhile, Michael bent over to examine the underside and back. His grimace deepened as he let out a worried grunt.

"What now?" she asked, still holding her hand up to the shuttle's heat.

"Look," he said.

She walked around to where he was. "What happened?"

"It melted."

In several places around the shuttle, spots of casing twisted into globs, resembling plastic that had gotten too hot. Some spots still had hardened magma on them.

"Oh, Michael!" Her hands flew to her mouth.

He placed a comforting arm around her.

"We could have been killed!"

His arm pulled her closer. "But we weren't. We're OK, and we stopped the leak."

"As far as we know! What if, what if that stuff comes down here and, and…"

He gave her a good squeeze, rubbing her arm to calm her. "We'll worry about that when the time comes. We've done the best we can for now, OK?"

She took a deep breath and nodded.

"Hey, I know. Let's go back to the control room and check on Brandon and Gus's progress."

Cynthia wasn't sure that was any better.

Seeing his wife's strained expression, Michael added, "Just think of the nose rubbing you can do to all those jerks who laughed at you about this." He extended his arm out in an encompassing gesture.

That idea gave her some of her strength back. She stood up straight and said, "No, I'll be professional about it."

Michael grinned, hoping she wouldn't.

"But as soon as that magma cools," she added, "I want a sample."

Captain Sanchez sipped his coffee as he started his morning out in the captain's office. *His* office. Two weeks into his first assignment, and it still hardly seemed real. He was now in command of the newest, largest cargo ship for Melize International Cargo Liners, the MICL *Emerald*. He started out for MICL seventeen years ago as a deckhand, and now … *now*, he thought with a smile, he was one of their captains.

Before he left for the control room, he ritually kissed the photo of his wife, Catalina, and their two sons, Felipe and Mateo. They wanted to be with him, a perk he had been looking forward to as captain, but not this time. Not on his first assignment. There would be others, he told himself. He wanted to devote his full attention to his first command.

He continued to sip his morning coffee as he walked to the control room. The ship's course felt smooth under his feet. Last night he had ordered the vessel to accelerate to 18 knots, much faster than the recommended speed. Recent economy and climate regulations forced MICL to urge their captains to go as slow as 12 knots, a whopping 14 miles per hour, but that wasn't a command; and he hadn't made the order to be rebellious.

The route assigned to the *Emerald* was far from new to him. He had traveled it at least twenty times during his career; it was that common. But it was for that very reason he had told his helmsman to increase their speed and divert from their given course, albeit only slightly. Pirates knew the original course well and prowled it often, especially this time of year. Carlos Sanchez wasn't taking any chances. His diversion would add less than a day to their journey and drastically reduce their chances of running into any pirates.

When he reached the control room, he acknowledged his working crew and then stared out the window to assess the weather and ocean, his mind on the real work ahead of him. There were reports to fill out along with many more hours, if not days, of admin work to finish before they next docked.

"Captain!"

Captain Sanchez's body stiffened mid-sip. He turned to answer, "Yes, Chief Officer Gonzales."

Gonzales stared out the windows of the control room, his face frozen in a state of panic. With one finger extended, his arm slowly raised until it pointed out in front of them. Sanchez followed it.

"Qué horror!" One reluctant foot at a time, Captain Sanchez approached the window.

The current before them leaned to the right, stretching out in an arc so wide and large he could barely tell it curved at all. His mug fell from his paralyzed hand and shattered on the floor. Black coffee flowed away from it. "Emergencia! Timon duro izquierdo!"

As the crew carried out his command, forcing the giant ship into the wall of the current, Sanchez ran to the starboard-side window. The sight made him grateful his family had not joined him. Past the white crest of the water, the ocean darkened into an ominous navy as it swirled into a whirlpool big enough to hold ten cargo ships.

CHAPTER 30

"Más! Más!"

"It's as fast as it'll go, Captain!"

Sanchez and his helmsman grabbed the nearest beam to keep from sliding into the bulkhead of the control room. No longer spotted with the tiny white peaks of the wide ocean, the outside wall of waters shadowed the vessel with their dark presence.

The engines screamed for relief as the ship's rudder failed against the impossible current. Even with the fallen cargo, the MICL *Emerald* was no match for the ocean's force.

Sanchez glanced out the window one last time, but it was futile. No light penetrated into the depths of the whirlpool that held them.

The floor beneath their feet groaned with the ship before the sound of fracturing metal entered their ears. The rudder had broken away. They stared at each other, their expressions a ghastly hybrid of comprehension and terror. As the ship lost its battle with the eddy and plummeted miles to the bottom of the Pacific Ocean, they knew their fight was over.

CHAPTER 31

Brandon heaved what little acid was left in his stomach onto the floor of the shuttle, where it jiggled around with the rest of his last meal. The violent current slammed them into the tunnel's wall with a bang.

"Sorry," Gus called out.

"I know," Brandon rasped between gasps for air. "Why is it doing this?"

"We're nearing the surface."

Several more bangs hammered the outside of the shuttle. The noises grew in intensity until Brandon felt the shuttle slow, but only in its forward motion. It continued to rock side to side, which made the challenge to keep standing greater than not throwing up again. He grabbed the podium for support, his legs bending as the floor rose and fell beneath them.

Movement from outside the windshield caught his attention. "What's that?"

Instead of the expected leak or bottom of a whirlpool, ahead of them lay shiny red metal which drew into a giant pointed edge near the center.

Gus's face puckered. "I believe it's a ship."

"Like another shuttle?"

"No. Like a sunken ship." He moved the shuttle forward a few more feet. "It's impossible to tell with the condition it's in now, but I would presume it was a containment vessel." His voice changed from intrigued to mournful. "And recent, from the looks of it."

"What do you mean?" Brandon asked, fearing he didn't want to hear the answer.

"I mean at least two dozen people just drowned."

The freshly painted hull spanned wider than the tunnel's width ahead of them and made Brandon's stomach heave again. Not from the motion, from the fear. "It's going to crush us, isn't it?" He watched as the outside edges of it scraped against the broken sides of the tunnel. Dirt and salt water poured into the tunnel with every jar.

"Not if we hurry." Gus stared out the windshield, just as mesmerized as Brandon.

The vessel inched further in. Brandon remained fixated on its ominous hull.

"Brandon." When he got no response, Gus shouted, "Brandon!"

Brandon turned to his uncle and, after seeing the expectant look on his face stammered, "Oh, right. Sorry."

With his legs now adjusted to the chaotic movement of their shuttle, and one hand still bracing his troubled, empty stomach, he side-stepped his uncle with a muttered, "Excuse me," and grabbed the projected tools.

He closed his eyes. "I can do this," he whispered to himself and then opened his eyes again.

The approaching ship was another boss fight. He had grinded his way to the top and was ready to take it on.

Sucking in his upper lip, he bit down on it, hard. If he could seal the smaller leaks around the outer edges, he would slow or even stop the current, and then he could worry about fixing the rest of it. *The rest of it*, he thought with a scoff. How anybody could remove a containment vessel from a hole in the bottom of the ocean, and plug what it left behind, was beyond his comprehension. "One task at a time," he muttered.

Gus gasped from behind Brandon's right ear. "I bet a bomb exploded!"

Brandon whipped around. "What?"

"An unexploded bomb," Gus answered matter-of-factly.

"Here? Now?" Brandon's voice broke in alarm.

"Oh, no no no." Gus waved his questions away. "Although…"

Brandon's face paled. "What do you mean, *although*?"

"Uh…" Brandon's terrified face forced Gus to rethink his words before saying them. "The ocean floor is littered with sunken war vessels, many of which still contain live ammunition, possibly even nuclear." He eyed Brandon's reactions carefully before continuing, "What has probably happened is that one of these ships' bombs exploded, which more than likely set off many more, resulting in a crater in the ocean floor. If Earth were structured the way most scientists claim it to be, that wouldn't be a problem. But since it isn't"—he stared out the window again—"you get this right here."

Brandon followed his gaze out the window. The cargo ship continued to jiggle from the force of the ocean's escaping water. "So when you say 'although' … you mean…" What color had returned to his face left again, taking more with it. "There might be more bombs that haven't gone off yet?"

Gus hesitated. He didn't want to lie to the boy, but he didn't want to tell him the truth either. "Y-yes," he finally said.

"Wouldn't that make what I'm about to do even more dangerous?" Brandon shrieked. His voice was starting to get hoarse. He wished they had brought some water.

Gus nodded. "Probably. Yes."

A chunk of ocean floor and rock, about the size of a car window, broke from around the ship's hull. It hit the shuttle with a deafening bang. As soon as it did, an alarm sounded, coupled with flashing interior lights.

Brandon looked to his uncle. The jolt had thrown Gus to the side of the shuttle, where he stood, bent over, eyes wide with fear, and grasping what he could for support. "Better do it now, Brandon! I'd rather blow up than drown!"

Brandon felt his jaw drop. "Are you *serious?*"

"It's quicker that way," Gus answered.

Stunned by his uncle's reaction, Brandon turned his head slowly back to the incoming current. Once again focusing on the task ahead, he took a deep breath and grabbed the holographic "welding" tool. He aimed it on the smallest rip he saw, where the shredded side of the tunnel met the looming vessel.

The distance between the shuttle and this hole of the tunnel was far greater than it had been for the earlier leak, but Gus was afraid to take them in any further. Brandon agreed. The current was already making him have to fight to keep his tool steady. He couldn't imagine having to fight it even more. Besides, if another piece broke off with them closer to it, Gus might not get his wish of being blown up.

Smoke and bubbles filled their view as the first shot left the welder. Brandon let go of the trigger to check his work before proceeding. He had to repeat that several times before he was confident enough to work without stopping.

As soon as he finished, he caught his breath and wiped the sweat from his palms onto his pants. Then he shook out his hands and wiped his face before grabbing the tool to work on the second section.

"Watch out!" Gus ducked down instinctively.

Brandon joined him. A second loud bang told them their time was running short. They both rose cautiously up and looked out the window. "Oh no," Brandon whispered.

"What?" asked Gus.

Brandon pointed to a tiny crack in the window. "That." The crack hadn't broken through to their side, but they both knew with the current they were fighting, the crack would grow into something far more dangerous.

With his eyes fixated on the new damage, Gus let out in a broken whisper, "Hurry."

Adrenaline made his hands shake, but Brandon grabbed the tool and got to work. He didn't stop to check for mistakes, he just went. Every now and then Gus would order him to stop, so he could gauge the progress, but Brandon hated to. When he did, the shaking of the approaching vessel he was trying to keep from crushing them came into view, causing his fear to spike.

CHAPTER 32

"I can't stop anymore!" The alarm still blaring, the inside warning lights flashing, seeing the front end of that cargo ship stare them in the eye was too much to handle. Brandon had reached his breaking point. He dared not even chance a glance at the once tiny crack in the window. For all he knew, it had grown into a dangerous valley.

"But what if we're off track?" asked Gus.

Brandon scoffed at the idea. His voice cracked several times when he answered, "I'm repairing the whole friggin' end of the tunnel! I can't miss!"

Gus disagreed, but said nothing. The horror in his nephew's eyes had sewn his lips together.

The shuttle shook with another bang. Gus responded, "Another piece of the ocean's floor must've broken off."

"I know!" Brandon shouted back. He figured he was over halfway done with the repairs by now, but couldn't bring himself to verify his estimate.

Several more clangs rocked the ship. The movement was so fierce it threw Brandon to the floor. Vibrations rolled through his body as the shuttle slammed into the tunnel wall.

When he pushed himself up, the crack in the window came into view. It had grown. The center had formed a well nearing the inside surface of the window. Brandon could see how thick it really was now — several inches from the looks of it. Veins grew out from the well like spiders' webs.

"I thought you said this wasn't glass," he said to Gus while his stare intensified on the growing problem.

"I said I didn't think they were glass. That doesn't mean they don't crack. Just be glad they're as rigid as glass is. Otherwise they would have buckled in long ago."

Brandon stood behind the podium, readying his tools. "One of the lights must've been hit."

Gus examined the outside through the windows. He let out a low, disapproving hum when he did. "It would appear several have."

Brandon swiveled his head to glance quickly through all the windows. Over half were dark on the outside. He wasn't sure if he appreciated the inability to see all that was flying past them or hated it.

The view ahead was clear. No more smoke, no more bubbles. "Let's finish this," he said.

Gus silently agreed.

Nearly all of the original structure of the hole had been destroyed which resulted in the repair work resembling a sewn Frankenstein more than smooth scar tissue.

"There's not much left," Gus said.

Brandon nodded.

"It shouldn't take long to—"

"Uncle Gus?"

Gus hummed a yes.

"Can you please be quiet?"

"Sorry."

Brandon sensed his eyes glazing over. He was losing his concentration. He shook his head and wiped his eyes to try and regain some of it. Then he grabbed his welder and pulled the trigger.

The massive surge of smoke and bubbles made it once again impossible to track his progress. Instead, he imagined a grid in front of him and guided the welder along it. As he did so, a slight sound caught his attention. It hadn't earlier due to it being so much quieter than the other noises which surrounded them: the hum of the shuttle's engines keeping them in place, the blaring alarm which had never stopped, the sound of shooting fire seaming metal. But now the seemingly less significant sound demanded everyone's attention. The crack was growing.

"What do I do?" screamed Brandon in alarm.

"Keep going!" But Gus's face looked worried.

A thin stream of water, no larger than a drip, formed on the inside of the shuttle window and ran down it.

"Uncle Gus?" Brandon tried to hold his tool steady. He was almost finished. If he could just go a little longer.

His breathing changed. No more in the background, it now took center stage, demanding and irregular. Hysteria was setting in, the kind of fear nobody can control.

Gus walked over to the leak and put his finger over it.

"Seriously?" Brandon screeched.

Ignoring his nephew, Gus left for the shuttle's control panel. While Brandon worked on welding the Pacific Ocean back together, Gus tried to keep them from drowning. He brought up the holographic display of the tunnel and pressed the blue square representing that section's pump. An odd sound, like a muffled buzzer, yelled at them, and the holographic representation of their section of the tunnel flashed red once.

Unable to figure out what the problem was, he pressed it again. And again. Several times he did this, each being followed by the "no no" buzzer sound until a computerized voice in the alien tongue said something to him. "I'm sure your explanation as to why you refuse to empty our water would make sense if I understood your language, but I don't!" He pressed it one more time in anger, this time holding his finger on it for several seconds without any hope it would change anything other than release a bit of his frustration.

The noises of Brandon working on the repairs came from behind him. He mustn't tell him what happened. If they were to have any chance of surviving, if they were to stop the world from collapsing in on itself, Brandon must have nothing but hope within him until he finished.

His body sagging with the realization of their probable fate, Gus made his way back to the leak and continued his fruitless attempt of holding back the ocean with his finger.

"It didn't work, did it?" Brandon asked, eyes focused on the task in front of him.

"What didn't?" Gus asked innocently, but the sadness in his voice was impossible to miss.

"The pump. That's what those buzzing noises were, weren't they?"

Gus stared at Brandon, still a child in his eyes. But he wasn't a child, he was a young man. He would have liked for his transition into adulthood to be less dramatic, but things like this wait for no one.

"No," he said. "It didn't work."

They remained silent after that.

CHAPTER 33

"Where are they, Michael?" After Cynthia retrieved a sample of the magma, she and Michael had returned to the control room, where they incessantly watched the flashing tunnel their son was in and tried not to wonder if he and Gus were dead.

"They have to still be in the tunnel, Cynthia."

She jumped from her chair and headed towards the door. "I'm going to go check the docking room."

Michael grabbed her wrist as she went past. "We already have."

She opened her mouth to argue.

"Twice," he said before she could utter a sound.

Pouting like a disciplined child, she plopped back into her seat and crossed her arms. "They should have been back by now." Tears distorted her words.

Michael placed an arm around her. Having his son off doing something deadly beyond all comprehension was bad enough. Having to comfort his wife while pretending he wasn't dying on the inside was the worst kind of torture.

"What was that?" Cynthia sat up, her ears perked.

"What was what?" Michael glanced at the map. The tunnel Brandon and Gus were in was still red, but no longer blinking ominously.

"Cyn— —chael. We're—"

"That!" Cynthia stood and rotated her head like a satellite dish attempting to follow the sound to its source.

Michael followed her. "It sounds like a radio."

"I need— —thia. Mich— Can you— —ear me?"

A weak flash of light told her where to look. Cynthia ran to the light. "It's Uncle Gus!" She pressed the one button that was flashing. "Uncle Gus! We're here! Can you hear us?"

"—es. Can you— —the tunnels?"

"What? You're breaking up."

"Can— control the tun—"

She mouthed the words under her breath. "Control the tunnels, control the tunnels. Oh!"

Michael jumped out of the way as she began a frantic pursuit for a way to manipulate the tunnels. "What are you looking for?" he asked.

"They need a way for us to control the tunnels." Her eyes landed on the holographic map displayed over the control panel specific to the tunnel Brandon and Gus were in.

Gus's broken voice continued to emanate from the intercom. Michael pressed the button. "Hold on, Gus. She's looking. She's looking!" He yelled his last words in case they didn't hear them the first time.

Cynthia hovered over the zoomed-in map, trying to learn what her son already had, how to use it.

In her desperation, she pressed every button, too quickly in procession, until the hologram in front of her became a twisted blur.

Two larger hands calmly placed themselves over hers. "Slow down," Michael said.

Cynthia's hands shook and her tears returned. The fleeting happy moment from hearing their voices collapsed into an oppressive worry. What if she couldn't find what they needed in time?

"It may be nothing," he assured her. "Be glad they're able to ask for help. It could have been a lot worse."

That image took the air out of her lungs, forcing her to spend several precious seconds regaining it. "Calm down," she breathed. "They're OK." Another breath. She closed her eyes and focused. Her breathing slowed.

"OK?" he asked, hands still on hers.

She nodded.

He released her and moved back across the room to the intercom.

Cynthia focused on the map again. It would be her research project, her next topic of lecture, her obsession. She used her hands to zoom in on the tunnel. "OK," she shouted to Michael. "I've got control."

He pressed the button. "Gus? Are you there? She's got control. What do you need?"

"Pump—"

"Pump," Michael repeated. "Pump what?" he yelled into the com. "We. Can't. Hear. You." He stretched his words out, enunciating each one in slow procession. "What. Are. You. Wanting. Us. To. Do?"

Gus's voice followed suit. "Pump. The. Water. From. The. Tunnel."

"Got that?" Michael called over his shoulder.

Cynthia nodded. She was concentrating too hard to do anything else. "Water. Water. Pump the water," she whispered to herself as her fingers probed the hologram from answers.

She zoomed in on the tunnel until only three sections were showing. "What are these?" Her eyes fixated on one of the thick lines separating the sections.

Michael walked over to her and leaned onto the panel. His lids squinted as he tried to see what she was talking about. "Oh. Bulkheads!"

"What?" Her face turned to his.

"Bulkheads. They keep leaks from spreading."

Michael watched as contemplation scrolled across his wife's eyes.

"Oh." She returned her gaze to the map. "Then that means…" She gasped. "Oh, Michael! They're underwater!"

He nodded soothingly. "Yes, dear. Yes. But they're in a shuttle. They probably just need us to pump out the water so they can collapse the bulkheads and return home. That's all." He said the words, but he didn't know them to be true. Granted, they were one possibility, but they didn't explain why the tunnel was still red or why their com was breaking up so badly. He kept all other options to himself. Right now, his goal was to do what they asked, pump out the water.

Cynthia rotated the map several turns. Frustration grew on her face until it became twisted. "I can't … figure … How am I supposed to do this?" she shouted. "Wait!" Her eyes widened in triumph.

She pressed one finger to one section, and held it. A brief second later, several icons lit up on the outside of the tunnel's map. Her vision shifted between them, momentarily overwhelmed with all the choices.

"Try that one." Michael pointed at an icon with a half circle on the bottom and straight lines shooting from it like rays.

She analyzed his choice then pressed it. A shimmering light ran up the sides of the tunnel while the computer's voice spoke in its ancient tongue.

"I don't think that was the right one," she said.

He grunted in disappointed agreement.

She scanned the icons again, forcing her eyes to slow down and read each one individually. One icon stood out when she did. It had several curved lines funneling into a cone, like a vacuum. Her finger touched it. There were a few seconds of nothing, then the icon flashed red coupled by another statement spoken in the computer's voice.

"Over here." Michael's finger grazed a similar icon, only its lines were wavy instead of merely curved.

CHAPTER 34

"Cynthia! Michael! Can you hear me?" Gus screamed into the com.

When the leak became too great for Gus to pretend his finger was anything but ridiculous, he went back to the control panel.

Brandon had said nothing.

As Gus browsed the buttons and projections, he tried a few. Alien words were said, sounds emanated from the unseeable speakers. But then one button, a small black button so far to the side as to go unnoticed until now, caught his attention.

It was the com.

At least he thought it to be. The clicking static that reminded him of a 2-way radio gave him hope that's what it was. Thankfully, he was right.

Cynthia's voice now came through, broken. "Uncle Gus! —here! Can you—"

The sound of his parents nearly swayed Brandon's concentration. He pushed it from his mind but found himself working faster. Hope, real hope, something other than the false hope of survival after fixing the disaster, had made its way back into his heart.

Gus answered them, "I can hear you, yes. Can you control the tunnels?"

"Where are they?" asked Brandon, unable to restrain his desire to know any longer. "Are they OK?"

"—king up."

Gus yelled his words more slowly. "Can you control the tunnels?"

"I said are they alright?" Brandon screamed at him.

Gus wanted to ignore him but recogized he wouldn't be able to. "Brandon wants to know if you're OK. Where are you?"

There was no answer.

"Uncle Gus?" A new panic came with Brandon's voice. "The hole!"

Gus glanced behind him. The small leak had now grown to nearly an inch in diameter. Water streamed into the shuttle. Due to the gravitational pull within it, the water, initially being pulled toward the center of Earth, fell to the floor of the shuttle in an arc.

Michael's voice drew Gus's attention back to the com. Brandon tried to regain his focus on stopping the Pacific Ocean from battering down on them. He continued the grid pattern he had started earlier. In the time they had spent talking with his parents, the steam and bubbles had cleared, allowing him a better view of where he left off.

While he worked, the water level within the shuttle rose until it entered his shoes. He screamed out in shock. "Gah! That's cold!"

Gus wore a worried expression. "This water is … near the bottom."

Brandon glanced over his shoulder at his uncle. Gus was hiding something from him. He chose not to think about it. The hole in the shuttle grew. Two inches, then three. He cringed to the side in an effort to avoid getting soaked by the continuously expanding, frigid waterfall.

He heard his father and uncle conversing again. "What. Are. You. Wanting. Us. To. Do?"

"Pump. The. Water. From. The. Tunnel," Gus answered.

Please, thought Brandon. Please pump the water from the tunnel.

"There." Brandon dropped the hologram and backed away from the podium. A minute or so later, the water ahead had clarified to where they could more easily judge his repair work. Only one or two spots remained. Quickly, he seamed together the remaining holes while still dodging the stream next to him. He was already starting to shiver and didn't need to add to his discomfort level.

The repair work was a mess, but it was holding. Gus draped an arm around his nephew, giving his shoulder a squeeze. "It's not as pretty as the last one, but it should last."

Brandon smiled, a mixture of pride and relief. No sooner had he done so, however, then his body shook violently. "It's freezing in here!"

"Yes," replied Gus. "And if your parents don't hurry, it's going to get a lot colder." Gus glanced around the shuttle a few times and said, "Here." He jumped up onto the bench and offered his hand to Brandon. "You'll stay warmer if you're dry."

They squatted side by side on the bench, too tall to stand. The water flowed in without resistance. Brandon felt his heart thudding just beneath his ribs. "What if they can't do it?"

Gus tried to swallow, but couldn't. "You saved them and countless others." His hand rubbed Brandon's shoulder. "That's what matters."

Brandon nodded. "What about all those ship people though?"

Gus turned to him. "What?"

"You know. The people on the boat that drowned. What about them?"

Gus sighed sadly. "There was nothing you could do for them, Brandon. They were dead long before we got here."

"No." He shook his head. "I know I couldn't do anything, but... I mean... I hate that they had to die but ... if that ship hadn't been there, what would I have welded to? Wouldn't that hole have just gotten bigger?"

"Yes," Gus answered grimly. "If they—"

The window shattered.

They raised their arms to shield their faces and instinctively turned away from the incoming shards.

Brandon took his last breath in the small pocket of air between his face and the back of his uncle's head before the incoming deluge took it away.

The cold water hit the back of his skull as intensely as a block of ice, slamming his head forward and knocking him senseless for a few seconds. His eyes protested when he opened them, but the survival impulse took control. He was otherwise numb. His fingers were touching his uncle's body. That he could see, but no sensations came from them.

Without thinking, he turned around to survey the damage. The lights were still working, making it possible to see within and outside the shuttle. Brandon faced the now windowless front of the shuttle and lowered his eyebrows with curiosity at what he spotted before him. Small shimmers of light appeared to be reflecting off the surface of water nearest the repair work. His body swam to it on impulse.

It was an odd sensation, traveling sideways to the empty window and then feeling the pull towards the shuttle once he exited it, but it was worth it. Using the hull of the shuttle, he shot himself towards the tip of the sunken vessel with all his might. He gasped for air when he reached the surface. After breathing was no longer the main priority, he pushed his hair out of his face and took in his surroundings. The air from within the shuttle had been thrust out by the force of the water and now formed a bubble at the top of the tunnel, which he was treading water to keep his head in.

Peering down at the shuttle, he realized Gus hadn't surfaced yet. He hadn't even made it out of the shuttle. Brandon dove back into the water and swam to retrieve him. The gravitational switch made it take a second longer as he was forced to find his bearings halfway through.

Brandon grabbed at his uncle, who was still facing the back of the shuttle. Gus's head swiveled around, his face filled with a horror Brandon never wanted to witness again.

Clumsily, Gus's numb fingers sought out Brandon's proffered arm. Brandon led him to the windshield and then used the shuttle's frame to pull his uncle free. After a single, loud gasp, Gus spluttered and coughed profusely before continuing his attempt to suck in enough oxygen. As he did so, Brandon noticed they were not treading water like he'd had to do earlier. They were standing on the front of the shuttle. The water level had lowered.

Great shivers convulsed Brandon's body when the air hit what was once covered by water. Slowly the frozen ocean receded. His parents had been successful.

"Thank you." Gus patted him on the back.

"You're welcome." They watched the water continue to lower. The bulkhead would be visible soon.

Beneath them lay a shuttle filled with water held in a gravity ninety degrees from the gravity of the tunnel it was sitting in. Gus knew it created a dilemma he needed to figure out how to work around, but he couldn't get past the oddity of it. "I guess I should have expected this, but it's still the weirdest thing I've ever seen."

Brandon laughed. It felt so good, he allowed it to continue as long as possible.

Gus let out a small chuckle. "What?"

"Nothing. That just didn't sound like you, I guess."

"What didn't?"

"Nothing," Brandon sighed. "I expected more of a… 'Due to the overt differences in the gravitational pulls of the…' Not 'weird'." He enunciated 'weird' but with a loving smile.

Gus shrugged. "Well, it is weird."

"I know." Brandon crossed his arms in a vain attempt to squelch the shivering. "So now what? How do we get back?"

Gus ran his hands over his hair, pushing it against his scalp, and wiped what was left of the water from his face. He then pulled his shirt away from his body, wrung out what he could, and used the driest part to wipe the lenses of his glasses clean.

"Technically, we could always scoop the water out with our hands, shoes, or whatever else we may have with us. But I believe it will be much faster if we open the door."

Brandon could only come up with one way to accomplish that, and that included getting back into the water, which he wasn't prepared to do yet. "I'm open to suggestions," he said with a false, secret hope.

"We should p-probably try the easy way first," Gus answered with a shiver.

"Yeeeahhhh. That would mean…"

Gus looked at him curiously, but Brandon didn't need an answer. He knew what it meant, and there was no way he was able to even dream of asking his uncle to do it for them.

"OK," Brandon acquiesced with a sigh. "Remind me where the button is?"

With his arms clenched around his vibrating body, Gus answered through chattering teeth, "O-over the door. Ind-d-dented."

Brandon gave a quick jerk of his head to show he understood and jumped into the shuttle. The change in gravity coupled with the ice cold water took what air he had held in his lungs away in a burst of bubbles. He forced his eyes open. The inside lights were still working. Rotating his body towards the door, he used his feet to push off of the holographic podium and swim near it. The button overhead was harder to push while underwater. The force of the water worked against him.

His lungs began to ache. Bracing his right hand against the framing of the door, he pushed against it until his feet felt firm against the floor. He then used his left hand to press in on the switch. He held it that way for one second before, unable to remain underwater any longer, he swam sideways to the surface.

"I don't think it's working," he gasped after gulping some much coveted air.

Gus scratched the side of his face in contemplation while Brandon held himself in place, his feet on the shuttle floor, his head leaning out of the empty window until his face broke the surface. His hands grasped the window's frame. The sensation, other than being frigid, was not uncomfortable. In fact, he considered it better to remain under than break the surface and be forced to acclimate to the temperature all over again.

"I bet it won't let us open it in the middle of the tunnel like this," Gus theorized. "I'm also willing to bet there's an emergency release somewhere, but where is the question."

"Do you think my parents can help us from the Hub?"

Gus grimaced. "Even if they could, we can't radio them. The com is submerged. I don't know about you, but I can't talk underwater."

Brandon frowned with him and racked his brain for ideas. Memories of laptops, automatic grocery store doors, emergency exits, and everything in between came to mind, but the shuttle reminded him more of a car than anything, which reminded him of his parents' remote key. "D'you think there's a remote? Like a car key has?"

Gus held his hands in surrender. "Again, even if there were, we can't do anything without it. Surely they wouldn't be stupid enough to keep something like that in the shuttle."

"That's true," Brandon said. Then his eyes widened and he threw himself back into the shuttle.

"Brandon?" Gus called after him. "Brandon!"

Brandon heard his uncle, but he couldn't stop now. The temperature had caused his body to start to numb again, and he needed his fingers fully functioning for this. The memory of the car keys had reminded him of a time he had tried to open the trunk. It wouldn't work. He was only ten or so at the time and didn't know any better. His father was the one who explained it to him. "You have to hold it, Brandon."

He had held it, and after several seconds, heard a pop.

Let's hope this works, he thought to himself as he made his way to the shuttle's door. A violent shiver ran through his body. He wasn't going to be able to handle another dive any time soon. Too numb to feel the way, his eyes had to guide his finger to the indent over the door. The knuckle turned white as he pressed it, and held it.

1 Mississippi. 2 Mississippi. Pain entered his lungs. He let out some air to ease it. The surface was just a few feet away. He could break it in two seconds if he had to. *5 Mississippi, 6 Mississippi. Come* on!

An urgent demand from his burning chest nearly made him stop. He released the rest of his air, hoping to assuage his body's need just a little longer. The sound of a latch opening nearly caused him to gasp. He thrust hard with his legs against the floor, pushing himself towards the water's surface.

But as the door opened, a current formed from the escaping water. It slammed him against the gap before he reached the surface and held him there. If his lungs held any hidden air reserves, they vanished in a small batch of tiny bubbles. The door did not open enough for him to pass through. He was held captive against it as the water rushed around him. The burn in his chest grew into agony, and the desire for air overcame the logic of being underwater. He inhaled.

Immediately, his body coughed to rid him of the poison, which in turn caused him to inhale again, and again, until he could no more. The last thing he remembered was the vague sensation of air on his scalp.

The sound of an opening latch followed by falling water caused Gus to lean over the edge of the empty window of the shuttle and worriedly peer into it. The lights were still on within it, but the water-covered shapes inside smeared together, like a river was flowing over them. Still, Brandon looked different than Gus thought he should.

"Brandon? Are you OK?" He knew shouting at him from outside the water was futile, but he couldn't help it. He was useless in the water. "Brandon!" Five more seconds, and he was going in, his inability to swim aside.

The five seconds came and went, but the thought of touching that frigid pool sent chills through his defiant body and made his joints ache prematurely. Angry at his body's attitude toward his nephew, Gus took one shaky breath, held his nose, and jumped in.

The gravity of the vessel pulled his legs behind him before his chest cleared the surface of the water. The shock of the cold coupled with the disorientation made him glad his nose was held shut. He opened his eyes and instantly wished he had removed his glasses before taking the plunge. They were nearly off at this point and not very helpful underwater anyway.

Brandon floated oddly next to him. Terrified for the worst, Gus wrapped his arm around his nephew and tugged. The tide of the escaping water fought him, but he refused to give up. By the time Brandon's body was clear of the door, the water's surface had fallen to their shoulders.

Brandon's face was pale. He wasn't breathing. The differing gravities made it difficult, but Gus managed to position Brandon so his upper body was bent over the edge of the shuttle. Water ran out of his mouth.

The shuttle was still over half full. Gus pulled Brandon completely out of it and turned him over to start mouth-to-mouth. He felt the grieving burn behind his eyes as the fear set in. Time passed slowly and quickly all at once. He was alert and clear thinking, but that made the seconds feel like minutes, and the minutes feel like hours. His fingers shook as he used them to pinch his nephew's nose, and his mouth contorted with the sob that was soon to take control of him.

One puff.

Brandon's chest rose.

Two puffs.

It fell after it rose this time.

Three puffs.

Brandon started to cough. Gus threw Brandon's head sideways, allowing the water to escape rather than choke him further.

Then there was no more movement. Gus debated whether he should resume his efforts. Before he could make a decision however, Brandon's lids opened, revealing dilated pupils that searched for a focal point. A second later, they closed as another round of coughing started.

Tears of relief and joy fell from Gus's cheeks as he watched his nephew push himself up and hack up Niagara Falls. Gus chuckled and rubbed Brandon's back. "Good job, Brandon. You did it."

Brandon gasped noisily. "Thanks," he choked out.

Gus leaned back, waiting for him to catch his breath and regain his strength.

Painful tears blurred Brandon's vision, but they weren't as painful as his throat and lungs were right now. "Holy crap that hurts!"

Gus chuckled.

"—you there?" A crackled voice caused Brandon to jump.

"You OK?" Gus asked him.

He nodded.

Gus reentered the shuttle. The water level was barely shin deep now.

Half wading, half kicking the water out of his way, he went over to the com. His words were purposefully slow and deliberate. "You. Did. It. Thank. You."

CHAPTER 36

"Uncle Gus? Brandon? Are you there?" Cynthia detected the frenzy in her own voice. If what she did had worked, they should have contacted her ages ago. She sat back, dread dominating her actions until she fell defeated into the chair, unable to call for them anymore.

"Gus! Brandon! Answer us, please!" Michael took over for her. He glanced back at the tunnel's holographic displays. According to them, their section of the tunnel was completely empty of water now. "Gus! Brandon!" He couldn't understand why they weren't answering.

"Stop!" his wife screamed at him. "Just stop." Her voice was weak, broken.

Her crippled face ripped through Michael's chest. The possibility of their son being dead was becoming larger by the second. Cynthia had always been his rock, the stubborn one. Without her, he knew he couldn't keep himself together much longer.

"No." He told himself and her defiantly. Then he took a deep breath and pressed the com button. "Gus! Brandon! Are you there?" He shouted the words into the com while staring into his wife's eyes, daring her to tell him to stop again.

"—Did. It." The faint half-words came through the com.

Cynthia didn't wait to hear the rest, she jumped to her feet and shoved her husband out of the way. "Are you OK?" In her rush, the words came out too fast to be coherent on the other side.

Michael held up a hand to his wife's chest and asked for her, slowly, "Are you OK?"

"Yes! Yes. We're fine. Were you successful?"

Cynthia burst into joyful tears and nodded her answer to the question. Michael choked on his next words. "Yes. For the most part anyway. We can talk when you get back here."

Cynthia nodded again, this time to herself. "Brandon, are you there?"

"Yeah, Mom. I'm here."

Fresh tears fell down her cheeks. "OK, Sweetie. I love you."

There was a pause. At first she thought he hadn't heard her, then his voice came through. "I love you too, Mom."

CHAPTER 37

"How do we get back?" Brandon asked Gus.

"We'll have to try using the shuttle and hope it works. We won't live long enough to walk back. Besides, the gravity would make it impossible. We would fall to our deaths."

Their situation sounded bleak, and just when Brandon had relaxed enough to enjoy his relief buzz. "What do we do about that?" He specified the open window.

"I suppose we could cover it with our clothes."

"With what, the duct tape we didn't bring?" Brandon's jovial sarcasm was a welcome reprieve to their recent experience. They smiled at each other.

"Have you ever ridden in a car without a back window?" Gus asked.

Brandon shook his head no.

"There's not much difference. The gravity of the shuttle is pulling us down, and the gravity of the Earth is pulling us in the direction we're going. Granted, it's not as fast of a pull as what we'll be traveling, but it's helpful nonetheless. Still, just to be safe, we should probably find a way to secure ourselves. If it did cause a vacuum and suck us out of here, like I said, the shuttle would be traveling faster than we could fall, so it would be an ensured death."

Brandon swallowed and searched for a seatbelt, strap, anything to attach himself to the shuttle. Not one. Finally he noticed the edge of the bench next to the door. He sat in the floor and leaned against the end of it. If he started to slide, he would grab hold of its edge and yell for Gus to stop.

Gus saw him take his position in the floor and clinch the seat cushion. "I'll drive slowly and stop at each bulkhead. Just in case. But we can't go too slow or we'll never get back."

Brandon nodded. He understood. He didn't like it, but he understood, and he accepted it.

With his feet angled behind him for support, Gus drove them to the first bulkhead. They weren't able to accelerate to much of a speed since the distance was so short. He opened the bulkhead and checked that the instruments had read correctly. The section was dry and safe for travel. Brandon stared at his knees. On top of everything else, he wasn't in the mood for nausea.

Gus moved on to the next bulkhead, more quickly this time. Without the protection of the back window, the sounds of traveling through the tunnel roared inside the shuttle. Brandon clinched his teeth against it. His lungs protested as the air thinned around him. They slowed for the next bulkhead. Air filled Brandon's next breath, satisfying his desire for more.

"Why is it doing that?" he asked Gus.

"Why is what doing what?"

"Why is hard to breathe unless we're stopped?"

The present task made Gus pause before answering. "Oh, remember the vacuum I mentioned? Well, the speed of the air outside is causing a slight vacuum on the inside."

Brandon's eyes widened.

"Nothing to worry about. It's not enough to pull us out, just enough to suck out most of our air. We should be fine. If I sense I'm about to pass out or anything, I'll stop the shuttle."

Gus's words weren't causing Brandon's anxiety to lessen any. "Is there not a way to stop it from doing that?"

"No. Not unless we go slower."

"How long would that take exactly?"

"I don't know. How many days do you want it to take?"

"Oh, ha ha," Brandon mumbled under his breath with heavy sarcasm. He didn't know why his uncle had to be so annoying at times, or why he thought he was funny when he so wasn't.

They continued speeding between bulkheads, checking each section for damage and residual water as they went. Everything appeared to be in order. When they got to the last closed bulkhead, Gus insisted they check the first repair job they did, just to make sure. It looked as perfect as when they had left it.

No bulkheads slowed their last leg of the journey, causing even Gus to battle the strain from the lack of air. He slowed now and then to let them catch their breath. When they at last made it back, Brandon had to force his fingers to release their clutch on the cushion. His knuckles were so white they almost glowed. The journey had made his knees stiff and his butt cheeks numb.

"You OK?" Gus asked, acting no more strained than if he had just driven back from a weekend at the beach. His appearance made Brandon feel silly for his reaction to his angst of being sucked out the back of the shuttle.

Before he could answer, Brandon's stomach growled loud enough to form an echo.

"Hungry?" Gus asked in all sincerity.

The growl was a welcome distraction. Happy not to discuss his own personal cowardice, he answered, "Starved."

"You should be. We've probably been gone several hours, and drowning's bound to take it out of you."

Brandon twisted his mouth in disapproval at what he believed was belittling such a tragic moment. Drowning. He had actually drowned. The event had certainly lived up to his expectations, but the aftermath had missed by a long shot. By his standards he should have a trophy or something, yet he didn't feel any different, certainly not any stronger.

If anything, he was weaker from the experience. He hoped that would pass once he ate and rested.

As soon as they exited the decontamination chamber, Brandon was smothered by his mother's hair while her arms squeezed him into a painful hug. "I'm so proud of you," she said in a hoarse whisper.

"Thank you, Gus." Michael drew Gus into a one armed hug and patted him on the back. He then waited for his wife to finish so he could welcome his son back.

Cynthia hugged her uncle in gratitude and relief of his safety. "So now what?" she asked once they released each other.

Michael pressed his lips down into a frown and huffed. "Now we talk. There's a lot to think about."

With a relevant glance to Brandon, Gus asked, "Can we talk while we eat? We're rather hungry."

"Oh," Cynthia blurted in surprise. "Of course. Sorry."

The journey in the elevator was drawn out and uncomfortable. Brandon didn't want to talk. He wanted to sleep, and the last thing he wanted to do was move artificially anymore. His motion sickness, slightly subdued by the excitement and adrenaline, was making a comeback. With a vengeance. His hands reflexively grabbed the pit of his stomach, and as soon as the door opened, he retched onto the hallway floor. Not much came up, just mainly some leftover water he had apparently swallowed while drowning.

"Hey." Michael caught his shoulder to steady him. "Are you alright?"

"Yeah," Brandon wheezed, standing up. "Just everything catching up with me." He caught a glimpse of the worry on his mother's face and knew she wasn't ready to hear about his mishap yet. He tried to silently share that information with his uncle and was relieved to see him nod infinitesimally in response.

When they entered the cafeteria, Brandon sat in one of the fluffy blue chairs in a corner and told them to get him whatever, he didn't care. Cynthia gave Gus a worried glance, but he assured her everything was fine and joined them in procuring some food.

Michael balanced his plate on his glass so he could carry Brandon's drink in his other hand. Cynthia held his plate between her two arms.

They handed him his food and sat in the chairs nearby.

Brandon grabbed a handful of random cubes and threw them in his mouth. He closed his eyes and moaned in content.

Michael, Cynthia, and Gus all gawked at Brandon in disbelief. He never thought he would have acted that way over blue and white food cubes either, but with as ravished as he was, salted cardboard would have made him happy.

He ignored their stares and noisily gulped his sweet, blue drink.

"How bad is the remaining damage?" Gus asked after washing down his first bite with half his purple liquid. The trip had drained him too.

Michael and Cynthia shared a fleeting, yet significant glance that did not go unnoticed.

"The immediate danger has passed. We were able to stop the magma—"

"Magma!" Brandon looked up from his plate and gawked at his parents with wide eyes. Magma sounded much worse than water.

Cynthia placed a hand on his knee. "It's OK, Brandon. We stopped it."

"Wait," he said. "Is magma—"

"Magma is under the earth's crust. Lava is when it comes out," Cynthia explained.

Michael continued where he had left off. "Right. We stopped the magma, but we weren't able to repair the damage it caused."

"Such as?" asked Gus.

"We don't really know," answered Cynthia. Her eyes darted once more to Michael, but he had his eyes locked on the table. "The map doesn't show us the surface in detail. At least that we can find," she added.

Michael didn't look up when he spoke. "According to the maps, it looked like we were under Wyoming."

Their silent communications had not escaped Gus's attention. "What part of Wyoming?" He slowly put a cube in his mouth, studying their reactions to his question.

Michael couldn't help but take a peek at Gus's expression before moving his stare to a far off cluster of chairs. "The northwestern part."

Gus's face showed no recognition. They would have to explain it to him when they were away from Brandon. Cynthia tried to convey that message to him by darting her eyes meaningfully at Brandon. Whether Gus took the hint or not, she wasn't sure, but at least he stopped asking questions.

Brandon stopped chewing and stared at his dad a moment, his jaw frozen is a sort of sideways chawing cow motion.

Michael smiled at the image.

"I have a friend that lives in Wyoming, I think. I don't really remember. He talks about it a lot anyway. Do you think he's alright?"

"I'm sure he's fine," Michael lied for the first time to his son.

Cynthia downed the rest of her drink to hide her rapid blinking.

Gus popped a red cube in his mouth and chewed. "What about Earth's internal structure? How permanent is the damage?"

Cynthia repositioned herself, took a deep breath, and shook her head. "We believe the internal structure is sound for the moment. Both tunnels have stopped flashing. There is still some minor damage, but it appears as though the earthquakes have returned to their normal rate and intensity."

Michael held up his hand. "That's not to say there isn't more work to be done, just that ... for now ... Earth's inner structure is stable again."

Brandon resumed his chewing and swallowed. "So now what? Can we go back home?"

Cynthia picked up her empty glass and looked in it. "Brandon? Would you mind getting me another drink?"

Brandon looked at her funny. She didn't normally ask for things like that.

"Get your mother a drink, Brandon," Michael said kindly. "She's tired."

In disbelief, Brandon took his mother's cup and went to fill it, all the while wondering what they thought he was if they were tired.

As soon as he was out of earshot, Cynthia leaned over to whisper to Gus, "Uncle Gus. Someone has to stay behind."

Gus's forehead creased in confusion.

"Most of the repairs are done, at least we hope the major ones are, but there are still minor areas of deterioration. We can't just leave those areas unfixed. That would be terribly irresponsible!"

Michael cleared his throat. "Right. They could grow into what we saw today." He shrugged, gesturing with his palms at the Hub in general.

Gus was listening now. He popped another cube in his mouth and chewed thoughtfully.

"Most of society would notice if we all four disappeared," Cynthia continued. "We can't all move here as a family. There's no one else. Brandon would be completely isolated from the rest of the world and—"

"It's OK, I'll do it," Gus answered the unspoken question.

Michael paused then said, "You'll do what? Exactly."

"You're right. Brandon can't stay down here forever, and he can't stay alone on the surface. I'll stay here, and you three can go back up."

Brandon was on his way back now and within hearing distance.

"Are you sure?" Cynthia whispered. When she and Michael had discussed their situation in the control room earlier, she had mentioned how her uncle would probably enjoy the isolation and work required, but she didn't want to force him into anything. And even though his offer sounded genuine and not obligatory, she had to know for certain he *wanted* to do it. "Uncle Gus, I don't want you to—"

He waved her away. "I'd love to," he got out between lip smacks from his chewing. He was popping his cubes like peanuts now and looking around the place with what she couldn't help but perceive as excitement.

Brandon sat in his chair and handed Cynthia's drink to her. She took it without any form of acknowledgement.

"A 'thank you' would have been nice," he mumbled, but no one was listening.

"I could enjoy this place." Gus nodded. "I mean, it needs a lot of work, but it's nothing I can't do. In fact, I'd love to get inside the mechanics of this thing and see how it all functions. Take it apart and put it back together again."

Brandon skimmed over each of their faces, searching for a clue as to what Gus was talking about. "What's going on?"

"Hmm?" Gus was still scanning the room with a dreamlike expression on his face.

"What are you talking about?" Brandon asked more forcibly.

Gus looked to Cynthia. He didn't want to say the wrong thing.

"Brandon," Michael started, "Gus is going to stay behind."

"What?!"

"It's not what you think," added Cynthia.

"I'll pop on the surface every now and then to let you know I'm still alive." Gus smiled.

"That's not funny," snarled Brandon.

"It's not meant to be funny." Cynthia gave her uncle a reassuring smile before addressing Brandon again. "We can't stay any longer than we already have. The major structural damage has been repaired, as far as we can tell, but there are still some minor areas that need fixing."

"As far as you know." Brandon enunciated each word pointedly. "What about all your scientist friends? Are you telling me they still won't believe you after you show them *this*?"

Michael and Cynthia stared at each other a moment, Cynthia chewing her lip and finger and Michael stroking an imaginary beard. If they told the scientists, they would come in with their teams. Then the government would get involved. They had both seen the end result of projects taken over by the government. Wars would break out. Which country would have control? Which country would use it to destroy the other?

Michael was the first to break away. "We're afraid the scientists might abuse it."

A quick glance told him Cynthia agreed with his answer.

"I don't understand," said Brandon.

"Scientists are … competitive," said Cynthia. "Besides, Uncle Gus would love it here, wouldn't you?"

Gus wasn't paying attention, his eyes continuing their wondrous examination of their current surroundings.

"Uncle Gus?" asked Cynthia. "Gus?"

"Gus!" Michael shouted.

He jumped. "Hmm? What? Oh, sorry. What did you ask?"

His response pulled Cynthia's lips into a reassured smile.

CHAPTER 38

Brandon begged and begged for one last night in the Hub. Not that he wanted to stay, quite the contrary. He couldn't wait to get back home. But his exhaustion was so severe, he didn't think his body would make the trek back up to the Grand Canyon, not to mention the hike after that.

However, his pleas were useless. One last time, Cynthia ensured her uncle wanted to stay, then they packed up, boarded the shuttle, and headed for the surface.

The hike up through the cave was so tiring, Brandon caught himself leaning against the walls with his eyes closed several times, and since some of those seconds were missing from his memories, he was pretty sure he had fallen asleep on several occasions.

When they finally neared the cave's mouth, Cynthia paused at its opening and deeply breathed in the air. "It's been a long time since I smelled that."

"We haven't been gone *that* long." Michael walked up behind her. "What's it been, a week?"

Brandon turned on his phone and held it close to the cave's mouth in hopes of a better signal. "Oh, come on! Tuesday?"

Cynthia groaned.

"Mom! I have a report to do!"

"We'll fix it somehow, Brandon," Michael assured him. "If I have to knock off an imaginary grandmother, don't worry about it."

Cynthia gawked at Michael in disbelief. Brandon continued to stare at his phone, worried about school.

A dark cloud was coming their way from over the other side of the canyon. "We better hurry," Michael said. "Looks like a storm's coming." He readied the rappelling gear.

His words made Cynthia forget about everything else and focus on the cloud. That was no storm, and she knew it. Michael probably did too. They would have to tell Brandon sometime, and soon.

Their trek up the Hopi Salt Trail was cold but gave them no trouble. As they reached the top, Brandon saw a large, whitish flake fall from the sky. "It's snowing!"

His parents followed his gaze up. "That's not snow," Michael said. His voice was grim.

"What do you mean?" asked Brandon.

"We need to go." Michael marched over to the rental cars. "Cynthia, you take that car. I'll take this one. Brandon, pick one and get in."

"What's going on, Dad?" Brandon approached the car Gus had driven them in.

Michael and Cynthia locked gazes. It was time. "Brandon," started Michael, "The magma wasn't just underneath Wyoming, it was underneath Yellowstone."

Brandon waited for more.

"Yellowstone is a super volcano, a caldera," said Cynthia. If it blew, which we think it did, it took an area the size of California with it."

Brandon's breath stopped.

"Look at that cloud." Michael pointed to the sky. The "snow" cloud billowed in their direction, threatening to surround them like a giant amoeba. "That's ash. It's going to envelope thousands of miles."

"You lied to me." Brandon glared at his father with a mixture of both anger and shock. "Sniper's dead, isn't he?"

Michael reached a hand out to Brandon's shoulder then pulled back at the last moment. "If he was anywhere near Yellowstone, then yes. He probably is."

"That's why you wouldn't let me stay another night! You *knew* this had happened!"

Michael nodded.

Brandon's chest burned. He wanted to yell at his father; he wanted to punch him. "Why? What happened? You said we fixed it!" He gasped. "Uncle Gus!" As the sudden realization entered his mind, he turned to race back to the trail.

Michael grabbed his arm and stopped him from going.

Brandon yanked away without success. "Let go!" He clamped his fingers around his father's wrist and tried to tear his hand from his arm.

"Gus is fine, Brandon," yelled Cynthia. "In fact he's probably the safest person on the planet right now!"

Brandon quit trying to escape but refused to release his grip. "What?"

Michael maintained his firm grasp of Brandon's arm. "Your mother can explain in the car."

Ash began to fall like flurries now. Brandon didn't want to wait. He wanted answers *now*. He jerked his arm away again but failed to release himself.

"We've got to *leave*, Brandon." Michael moved his head in closer to his son, refusing to back away from his anger. "I understand you're mad, you have every right to be, but we need to leave *now*. If we get caught in that cloud…" He shook his head.

Cynthia's face was worried. "Get in the car, Brandon."

Brandon scowled at his father. He wanted answers, but something about their expressions told him the danger was real. As soon as he thought Brandon would cooperate, Michael relaxed his fingers. Brandon jerked away, his lip turned up in a snarl.

The locks on the car Cynthia chose to drive clicked, and Brandon walked over to it. Refusing to look at or speak to anyone, he opened the back door and slung his bag inside. He slammed it shut and threw himself into the front seat. Cynthia was already there. As they buckled, they heard Michael's tires spin on the loose dirt.

Cynthia turned the key. The engine groaned in its attempt, but it would not start. The ash was falling heavily on the opposite side of the canyon. And it was coming their way. Brandon saw his mother's face turn to panic, and he forgot about being angry. "What's wrong?" he asked.

She turned the key again. "If we don't get out of here before that ash hits, we won't have an engine to use."

Two more turns, and the motor revved normally. She didn't wait for it to warm up. She slammed it into reverse and skidded her way to Michael who was waiting at the end of the road for them.

Where are they? Michael thought. One minute longer, and he was going back for them. He shook his free leg up and down, rocking the car as he did. Something moved into the rearview mirror. It was them. He mashed his foot on the gas pedal and sped away.

Brandon knew better than to bother his mother with questions at the moment, but the silence magnified his emotions. He turned the dial for the radio.

A DJ's voice came through the speakers. "—flights cancelled as the ash encompasses all of Omaha. Other planes are being brought in to aid the fleeing victims."

Unsure Brandon could handle it, Cynthia reached up to turn it back off but was quickly slapped away by his hand. "Leave it."

She understood and accepted that he was upset, but disrespect was intolerable. Her glare informed him of such.

"Please," he added, hoping she would just let this go and drive.

The DJ spoke again. Cynthia turned her concentration to getting them out of there. "Pilots and airports are volunteering their planes and time to bring in survivors. There is not a complete death toll yet, but estimates are near two million. Experts believe that number will grow from delayed reactions."

Brandon's jaw fell. Two million. It was too much. Two million people wouldn't fit in … in… He tried to imagine an entire state exploding into space and couldn't.

A second DJ responded, "That's sad news. That really is."

The first DJ continued reading the report. "According to the latest, most of Montana … Idaho … and the entire western half of Wyoming have been destroyed. They do not expect any survivors."

Brandon's breath hitched in his throat. "Do you think any of them had time to escape?" Being mad seemed silly now.

Cynthia's fingers tapped her lips in a thoughtful sort of way. She picked up her phone and tried to turn it on, but it was almost dead. With an exasperated huff, she tossed it in Brandon's lap and said, "Plug that in for me, will you?"

He didn't move. "Mom?"

"What, honey?" She hadn't meant to be rude. She was too engrossed in trying to get them to safety to listen to what he said.

He asked the question again. It was harder the second time. "Do you think any of them had time to escape?"

She blinked. "Any of who?"

He sighed, annoyed with her lack of concentration. "Any of the people they're talking about?"

Cynthia pressed her lips together hard. She doubted very seriously any of them did. The radio didn't say exactly what happened, but she could guess.

One of the DJ's said, "You know, my wife and I were just talking about taking a trip up north and even visiting Yellowstone. I guess it's a good thing we hadn't yet."

"Yes, Bob," replied the other DJ. "It sure is."

Cynthia closed her eyes for the briefest of seconds before watching the road again. When she opened them, she thought she saw Michael's car swerve slightly.

Michael jerked the car back in his lane. The news had dumbfounded him for a second, causing him to allow the car to drift off course. So Yellowstone *had* exploded. Their worst fears were confirmed.

Questions flew from his mind much like the survivors must be fleeing their homes. How much damage was done? How many more will die? How much food will be lost, soil damaged, land made uninhabitable?

He decided to call Cynthia. Luckily, he had remembered to plug up his phone when he got in the car. She answered on the first ring. "Hello?"

"Hey, um…" He hesitated, not sure how to tell her.

She didn't need him to. "If you're talking about what's on the radio, we heard."

Silence filled both cars for nearly a minute. It was Michael who broke it. "We need to get home. Fast."

"I know."

Another, shorter minute of silence passed before Michael said, "It doesn't look like we're going to be able to fly. Do you have the number for the rental agency?"

"I'll take care of it," she assured him.

"OK," he answered. "Love you."

"Love you, too." She smiled.

"Tell Brandon I love him."

"I will," she said.

"Bye."

"Bye." She hung up the phone.

The phone lay in her outstretched hand unnoticed for several seconds. Finally, she placed it back in the cupholder so it could finish charging. "No, Brandon. I don't think any of them had time to escape."

As Brandon stared out the window, stunned from it all, Michael and Cynthia pressed their accelerators to the floor.

CHAPTER 40

"Thank you, sir." Mr. Stockton took Brandon's completed research paper without emotion, although it was hard to tell in the dimmed rays of the obstructed sun. The flickering rectangular fluorescent lights of the high school did little to illuminate details.

The ash of Yellowstone had spread immeasurably over the last weeks. Even in Georgia, over two thousand miles away, the sun cast a blood-red shadow in the sky. The death toll stopped at three million, mainly due to the inability for body counters to reach most areas. Transportation remained a standstill in the entire northwestern US and southwestern Canada.

Brandon returned to his seat, passing several spaced out students along the way. Nearly a tenth of the student population had suffered panic attacks and depression so severe they had to be hospitalized after the explosion. Now they popped pills which made them a zombie, but at least somewhat functioning. A set of "temporary" counselors now worked from permanent offices set up in the library. Only the most dire cases were allowed to visit them, and those were enough to cause lines. A very few families had moved to Mexico or Europe in attempts to "survive the apocalypse of America." Those left, like the once jovial, nonchalant boys like Kevin and his friends who used to play jokes and make others laugh, now sat silent and restrained. Ms. Gordon once commented to another teacher how their change in behavior disturbed her the most, until she realized the whole class was listening to her disclosure.

As the rest of the students took their completed papers to the front when called, Brandon thought about his family's attempt to return to normal after their excursion. When they first came back to the surface, he tossed his original subject choices aside and decided to write his report on the quakes, Yellowstone, the whole mess, especially since he was there and saw it all firsthand. But his parents said it probably wouldn't be a good idea, and they were right. Not only was he too close to what happened and would have a hard time writing a paper expected of a person ignorant of the true structure of Earth, nearly every student and their brother tried to write on the recent events, and with Mr. Stockton's current depression induced apathy, he allowed them to. So instead, Brandon wrote on the legend of the Hopi Ant People. Still close to home but not at all divulging.

He wished he could tell them. He wished he could tell everyone there was somewhere safe for them to go, somewhere with plenty of food and where the ash couldn't touch them, but he knew better. Pandemonium would ensue. Fights would break out. People would die. There was no way anyone, especially an already spread-too-thin government would be able to control that amount of chaos.

Telling them wouldn't help much anyway, even without the mass hysteria. No one had heard from Gus since that first weekend after they returned home. He had come to the surface to call that Friday night on what was supposed to become a weekly ritual for the family. They would receive updates from each other, Gus hearing about their week, them hearing what all he was working on at the Hub. But their first telephone conversation had been their last.

The ash lingered in the Grand Canyon air like a flu virus in December. It was so thick during that one phone call, Gus hacked and coughed until he was forced to return to the Hub. Before he left however, he mentioned trying to find another outlet to the surface, but so far that hasn't happened, at least not to their knowledge. Brandon worried it never would. Whenever he asked his parents about his great uncle, they assured him he was fine and not to worry, but ever since his father lied about Yellowstone, he had a hard time believing them on things anymore.

No one said a word when the bell rang; they all walked to their last classes for the day in an eerie silence. The only noises Brandon heard in the hallways were lockers shutting and footsteps, many many footsteps. But no voices.

Spanish, his last class, was now one of his favorites. Students talked their, his teacher made sure of it. She stubbornly refused to let any of them use the current situation as an excuse. He loved her for that. It was the only time he heard their voices, the only time he could tell how they really felt.

As the last bell rang, students donned their masks and headed for the doors. Brandon didn't wear his every day. He thought it silly to since he had every intention of going back to the Hub someday, hopefully when school let out for the summer. When he didn't wear his mask, people stared at him. Teachers fussed. One time they even sent home a paper for his parents to sign. His parents told him if he didn't conform to current societal expectations, it would cause suspicion. He had rolled his eyes at them at the time but wore it more often since. Maybe it was the memories of Gus hacking on the phone, maybe it was peer pressure, but for whatever reason, he wore it today.

The ash sprinkled edges of grass blades, making it look like it had been snowing in April. Some places were worse than others, whether from the wind or where homeowners swept the piliing ash from their roofs. Brandon scraped some of it with his shoe as he walked past.

Once he got near Gus's house, he pulled a key from his pocket and used it to open the front door. The displacement of millions of people, domestic refugees they were called, had reached every corner of the country, even southern Georgia, and some of them had become desperate. Crime in the country skyrocketed, especially break-ins and squatting. In the hopes of preventing this from happening to one of their own homes, one of Brandon's chores was to spend time in his uncle's house every day after school before his parents came and got him.

He locked the door behind himself, including the bolt and chain, and sat on the couch in front of the already on TV.

"—with the inability for atmospheric vehicles to fly through the area, the extent of the damage will have to remain a mystery. Thanks to mapping apps however, we're able to show you live satellite footage of what the area looks like from above the earth's atmosphere."

A typical satellite picture of North America filled the screen. Weeks ago, Brandon would have never known the difference between what he was being shown and normal cloud cover of the land. Thanks to daily news reports, he, along with the rest of the US population, were practically experts.

The weather-, now volcanic-ash-man, smoothed his tie with one hand while gesturing on the map with the other. "Not much spread since last time, folks, but"—the map zoomed out to include the east coast—"the Jetstream has now pulled it as far as the Atlantic Ocean, sparking concern from environmentalists as to the effect it will have on marine life." His fingers ran along a thin, grey cloud which trailed out of the general mass, down to the southeast, and off the eastern coast of the US.

Brandon paused the TV before it had the chance to change to the next report. A silver and grey rainbow stretched across the affected area like a blossoming hurricane. Slight patches of almost white told him real clouds were mixed in with the ash. Maybe it was rain, he thought. Maybe the water would bring the ash with it to the surface and clear the air some.

The only places in the continental US unaffected were the southwest and the northeast. The Jetstream had brought it diagonally across the country as though the finger of God had drawn it there. Brandon traced it with his own finger. If the Jetstream moved, it could spread to New England too. Three-fourths of the entire country would be in trouble. Big trouble.

He sat back on the couch and resumed the program.

"Back to you, David," The weatherman said to the camera.

"Thanks, Clarence." A clean-cut man with an over-priced suit and a grim expression turned from the side facing the weather area to the camera and quickly changed his grimace into a fake smile. The channel's emblem draped behind him. "Today marks two months since our last quake. The quakes, which started nearly eight months ago have vanished as mysteriously as they appeared. Here to tell us more is Marjorie. Over to you, Marj."

"Thanks, David." A middle-aged woman with too much make-up and a tight red dress stood in front of a university. "I'm here outside the Science Center of Pennsylvania State University, ranked number one for its geology program in 2014 by US News, with geologist Acharya Kumar." She turned her stare from the camera to the man standing next to her. "So, Professor Kumar, what is the reason behind the cessa— the cessation of the quakes?"

Brandon squinted at the TV, now focused on Professor Kumar, an Indian man in a pale blue dress shirt. He knew that face. Cynthia or Michael one had pointed him out once, recently in fact.

Kumar answered Marjorie, "When the eruption of the caldera of Yellowstone took place, we focused our attention on it and what it meant for Earth's near future. Now that it has calmed, and we are left with just the aftereffects, as terrible as they are, we have once again been focusing on the quakes. Which, as your colleague just stated, have stopped."

"And what have you discovered, Ach— Professor Kumar."

The professor ignored her terrible pronunciation. Brandon stiffened with the realization of where he recognized him from. He had been one of the scientists his parents first told their theory to. Even more interested than before, Brandon moved to the couch's edge and turned up the volume to the television.

"This was just a hypothesis at first." He waved his hands is a dismissing motion. "But enough time has passed now, we can safely say the explosion of Yellowstone is to blame for the quakes."

Marjorie's brows disappeared into her hair. "You mean we should be expecting more of them?"

"Oh no, no, no!" the professor chuckled. "When a volcano nears eruption, many quakes can and do occur. And they show all the signs of the quakes we recently endured, including strengthening up until the actual eruption. Once the pressure is released, the quakes return to their normal strength and frequency."

Brandon snorted. Granted, their story wasn't a bad one, pretty good actually. Lucky for their story his parents didn't repair the tunnels in time to keep Yellowstone from blowing up the western half of the continent, he thought with caustic sarcasm.

"Thank you, Professor Kumar. Back to you, Dave."

The screen switched from in front of the university back to the news station. "Thanks, Marjorie. A new protest has broken out over the—"

Brandon didn't care what trivialities the ignorant were fighting over now and started to mute the TV before remembering his instructions. He glanced at the clock. Still another hour before his parents would knock on the door.

He pulled out his laptop. Gaming had slowed to a standstill. Sniper hadn't been the only casualty. Many players had lost their lives, but even more had lost their homes. Servers were down, and what few remained were unreliable. Recreation was on the back burner for nearly everyone.

Now, instead of chatting with people who ranged from school friends to across the world, he wrote. Gus may not have contacted them since that first weekend, but they hadn't given up hope that he would, and they needed a translator for when he did. Their first week back, after he got caught up with his schoolwork, Brandon spent his afternoons and evenings adding his father's cuneiform dictionaries to his own laptop and downloading translation software to use as a backbone for his own. The basics of his program were finished. Now he just had to finish adding all the words, all who-knows-how-many thousand of them. He spent the next hour alt-tabbing between his program and one of the dictionaries until he had added another fifty. At this rate he'd be done in… He slammed his head back into the couch and sighed. He didn't want to think about how much longer he would be at this.

When his parents arrived, Brandon packed up and left with them, leaving the lights and TV on. They would turn them off at bedtime and then back on again the next morning. It helped keep up the appearance of someone living there. With their masks in place, they walked over to their house.

"How was school?" Michael asked after they put up their stuff and were setting the table for supper.

"I turned in my paper today." Brandon shrugged. "That's it really."

Michael sat in his usual chair at the table and pulled himself closer. Cynthia and Brandon followed suit. "We still haven't heard from your uncle Gus," Michael said customarily while flicking his napkin to the side before placing it in his lap.

They ate off the good dishes and used cloth napkins with nearly every supper now. Waiting for a special time seemed silly anymore. Brandon picked at his broccoli with his fork and wondered how much longer they would have access to fresh fruits and vegetables. The news had mentioned something about which foods came from which area and would therefore soon be in limited demand or unaffected, but he couldn't remember the list. He was sure one of his teachers even assigned a report on the subject. He wondered if maybe he should've paid more attention.

"How was work?" he asked.

While Brandon's absence was easily excusable, even forgotten, his parents' were not. They left a full week prior to when he did and nearly lost their jobs because of it. Those jobs provided them a much coveted access to research and testing facilities they wouldn't otherwise have. They managed to convince the university, somehow, to let them stay in exchange for what they often referred to as "community service". This included extra tutoring for all of their current students and other activities the dean thought essential for them to retain their positions.

Brandon knew why they weren't telling anyone, especially the university, but the burning secret in his chest became even more unbearable when he thought about what his parents had to go through just to keep up the pretenses.

Their family had grown closer due to their experience and as a result, didn't need to talk as much about the little things. If something came up, they shared it. The days of pulling answers out of each other were over.

The house phone rang. Everyone froze with their forks in the air and stared at it, wondering if the sound was real.

It rang again. Cynthia jumped to answer it. "Hello?" Her heart thudded in anticipation until her face warmed from the racing blood.

"Cynthia!" Gus's voice sounded from the other end. "How are things?"

She gasped, her breath catching as she did. Tears burned behind her eyes. "Uncle Gus!" she squeezed out in a whisper.

Michael took the phone away from her. "Hold on, Gus," he said into it. "Let me put you on speakerphone." He pressed a button and then placed the receiver in the middle of the table. "OK. Go ahead."

Cynthia stood next to the table, chewing her nail. Michael's arm went around her shoulders and rubbed them soothingly. Brandon stayed put. They all three stared at the phone with silent expectancy.

Gus's voice came through, but it broke up frequently. "I've found — exit. —phone signals are — weakened — ash."

Michael nodded. Brandon stopped staring at the phone and with a confused face, looked to his father for an explanation.

"The ash is blocking the cell signal. That's why he's coming in so poorly," Michael explained quietly.

Brandon nodded.

"What?" screamed Gus. "I can't hear you."

"I was explaining to Brandon about the ash and the phone signal," Michael yelled back slowly.

"Oh. OK." Gus slowed his speech in return.

Cynthia wiped her eyes and cleared her throat. "Where is the new exit?"

"I'll text you the instructions." There was a short pause. "How bad is the damage?"

Glances flew across the table between the three of them.

"It's bad, Gus," said Michael.

"It must be," Gus answered. "I can't find a hotel room anywhere, and there are signs all over the place for dom-refs, whatever those are."

"Domestic refugees." Michael almost chuckled over Gus's reaction.

Cynthia and Brandon both smiled. "They've been displaced by the eruption," Cynthia added.

"I've discovered a new food cube. Orange! It tastes just like oranges! Shame you didn't have it while you were here."

Brandon could hear the loneliness in his uncle's voice and pitied him.

"Oh, Cynthia! What did your samples tell you?" Gus asked.

"Nothing unusual. The dating was off, of course, but given what we now know about Earth's origin, dating any of it seems pretty silly."

There was a moment of silence on Gus's end of the phone. "When do you think you'll be coming back?" he eventually asked.

No one spoke for a few seconds while Michael thought about his answer. He wanted to go now. They all did. But they couldn't. "We'll have to wait until summer, Gus. Brandon's got school, and the university isn't very happy with us. If we leave before this semester's over we'll lose our jobs. And we're not ready to do that yet."

"I understand." Gus coughed.

Cynthia fidgeted. "Are you wearing a mask?"

"A mask?" He coughed again. "No. Why?"

She slammed her palms onto the table and took a deep breath, ready to tear into her uncle for being so irresponsible. Michael placed a hand in front of her. "The ash causes pneumonia, bronchitis, and even cancer in some people."

"I'm not going to be around long enough to get cancer from it, Michael. I'm already over seventy."

Cynthia bit her lip to keep from saying anything.

Michael ignored her. "What about repairs? Have you had to do anything else?"

"Just a few things here and there, nothing major. What about you, Brandon? How's my translator coming?"

"I've got the program written." Brandon smiled. He missed their conversations. "Now I'm just adding in the words."

"Excellent!" Gus screamed with excitement, which caused him to double over with a large coughing fit, ultimately ending with several disgusting sounds.

Brandon turned up his nose and dropped his fork onto his plate.

"You need to get back to the Hub, Uncle Gus," Cynthia yelled into the phone.

Another cough forced its way out. "OK. OK."

"Be careful!" she yelled. "We love you!"

"I love you too!" Another cough. And then a click.

The kitchen went silent. Michael returned to his seat and continued to eat. Cynthia also returned to hers, where she silently twirled the fork handle in her fingers.

A question burned inside of Brandon. He had asked it before, but of course no one had the answer. He wondered if his translating program would clarify it for them when they returned to the Hub.

They all three jumped as each of their phones vibrated with message alerts. Gus had sent them the address and instructions for the gateway just as he'd promised.

"Interesting," said Michael.

"Indeed," replied Cynthia, a little more cheerful.

Brandon dipped one eyebrow. Even though his parents obviously understood where the message was referring to, he didn't have a clue. Maybe he could map it on the internet later.

"We'll plan a trip as soon as school's out." Cynthia smiled at Brandon and took a bite of food, her hunger returning now she knew how to reach the Hub again, and that Gus was safe.

The question nagged Brandon again. As his parents resumed their silent eating, each ruminating on their own thoughts and concerns, he found it harder and harder to ignore. He swallowed, and tapped his fork tines unknowingly against the edge of his plate. Michael stopped ruminating and stared at Brandon's fork until he stopped. Brandon stared back at him. He couldn't contain the question anymore.

"Who built it?" he asked.

"Who built what, honey?" Cynthia answered, not realizing the question was not meant for her.

"Earth."

ABOUT THE AUTHOR

Ms. Cauldron writes books for all ages. While fantasy and science fiction usually pique her interest; humor, character conflict, and smart aleck dialogue are her go to's.

She currently resides in eastern Cupola with 12 gramwhats, 3 cats, and a herd of domesticated moths where she spends her free time watching conspiracy videos.

https://nippi1.wixsite.com/nacauldron/

www.ingramcontent.com/pod-product-compliance
Lightning Source LLC
Chambersburg PA
CBHW070616300726
48975CB00006B/1830